The Hookline Books come from
which is judged by book groups.
winner

Reviews:

'*A delicate and unusual novel that explores the precariousness of
relationships with precision and insight.*'
Livi Michael

'*A beautifully written book, in which an unusual relationship is
closely observed and rendered with great sensitivity. Bryony Doran
looks beyond surface appearance, to reveal the workings of her
characters' hearts with honesty and compassion.*'
Judith Allnatt

'*Bryony Doran has a poet's eye for detail - this unusual novel
lingers with you long after the last page has been turned...*'
Berlie Doherty

'*The China Bird is a real triumph... a literary classic which should
be, and must be, eagerly consumed by readers of all tastes.*'
Rob Around Books

'*The China Bird defies categorisation. It is very well written in a
detailed literary fashion, but it is also quite sexy - or so it seemed to
this reader.*'
Alan James Brown

The China Bird

by
Bryony Doran

Hookline Books

Published by Hookline Books, 2009
Reprinted 2010

Bookline and Thinker Ltd.
Suite 231
405 King's Road
London SW10 0BB
Tel: 0845 116 1476
Email: editor@booklinethinker.com
www.booklinethinker.com

A CIP catalogue for this book is available from the British Library

This book is a work of fiction. Names, characters, places and
incidents are either a product of the author's imagination or are
used ficticiously.

ISBN: 978-0-956517739

Cover design by Donald McColl

Printed and bound by Lightning Source UK

For Bill Allerton with much love and thanks

Bryony Doran was born in a Youth Hostel on Dartmoor. She grew up in Cornwall and studied fashion at Manchester Metropolitan University. In 2004 Bryony graduated from Sheffield Hallam University with an MA in writing. She has one son and lives with her partner who is also a writer.

CHAPTER ONE

Edward hoards his mother's letters, not opening them straight away, but sometimes savouring what might be. He stacks them upright, and every morning when he opens his drawer for a neatly rolled pair of socks they tilt towards him in greeting. He laughs to himself, knowing how frustrated Mrs Ingram will be when she finds a letter still sealed. He could take them to work or lock them in his suitcase, but he knows that if she reads them, they will have between them an unspoken language of common knowledge.

He wishes he didn't set such store by his mother's letters and that, after his father's death, he could have distanced himself from her totally. Usually she writes in intricate detail, painting pictures of her everyday life and of her garden, but the one he has opened today is a request. She wants him to accompany her to a funeral; a whole day in her company. He isn't sure he can manage that.

From the wardrobe, Edward takes a jacket hanger of lightly varnished wood. He pokes gently with the end of the hook at Mrs Ingram's cat, asleep on the bed. She ignores him. He drops the hanger onto the bed and turns away, beginning to peel back the left lapel of his jacket, slowly levering it over his lowered shoulder until it drops from his arm then, using his free hand, he pulls at the other sleeve until the jacket falls onto the bed. He sits down next to the cat and knobbles her jaw with his knuckle. He is distracted by the light from the window, where it illuminates the hidden water marks on the lining of his jacket. The cat purrs, stretches, claws at the jacket.

'No you don't!' He snatches his jacket away and, holding the hanger aloft, drapes it around the varnished wood. The hanger, which is perfectly symmetrical, does not fit. This is a jacket that has been crafted and moulded to fit his twisted body.

Under his mattress Edward has a set of pink cardboard patterns, drawn and cut for him by his Uncle Ruben.

'This, my lad, is a special formula just for you. Hold on to these patterns and you can always get a jacket made to fit. No off-the-peg rubbish for my nephew.'

He had draped his tape over every part of Edward's body, taking a measurement of every dimension.

'Is it accurate, Uncle Ruben? Your tape looks a bit bandaged.'

Uncle Ruben had smiled, shown his brown, crooked teeth. 'Keep cutting it with these blooming things,' he'd said, waving an enormous pair of black handled shears. 'But never worry, my lad, your Uncle Ruben makes compensations. It'll fit you like a glove. You'll see.'

Edward remembers being pinned and pulled in every direction. The sight of Uncle Ruben manipulating the shape of his back into the jacket, steaming, moulding, pulling, and the warm comforting smell of wool, mixed with the scent of old fish heads carelessly thrown under the bench; pickled herrings from Uncle Ruben's favourite lunch.

As he hangs his jacket in the shade of the wardrobe, Edward fingers the leather buttons on the cuff. Neither he nor his mother have ever informed Uncle Ruben that he had left home and so, once a year on his birthday, a letter arrives for him at his mother's house. She slips it unopened into his birthday card. Mrs Ingram doesn't know that he gets letters from Uncle Ruben, post-marked New York. He always takes these letters to work and stores them in his desk drawer under lock and key.

Edward has never written back. He considers his uncle's letters a peace offering, something owed to him. All through his childhood he'd said, 'You're my favourite nephew. The person I treasure most in all the world.' And then, when Edward asked for his help, he'd announced that he was off to find his fortune in America.

'Never mind, lad,' he'd said. 'Don't worry. Things have a way of working out.'

He'd laughed then, slapped Edward on the shoulder and asked him if he was going to miss his favourite uncle. Edward pointed out to him that he was the only uncle he'd ever had.

CHAPTER TWO

Angela gets off the bus in the centre of town. She looks up at the town hall clock: half an hour until she starts work. She enters the Central Library and wanders without thought, dancing her fingers along the spines, absorbing the grandeur; a cathedral of books.

She pauses at the Art and Oversize Book section. Pulling a large volume on Degas from the shelf, she flicks through the pages from front to back, looking for inspiration. She strokes a picture of a woman drying herself, a moment of great intimacy captured by the artist. She slaps the book shut and runs her hand along the spines again until... Egon Schiele. His work has a visual truth, a style she envies. The models are jagged, thin, distorted images. She studies his use of the black crayon outline, colours carelessly spilt across black lines.

She scans the text: *Schiele set about dismantling conventional idealized images.* A picture of a baby, screwed up and ugly, stares back at her. *The artist was determined to show that his task was not to show the splendour of humanity but its pitiful wretchedness.* There is something in this that she is seeking, and yet, it is not quite this, she doesn't want to turn beauty into wretchedness... more... well..., she scans further down the page, *Schiele despaired of his uncultivated teachers and fought against their constraints.*

She smiles to herself, thinking back to the conversation she'd had earlier when her tutor asked if she'd thought any more about her dissertation. Why was he so against her doing life studies, for Christ's sake? Just because it wasn't the in thing to do. What did she care? But she does. She can still feel the iciness of self doubt at his words, still remember how he drew heavily on his cigarette and then, in that pretentious way of his, threw it half-finished onto the step, grinding it with his moccasin, all the time building up the dramatic effect.

'And what medium will Madam be using for this innovative idea of hers?'

She remembers the sarcastic edge in his voice. She'd begun to get angry at this point. 'Charcoal, actually.'

'And to think,' he'd muttered, 'you're so talented and you're going to throw it all away.' He moved up one step, became level with her. 'You know how good you are. You don't need me to tell you that. But to get on these days you have to create a concept, something really off the wall, not just life drawings, or painting. It's no longer enough. Can't you see that?'

She wasn't sure of his motivation. Who was he trying to help? He was a talented artist himself. Couldn't he see that she too wanted to hone her skill, express herself through her drawing? She'd had enough of toeing the line, three long years of it.

As if he'd read her thoughts, he'd said, 'Just toe the line for a bit longer, eh? Get your degree. No, get a first, you'll walk it. Then you can do what you want.'

She laughs to herself, slotting the book back into its space, remembering her parting shot: 'My art's not about passing exams.' And how, all the way into town on the bus, she wished she'd bitten her tongue. She wants a first more than anything. She wants to go on to study further. She wants to go to London, to the college that had first offered her a place to do a degree. Out of hundreds of applicants she'd been offered one of only ten places. But she'd had to tell them she couldn't go, explain her personal circumstances. They'd written, told her how disappointed they were, what a rare talent she had, and to apply for an MA course with them once she'd finished her degree. She can still feel the glow of this promise in her chest.

She glances down at the books on the bottom shelf and sees a fat volume on the life and works of Toulouse-Lautrec. She pulls it out with both hands and opens it on a table.

The centre is a collection of glossy plates, but that's not what attracts her. She is fascinated by the photographs of the man himself. Dwarf-like, he has the appearance of neither man nor child. His full upper and thin bottom lip lend him a duck-like appearance, while his shoes appear to curl up at the toes, like those handed down from an elder brother.

She sketches his outline on her pad. He dresses cleverly in a three-quarter-length coat so she cannot quite gauge whether it is his legs or his torso that are too short. A tall top hat only adds to the incongruity. She sketches him again as he might appear nude, giving him heavy hips and short legs, a stance she finds strangely appealing.

The Town Hall clock strikes twelve. She leaves the book open on the table and makes her way to the main doors, humming quietly to herself. She skips down the stone steps and hurries along the street to Henry's; a restaurant on a busy corner. As she works the tables, she notices for the first time how, from the inside, the large windows of old-fashioned glass distort the figures of passers-by.

CHAPTER THREE

Edward watches the crows circling the fine black lines of leafless trees etched against the pewter sky. He hears the first thud of earth on wood and stares down at the coffin. The brass nameplate is already tarnished by the wet soil. He shivers, wishing he hadn't come.

On the journey over he'd asked his mother how they were related to the dead woman. The train was pulling away from Huddersfield station. He'd waited for an answer, watching the station clock grow smaller and smaller. 'She was a distant relative. Far too complicated to explain,' was the only reply. He'd forgotten how his mother coveted secrets. He tried again, 'So her name was Claudette Mason?'

He received a slight nod of the head, and noted that she was wearing her pewter pearls, the diamante clasp resting on the prominent vertebrae at the back of her neck as she turned to look out of the window. He persisted, 'You ask me to take a day off work and come to a funeral with you, but I'm not to be furnished with any of the particulars?'

She turned then, she must have heard the pique in his voice, 'I appreciate you coming, thank you.' She spoke with a measured politeness, 'I didn't want to come on my own.'

He tries to keep the sarcasm out of his voice, 'Unusual for you, Mother.'

'I didn't know her that well. We wrote mostly. She was an interesting woman.'

'And we were related?'

'Yes, but I don't remember how. It's not important anyway.' She leans back in her seat, closing her eyes against the sun.

Edward smiles to himself. Surely at forty-nine he should have learnt how to handle his mother.

Edward digs his stick firmly into the mud and studies the faces of the other mourners. Across the grave is a girl in her early twenties. Her hair is dyed a garish purple and is scraped into a short ponytail at one side. Her skin, by stark contrast, has the luminous quality of white jade. She has her arm around the shoulders of an elderly woman who is dabbing her cheeks with a screwed up tissue. The girl, a frown furrowing her brow, is staring straight across the grave at his mother, who is unaware of the girl's scrutiny.

Edward can feel his mother's claw-like grip tighten on the inner crease of his elbow as they move away from the graveside. It occurs to him that, almost without him noticing, she has become frail. The closeness of her bothers him. He can smell her scent – Lily of the Valley. Fumbling for his handkerchief, he disengages his arm and moves aside to blow his nose. He hears a gasp and, turning, sees his mother, as if in slow motion, fold to the ground. Before he can react, Mr Cole the solicitor is there, grasping her elbows from behind, easing her gently to her feet.

'Mother! Are you all right?' His words sound polite, distant.

She examines the side of her camel coat, now streaked in mud. 'Yes, no thanks to you.'

'Maybe you should get a stick, Mother.'

'I don't think so.'

The solicitor interrupts, 'Now, are you sure you're all right?' He takes his handkerchief out of his pocket, 'Would you like me to wipe your coat down?'

Edward turns away towards the car. Let him look after her.

Rachel closes her eyes and listens to the soft purr of the limousine as it makes its way beyond the cemetery gates. Suddenly she feels so very tired. The fall has shaken her more than she cares to admit. All she wants to do now is go home and sit with her cat in the chair overlooking the garden. At this time of day the sun will be stealing into the back room. The cat will be sitting there now. She smiles to herself, realising how little she, like the cat, wants from life nowadays, but how differently she would do it if she had another chance. How she had envied Claudette her life with its veneer of culture, the paintings and books that mapped the history of her life. She gazes out of the car window and watches the sun shaft through a break in the clouds. It glances off the flat surface of a distant reservoir. Under that thin layer, had their lives turned out to be so very different?

CHAPTER FOUR

'Sorry. I've been staring at you all day. I'm Angela, by the way. Angela O'Donnell.'

Edward looks up and sees the girl with purple hair address his mother.

'It's just that, I'm sure I know you from somewhere.'

His mother shrugs, 'I've never seen you before in my life.'

'We're from Sheffield,' he says, by way of an apology for his mother's bad manners.

The girl glances over at him. He shakes his head at her and pulls his mouth into a long thin line. She flashes him a smile.

'I'm a student at Sheffield,' she laughs, 'I wonder, do you ever go to Henry's on Burgess Street? I work there as a waitress. Maybe that's where I've seen you.'

Rachel gives a quick shake of her head and scowls, 'No. I've never heard of the place.'

Edward notes the sharp tone in her voice.

The wake is being held in a dreary pub high up on the winter moors. It is full of people he doesn't know, just like his father's funeral twenty years earlier, where people had nodded and smiled, and not known what to say.

He remembers the desolation he had felt back then. His father's life had slotted so tidily between his own and his mother's so that, all too late, he'd realised that the true beauty of the man lay in all his quiet ways. Even in retirement he was still the first up, enjoying the silence of early mornings, alone with his crossword and cup of tea.

Barely a week after his father's death, Edward was overcome by a desperate need to leave home. The lie that had been his parent's marriage seemed to resound throughout the house. All that was familiar to him only heightened the absence of his father. He felt no guilt at leaving his mother; it had been his father who had needed him as a foil against her. He hoped that if he left home his grief would ease and he could learn, like a child taking its first steps, to move forward into a new life.

Janice, a colleague from the library, told him about a Mrs Ingram who was looking for a lodger. Her mother and Mrs Ingram played bingo together on a Saturday night. When he told his mother that he was moving out, he was piqued to find that she seemed rather pleased with the idea.

It wasn't until the day he was leaving and they were sitting down to Sunday lunch that he had any misgivings. Maybe her bravado was all a front. His mother had soon relieved him of that notion. She put down her knife and fork, laughed and said, 'Thank God, I won't have to cook another Sunday lunch ever again.' She must have seen the look of dismay on his face, but she just shrugged, 'I only ever did it for your father, but what's the point now? It always seemed a waste of a good day to me.'

Half in jest, Edward had replied, 'And here was me thinking I still might come for my Sunday lunch.'

She'd suddenly sat upright, a look of irritation on her face, 'You can forget that. Your father was a good man, but now I want to live my own life.'

A good man! What a damning statement, Edward thought.

He had gone back three weeks later and been puzzled to find the wheelie bin filled to gaping on a Sunday. Bin day was Friday. What had his mother been doing over the weekend? Something in the bin caught his eye, and he flipped the lid open with his stick. It fell against the side with a dull, plastic thud. Instantly, he recognised the scuffed-leather soles of his father's best ox-blood brogues. Incensed, he flipped the lid back over and wheeled the bin down the drive and along the quiet Sunday street until he came to a path that led down to the river. It was awkward over the rough ground but his anger gave him strength. He pushed the bin through the sparse willow thickets, past the suspended tyre that dangled out over the river and to where the bank became less steep. He tried to tip the bin out onto the path but it was too difficult for him. He tried again and it veered off crazily down the bank toward the river, his father's shoes tumbling down into the brown water. He caught sight of a paisley scarf that his father wore on special occasions, and a grey worsted cap, long past its best, that he'd worn when he went to his allotment. He tried to descend the bank to retrieve the cap, but the ground was too slippery. Caught in the cleft of a tree root he spotted his father's false teeth; the ones the undertaker had pestered his mother so hard for, and what he'd taken to be a branch had a rubber ferrule on the end. It was his father's walking stick. How could she have thrown out his father's stick? It was the first time Edward had cried since his father's death.

He'd never gone back to the house. When he first left he'd thought that he would return for the rest of his things bit by bit and now, all these years later, he wonders if they are still there. He should have asked his mother a long time ago what she'd done with his belongings. Maybe he should ask her now, but she'd been edgy, especially after her fall. He could go to the bar, get her a drink, make it a peace offering.

The girl with the purple hair is standing at the bar. She has her back to him and is chatting with two workmen, who lean over their beer and cigarettes.

He listens to their conversation.

'Slummin' it a bit aren't you, love? Don't usually see the likes of you in here.'

'Oh, even the likes of me occasionally goes for the odd bit of rough.'

The workmen laugh loudly. Edward is surprised to find her so forward. Sensing a presence, she turns. He is gratified to see that she has the grace to blush.

She smiles at him and shakes her head, her sideways ponytail bobbing up and down. 'You know, it's really frustrating. I wish I could work out where I've seen your mother before.'

'I'm sorry I can't help you,' Edward hears himself reply, 'and I can tell you now, if my mother does know, I doubt very much she'll tell you.'

She has a very direct gaze and, as he stares back into her eyes, Edward sees that the irises are a pale grey, rimmed by a fine black line. Up close, her skin has a wonderful, translucent quality. A fine vein runs down the side of her cheek and he has an almost irresistible urge to put his hand up to it and trace the faint blue line with the tip of his finger. She smiles, and he notices that her teeth are like fine porcelain.

CHAPTER FIVE

In the far distance Angela can just make out the glint of lorries on the motorway. The cottage is different without Claudette; all her things are still in place, but now it feels like the home of a stranger.

She runs her eye along the pictures. Earlier she had collected them from around the house and now they are leaning against the wall; thick oils of bleak landscapes, a coppice of leafless trees, wild horses caught in the colours of a deep red sunset. Best of all she likes the figures in charcoal; clumsy silhouettes against the light, as if existing between two worlds, women and children standing on a skyline, swarthy, the light behind them fading to mauve.

Why was she so surprised that Claudette had bequeathed her these pictures and her books? Surely it had been Claudette who had fought her corner when her gran had been opposed to her going away to art college? Claudette had found the perfect compromise by suggesting that, after her A levels, she should attend the local tech college and do her foundation year there. Break her gran in slowly, so to speak. She remembered the time she had gone with her gran to show Claudette her school report. It was the only time she ever heard Claudette and her grandmother argue.

'She's not going and that's an end to it.'

'Elsie, my dear friend, the girl has a gift. You know she has. Let her go with good heart.'

There had been a silence, and then Claudette's voice again, hardly audible. 'History will not repeat itself and she's far more talented than her mother ever was.'

Her gran had not replied. The vacuum cleaner was switched on instead.

Angela looks over at the old woman who is standing at the doorway into the kitchen, deep in thought. Her poor gran, she had always been so anxious for her, especially when she'd finally realised that her granddaughter was not going to be dissuaded from her studies. That first year of A levels had been a good time, one of the few times that she ever felt she belonged. She'd found her first boyfriend; a Jewish boy in the year above, called Jeremy. His parents weren't that pleased at him going out with a gentile but she wasn't bothered by that. She had liked him, really liked him. They had explored each other's bodies, tentatively made love. She hadn't known what to make of it all. She'd felt there was still a world that hadn't opened up to her yet. At the end of that year he'd gone away to university and their relationship had fizzled out. She was sad at first, but then soon got over it. She wanted to concentrate on her work. She hadn't had another real boyfriend since, only Dan, a mature student in her year, but that was little more than a casual arrangement.

'The place could do with a good clean.' Her grandmother wipes a finger along the top of the dresser.

Angela turns to look at the portrait of a man still hanging on the far wall, 'Pity she didn't leave me him, too. I've always rather liked him. Who did the solicitor say he was?'

'Richard Appleyard, I think. A good Yorkshire name that, Appleyard. I once asked Claudette who he was, she just laughed, said it was her English brother. She didn't elaborate.'

'And why would she leave it to that old woman?' Angela peers up at the portrait. 'Rachel... Rachel Anderson, wasn't it? Not Appleyard.'

'Mrs. Anderson to you, young lady.' She puts an arm around her granddaughter's shoulder. 'It's a mystery to me, lass.'

'You know, I'm sure I've seen her before.'

'Well, I've certainly never met her.' The old woman crosses the room, 'She must have been some relation of Claudette's. I'm not sure she ever came here, not to my knowledge anyway.'

'And did she say,' Angela nods at the portrait, 'that he was her father?'

'Apparently. But she was a bit frosty, wasn't she? Didn't volunteer much, her son was friendlier though.'

'Yes, he was. In fact I found him quite fascinating.'

'How do you mean?'

'Well, did you notice how precisely he was turned out? I don't know why, but you never expect someone who is deformed like that to pay so much detail to their appearance. I mean, thinking about it, he had great style. From the way he'd got that sort of reddish hair of his slicked sideways so you could see nearly every comb mark, down to the hankie in his tweed jacket, and those fantastic old brogues he had on. And did you see how he kept compensating for his mother's rudeness? But in a way that she never quite latched onto.'

'Well, someone had to, didn't they?'

'I quite liked her.' Angela leans on the windowsill, her back to the window, 'She had a sort of defiance about her. Not like an old person.'

'Rudeness more like, I hope she shows her gratitude when you take her the portrait.'

'I might be able to find out more info for you.'

'What makes you think I want to know her business?'

Angela doesn't answer. She is scanning the bookshelves for one particular book. It isn't in its place. There is a gap where it should be, like a missing tooth. Claudette had never liked her looking at that book. She frantically scans all the shelves. It isn't there.

Her grandmother has wandered upstairs.

'Gran?' Angela shouts up the stairs. No answer. She finds her looking out of the window in Claudette's bedroom. Her shoulders are shaking.

'Please Gran, don't cry.'

Angela scans the room. The bed is unmade. On the bedside cabinet stands a carafe of water, a film of dust coating the surface.

Her gran blows her nose, 'Sorry, lass. I was thinking about her dying here all on her own. What a way to end a life. I knew I should have come that week.'

'But Gran, you weren't well.'

'Still, no excuse. I should have come.'

'Why did she never come to visit you? Why was it you that always had to visit her?'

Her grandmother strokes Angela's head, tucking a stray bit of hair behind her ear, 'You'll learn that friendships aren't always equal. I went to her as a cleaner and we became friends. But for both of us it felt better leaving things the way they were.'

Angela hugs the old woman close, breathes in the cloying scent of talc.

It was only two weeks since they had learned of Claudette's death. She'd returned home to find her gran sitting in her grandfather's winged chair. That alone made it obvious something was very wrong. Since her granddad had died the previous summer, no one, except visitors who didn't know any better, sat in that chair. Tears were streaming down her gran's face, and in her hand she held a letter. She handed it to Angela.

When her grandfather died, Angela felt as if someone had pulled away a blanket and exposed her to the outside world. With Claudette, it was as if she had lost the only person who had ever truly understood her.

'I need to blow my nose,' her grandmother says, gently pushing Angela away. 'Unless,' she tries to laugh, 'you want it all over your nice new jacket.' She sits down on the edge of the bed and retrieves a handkerchief from up her sleeve.

Angela smiles and wipes the shoulder of her black jacket, 'I think it's survived. Gran, have you seen that signed book of Claudette's? You know, the one with charcoal drawings of gypsy people?'

'It's there, look!' Her gran points to a book face down on the bedside cabinet. It is open at the photo of the artist. She takes the book from Angela and stares down at the photo. 'She always said she was happy with Mr Mason, but I don't know. I think she might have been better going back to France.' She strokes the photo of the artist. 'She seemed like such a fish out of water. Especially up here, miles from anywhere.'

'I'd love to live up here.'

Her grandmother sighs, 'Come on, we'd better get your things packed up.'

Angela checks the other books in the bedside cabinet. Tucked away at the back is a leather bound photo album. Each photo has an inscription in French. Angela picks up the album and, tucking it under her arm with the gypsy book, she follows her grandmother downstairs.

The art books take up six large boxes.

'Wherever are you going to put all them?' Her grandmother grumbles.

'My bedroom, of course.' Angela pulls off a length of bubble wrap and wraps it around another picture.

'And what about the pictures? You're not going to keep them all, surely? You could sell some. Help pay your way through college.'

Her grandmother is sitting in a chair next to an empty fish tank. Angela wishes that she could make her understand how much Claudette's legacy means to her.

'What happened to the guppies?' she asks.

'Oh, they went a long time ago. Too much trouble.'

Angela pulls off another length of bubble wrap and lays it out on the floor. She places the portrait of Richard Appleyard face upwards on the bubble wrap. She looks down at him. He is leaning back in a chair, arms folded across his chest. The features of his face have a delicacy bordering on the feminine. Even his fingers are long and slender. But the eyes are what Angela keeps returning to. The eyes stare directly at her; eyes that show a dry humour and a keen intelligence. Angela smiles back, then she remembers where she's seen Rachel before.

She had been the first model Angela had ever drawn, in her first week of college, her first life-drawing class. She remembers being fascinated by this old woman, naked except for a pearl necklace. She had always worn a necklace. Not always the same one, but always a necklace. Angela once heard a student complaining about it to their tutor, but the necklace had remained.

Angela had admired the old woman's breasts; unbelievably they still had a girl-like roundness to them. The pubic hair was completely white, bound in small curls like the permed hair on her head. Her hips also had a roundness to them; a sexuality that Angela once thought disappeared with old age. The only notable signs of age were on her limbs; the skin on her thighs mottled with thin vermilion thread-veins, her hands and her arms dotted with liver spots. Angela remembers how the necklace fell differently according to her pose, and how it illuminated the underside of her jaw.

CHAPTER SIX

Rachel stretches her arm over her shoulder and fumbles to undo the covered buttons at the back of her neck. She slips the silk blouse over her head and lays it flat on the kitchen table. She bunches a tea towel and runs it under the cold tap, dabbing at the yellow stain on the neckband. The mark is stubborn and only a small amount soaks into the tea towel.

'Damn! I should have used sticky tape before I wet it. Why didn't I think?'

She shivers, lifts the thin lace strap of her white bra back onto her shoulder, runs cold water into the Belfast sink and plunges in her blouse. It bobs to the surface; the white fabric mirroring the white porcelain, a bright yellow scar spreading into the clear water.

She rests her hands on the edge of the sink and observes herself in the mirror hanging on a nail hammered into the window frame. Putting both hands behind her back she unclips her bra, and lets it fall down her arms and onto the floor. She breathes in and holds her shoulders back, willing her breasts to rise with her rib cage. She cradles them gently, lifting them higher up her chest, allowing her string of pewter pearls to tuck into her newly formed cleavage. The pearls look dull and lifeless against her dry, crinkled skin.

Lifting her hair from the back of her neck, she unfastens the diamante clasp of her necklace and runs the pearls through her fingers. The smallest ones at the ends are cool, but the king pearls in the centre glow with warmth, as if they should have their own heartbeat. She runs the warm pearls over her front teeth and feels their secret roughness and knows they are a treasure to be prized. They were hers by right, or they would have been, after her aunt had died. Her uncle knew she'd taken them. He'd caught her admiring herself in the biscuit tin lid, propped against the wall in the shed where the farm hands drank their tea and the yard dogs slept.

'You don't need those, lass.'

Rachel had turned bright red.

'A fine looking girl like you doesn't need trinkets.'

'I only borrowed them.'

He stood behind her, said quietly, 'Lift up your hair.'

She scooped her black hair up into a ball at the back of her head.

'How old are you now, lass?' he whispered.

'Nineteen next, uncle...'

He kissed the back of her neck, his moustache tracing her skin like a spider's legs. She watched her blurred vision in the biscuit tin lid, her hands still holding her hair in place.

Her uncle brought his hands round to press tight into her belly and she let out a low, soft moan.

'Undo your blouse,' he whispered.

She closed her eyes, left one hand to hold her hair and started to undo the pearl buttons. Under her blouse was a huge, white, lace brassiere.

'Undo it.'

For this, she needed both hands. Her uncle pulled her blouse off and down her arms, then cupped her breasts gently in his rough hands. He put his chin on her shoulder; his stubble scratching her bare skin,

'There, that's how pearls should be seen.'

She arched back her head, stuck out her bottom and exulted in the power of her body. Her uncle rubbed himself against her, twisted her hand behind her back and pressed it against the front of his trousers. She felt something hard, violent. Suddenly she was afraid and tried to pull away,

'Uncle! Please!'

He turned her around and looked at her with a puzzled expression. 'What's the matter, lass?'

'What was that?' she said, pointing to his groin.

He laughed softly, 'Do you mean to tell me you've never been serviced?'

'What do you mean?' she whispered, picking her blouse up from the straw.

'You know, like the bull does to the cow, like the ram does to the sheep.'

'I don't know what you mean.'

'Well, I never. A little prick-teaser like you. I thought you would have had a string of men. Sex, Girl, I'm talking about sex. What you felt was my prick.'

Rachel put her blouse on and started to button it up, 'I never knew.'

'Would you like to?'

She blushed, angry with herself for the colour in her cheeks. She looked up, defiant, 'I have a boyfriend.'

'What? That George fellow? Well, he hasn't serviced you. That's obvious. I should say you're well ripe for it.'

She picked up her bra from a straw bale and shook it, 'I'd better get back. I'm supposed to be baking bread.'

She turned towards the door.

'Rachel?'

She looked back. He held out his hand, 'The necklace.'

Reluctantly she undid the clasp and dropped it into his large, open palm. He held them up to her face, 'They suit you well. Would you like them?'

'Would you really give them to me?'

'Your aunt has no use for such a lovely necklace, but you... ' he shook his head, 'they'd bring you pleasure, wouldn't they?'

She nodded.

'You could give me pleasure,' he said.

'How?'

'I'm out rabbiting tonight and, when I get back, I'll be in here skinning them.'

CHAPTER SEVEN

'Spare any change?'

Angela turns to see a beggar squatting against the sheltering wall of the Town Hall.

'Spare any change?'

She shakes her head and crosses the road. The girl, about her own age, had looked scared; not lifeless like they usually were, but scared. Angela stops and retraces her steps. She undoes the front pouch of her rucksack and takes out an apple,

'Here.'

The girl looks up and then back down at the bowl on the pavement.

'Here, take it.'

The girl reaches out and takes the apple. Angela turns away. It is then that she notices Edward, bent heavily over his stick, making his way along Surrey Street. He stops at the pavement edge and darts his head in what seems an almost furtive fashion from side to side, checking for traffic. Angela partially closes her eyes. In his black overcoat Edward appears like a thorn tree in winter. His stick, one single stem, his legs another, and his head and back the nub where the branches have woven together to be moulded and shaped by a harsh wind.

'Hey!'

Angela turns.

'I don't want your apple.' The girl throws the apple for Angela to catch. She ducks and it falls to the ground, smashing against the edge of the kerb and splitting into two almost perfect halves.

'I need money.'

Angela snorts, 'Tough, I'm just on my way to work to earn some. Shall I bring you my wage packet after?'

The girl shrinks back against the wall, curling deeper into

herself, closing her out. Angela turns away and searches the crowd
for Edward. He is nowhere to be seen.

Edward stands at the pelican crossing and presses the button. He
closes his eyes and waits for the beep, beep to tell him it is safe to
cross. He hears it, hears the halted cars revving their engines and
smiles to himself as he presses the button again. When the green
man flashes for the second time he crosses the road and stands
outside the restaurant window. He tries to peer in but he cannot see
past the tall ferns in the window. He has been here before with his
mother, he is sure he has.

Edward pushes open the door and enters the restaurant. The
ceilings are high and the noise of the place disorientates him. He
glances round, searching for an empty table.

'Hello. Fancy seeing you here, I was just thinking about you.'

Angela is standing in front of him holding an empty tray.
When he looks down at the tray she drops it to her side and, as he
looks into her face, she says, 'I saw you on Surrey Street a bit a go.'

'Did you?' He smiles, 'I thought I'd come and see you,
apologise for my mother's behaviour.'

'Let's find you a seat. Look, there's a free table over there.'

She guides him over to a table and waits as he removes his
coat and sits down.

'Right. What can I get you?'

He ignores her request and asks instead, 'How are you?'

'Okay,' she smiles.

'I nearly didn't recognise you with your hair dyed black.' He
fingers the edge of the menu and watches as she pulls her hair into
a bunch at the nape of her neck.

'My gran,' she shrugs. 'She didn't like it. This is a
compromise.'

'You said you were an art student. Is that right?'

'Well remembered,' she slides into the seat opposite him,
'Final year. I'm supposed to come up with an idea for my
dissertation, but I don't seem to be able to get my head around it.'
She gets up, 'What can I get you?'

'I'll have a coffee please.' He pauses, 'Maybe I could help? I
work in the library.'

She puts her pad back into her apron pocket, 'Funny that,

I've just been in the library. I went in to see if they had any different art books than at college.'

'And did they?'

'They had a nice one on Degas.'

'I could look downstairs in the basement; see if they have any unusual ones.'

'Thanks, but it's not books that I'm really looking for. I need a life model.'

'A life model?'

'I'm still looking for the right person.'

'And are live models so difficult to find?'

'Yes,' she laughs. 'You see, I'm not really sure yet what I'm after.'

He watches as she returns across the floor with his coffee, holding a small tray on the palm of one hand. 'Edward? You don't mind me calling you that, do you?'

He shakes his head, 'No, of course not.'

She places the coffee carefully on the table in front of him. 'I want to ask you something. But please don't take offence...'

'Ange!' A waiter from across the room calls her. She grimaces, 'Sorry, I'll be back in a minute.'

He catches sight of her working the tables at the other side of the room. She has a great fluidity of movement, her body seeming to move from the waist; her hips swaying from side to side. It is a very natural movement. Undulation, he thinks.

Yes. She undulates.

Please don't take offence. He keeps recalling the words. What can she want?

She smiles at him apologetically from across the room and shrugs her shoulders. He is putting his coat on when she eventually returns.

'Sorry about that.'

'What is it you wanted to ask me?'

'Oh. It wasn't important. I forgot to ask you how your mother is. Will you tell her I'll have her picture soon? I'll give her a ring about bringing it round.'

He picks up his stick. 'Tell me,' he hesitates, 'What did you really want to ask me?'

She laughs, tilting her head away from him like a nervous animal. 'Really it wasn't important.'

He observes again the vein that runs like a shadow-line down her cheek. 'You can't say, '*I want to ask you something but please don't take offence*', and then just walk away.'

She bites her bottom lip, looks directly into his eyes. 'I was wondering...'

'Go on.'

'If you'd consider it.'

'What?'

She laughs nervously, 'Have you ever considered being an artist's model?'

He hears his voice squeak in astonishment. 'Me?'

She nods.

'What? Your life model?'

'That's what I had in mind.'

'Well,' He gulps. 'Why me?'

Her boss calls out from the kitchen, 'Ange!'

He catches her arm. Her skin is covered in a fine down. She looks down at his hand on her arm. He lets go. 'Tell me, I need to know. I mean, I'm hardly something out of a Degas painting, am I?'

'I saw you earlier while you were waiting to cross the road, and, well, I just knew.'

Edward shakes his head, frowning. 'I don't understand. What do you mean?'

Her boss is beckoning her. She starts to back away. 'Sorry, I really have to go.'

Dazed, he sits back down on his chair. The inside of his head feels like cotton wool. She hesitates, 'Are you all right?'

'You didn't answer my question. Why me?'

'If I knew, I'd tell you.'

He stands up, and she halts a moment,

'Can you come back on Thursday? I'll see if I can think of with a better explanation.'

He nods, and watches as she walks away.

CHAPTER EIGHT

The mid-afternoon sun is moving round to the back of the house, a last sliver just catching the front step. Stretched full length along it is a huge ginger tom, soaking up the warmth from the stone.

Angela looks at her watch. Three o'clock? She undoes the drawstring of her rucksack and gets out her diary. Yes, she was right. 3 o'clock, Wednesday.

She sits down next to the cat and watches as it stretches all four legs out straight, opening and closing its claws as it does so. Angela studies the intricacy of shade and marking. Ribbons of exquisitely defined stripes encompass its body from head to tail. A proper marmalade cat, she thinks. It lifts its head and meows at her, showing the ridged pink roof of its mouth. She turns away and, stretching her arms above her head, glances again at her watch. The cat stands and arches its body upwards, rubs itself against her, purring loudly as it looks for a lap to climb on to. Angela hunches herself forward and grasps her knees, elbowing the cat,

'Bugger off!'

'Don't you like my cat?'

Angela shades her eyes and looks up. Rachel is standing at the bottom of the steps.

'I didn't hear you come in the gate.'

'That's because you left it open, young lady.'

The cat jumps down the steps and rubs its body around Rachel's stockinged legs. Angela ignores her remark about the gate,

'You look very nice. Have you been out to lunch?'

Rachel picks up the cat and it nuzzles the top of its head into her chin,

'Yes. I'm sorry I'm late. I was enjoying the sun so much I forgot about the time.'

Angela stands up, yanking her rucksack onto her back, 'I've brought the portrait.'

'I hope it's not in there.' Rachel says, nodding towards the rucksack.

Angela points towards the door, 'I've propped it up over there.'

Rachel puts down the cat and, opening the clasp on her bag, gets out her key, 'Would you believe this will be the first time I've clapped eyes on it?' She opens the door. 'Come in,' she says, 'and bring the portrait, will you?'

Rachel leads her past the kitchen and into a sunlit room that overlooks the garden at the back of the house. Angela can smell the aroma of freshly baked cake. While Rachel goes to make the tea, Angela surveys the room. At mid-height along two sides runs a bookcase, tightly packed with books. On another wall, standing alone, is a taller bookcase filled with over-sized books. She moves nearer, art books, a good selection.

Rachel carries a wooden tray through from the kitchen, 'Can you lift the flap please?' She nods at an oak table placed against the wall opposite the French windows. Angela lifts the flap and pulls out a barley-twist leg, smoothes her hand across the top of the oak table and smiles at Rachel, 'You've got some lovely things. Your house reminds me of Claudette's.'

Rachel smiles, pleased by the comparison, 'Thank you. I shall take that as a compliment, though I'm not sure it's fully deserved. My house doesn't reflect my life the way Claudette's did. Though I suppose that's not strictly true either, maybe it does. My life has been rather dull.'

'How can you say that? What about all your books?' Angela gestures to the bookcase in the corner.

'You know, the strange thing is, I only started collecting them after my husband died. Not sure why, I don't think he'd have said anything. Maybe that's why,' she tails off.

'I wish I had half as many books,' Angela laughs, 'Though I have, haven't I? I've inherited all Claudette's.'

'How well did you know her?'

'She was my Guardian. Well, sort of. If anything had happened to my grandparents she promised my gran she would look after me.'

Angela remembers guiltily the rows she had with her gran, mostly about spending all her time drawing instead of getting on with her homework, and how she'd wished she could go and live with Claudette,

'She was always really good to me. At Christmas and birthdays she used to buy me a book on art, or some paints. One year she bought me a set of badger-hair paintbrushes. Gran was very cross, said she shouldn't go spending her money. When I was about ten she called at our house, the only time she ever did, and said she'd come to take me to an art exhibition in the centre of Manchester. I think it was already arranged with my gran but she'd never mentioned it to me, probably hoping Claudette wouldn't turn up. I remember being blown away by the colours. I'd never seen colours like that before.'

'Who was the artist?' Rachel asks.

'Van Gogh, fancy, I had completely forgotten that.'

'So, you're studying art here in Sheffield?'

'Yes. I was offered a place in London, but my grandparents were upset about me going so far away.'

Rachel glances over to the art books in the corner, 'At least you got to go somewhere. It was always my dream to study art.'

Angela tilts her head sideways and studies Rachel's face, 'Have you ever thought of being an artist's model? You've got the bone structure.'

There is a glimmer, a slight hesitation, 'No, no, I haven't.' Rachel lifts a willow pattern cup from the tray and pours milk from a jug and then the tea from the pot.

Angela picks up her cup. 'I love willow pattern. My gran used to have it. I used to make up stories about the figures on the bridge.'

'What happened to them, did they get broken?'

'She threw them out, got something more modern. I think the world of my gran, but neither my granddad nor I could ever understand why she always wanted new things. I like having old familiar things around, but she gets bored with them.'

Rachel slices into a square block of ginger cake, 'So you were brought up by your grandparents?'

She puts two pieces on a plate for Angela. The tea is strong and milky, just the way Angela likes it. She takes a bite out of the cake and nods. Rachel replaces the knife quietly on the plate, 'What happened to your parents?'

Angela takes a sip of her tea and asks, 'Aren't you going to look at the portrait?'

She sees a brief smile pass across Rachel's face, 'Would you unwrap it for me?' she asks.

Angela gets up, 'Yes, of course.'

'No. Finish your tea first.'

Angela nods over towards the book case, her mouth full, 'I see you've got an Egon Schiele book. I really like his stuff.'

'I don't.' Rachel gets up and pulls the book from the shelf. 'In fact, I'd better remember to take it back. Edward lent it to me.'

'Why don't you like him?'

'Oh, well,' Rachel opens a page, 'Look at how grotesque he makes the figures. Why can't he draw beautiful people?'

Angela touches the open page. 'But these are real people.'

Rachel takes another book from the bookcase. 'Do you know the artist Degas?' she asks.

'Yes, I love his strutting ballerinas, but I think they're a bit superficial.' She pauses, 'like people moulded to be beautiful, somehow.'

'I don't agree.' Rachel shakes her head. 'Why do you young people prefer ugliness? Do you find beauty so superficial? I don't think ballet is artificial. If it were it wouldn't awake such strong emotions in me.'

'Well, there you have the advantage over me. I've never been to a ballet.'

'Never?'

Angela shakes her head.

'Would you like to?' Rachel enquires, looking into the girl's face.

'I'd love to. It's just, well, I never went as a child. My gran would never take me. I think she found it all too posh. And since coming to college... ' she shrugs. 'I never seem to get round to it.'

'Would you like to come with me? Let me take you, as a thank you for bringing me the portrait.'

Angela puts her head to one side, 'Are you sure? I'd love to.'

Rachel cuts more cake, 'It would be a treat for me to go with someone else and,' she smiles, 'It would give me a chance to show you what sensuality really is.'

'Can I ask a question? Why did Edward bring you the Schiele book if he knew you didn't like that kind of art?'

'I sometimes think he does it just to annoy me. He can be a bit funny like that.'

Angela nods, a smile touching the corners of her mouth. Edward hadn't come back to the restaurant the following Thursday. It had been a whole week before she'd caught sight of him hovering by the door.

After they clear the tea things, Angela puts the portrait on the table and carefully peels back the layers of brown paper and bubble wrap. She watches for Rachel's reaction and sees she is quite overcome.

'Who was he?' Angela asks, her voice barely above a whisper.

'My father.'

'Yes I can see that, you have his eyes.'

'He is very young here, you know? This must have been painted before he was married, and yet...' Rachel looks down at the date next to the signature, 'It says 1939, how puzzling.'

Angela examines the signature, 'I think it was painted by Claudette's lover. Maybe he did it from a photograph.'

'Claudette had a lover?'

'When she lived in France, before the war. My gran told me.'

'Oh, I see! I think you're right,' Rachel muses, 'We did have a photo like this.'

'Talking of photos, I sort of, by mistake,' Angela grins, 'Took a photo album as well. I'm sure there are some photos of him,' she nods at the portrait. 'I'll bring it round if you'd like to see it.'

'I'd be fascinated. You know,' Rachel picks up the portrait and holds it at arms length. 'I think I'm going to enjoy having him around.'

'I do wish I could remember where I've seen you before,' Angela says again, looking at the old woman. This time, Rachel's features remain totally impassive. Angela glimpses again the artistic potential of her face. Maybe she could be persuaded to model if Edward wouldn't agree.

Rachel shakes her head and smiles. The cat tries to jump up onto Angela's lap. She shoos it away.

'She likes you.' says Rachel, 'Strange that, how cats always like people who don't like them.'

CHAPTER NINE

Edward surveys the sunlit studio. It is devoid of furniture except for a small knitting-chair like his mother once had. The chair is upholstered in a worn, orange-flecked fabric. At the back of the room is another chair, an orange plastic one with black metal legs. The floor is covered in cheap, petrol-blue carpet. He sits back in the knitting chair and closes his eyes. After his second visit to the restaurant, it had taken him a week to pluck up enough courage to go back again. He'd been in two minds whether to return at all, but her request had intrigued him.

She'd intrigued him.

He can hear her now, setting up her drawing equipment. The sun from the skylight has warmed the fabric of the chair and the warmth is soaking into his body. He feels as if he is part of a surreal dream in which this girl has come into his life and spirited him here to this studio.

'Just come along to the studio, let me make a few sketches, see how you feel,' was how she'd phrased it. She'd taken a ten-minute break, bringing two coffees to the table. He'd watched as she'd warmed her cheek with her cup.

'I came to the library to see if I could find you last week.'

Euphoric was how he felt. There was something about this girl, something in her manner that gave him a sense of release and, for the first time in years, he'd wanted to sing. He had completely forgotten to ask her why she wanted to draw him.

He opens his eyes and notices a fine wire mesh running through the glass of the skylight. His stomach is churning. He presses his hands to it to stem the noise and it makes a loud gurgling noise. He looks over to see if Angela has noticed.

She is kneeling on the floor, unrolling a tube of paper, her hair falling across her face. He observes that she has a hole in the sole of one shoe. As if sensing his scrutiny, she brushes her hair away from her face, looks up and smiles.

He smiles back, 'It's so lovely here in the sun.'

'Not too hot, then?'

'Nope.'

She stands up, drags the plastic chair from the back of the room and places it opposite him before sitting down. 'Right, let me just clip the paper flat and we'll begin, shall we? Just relax and try to keep still.'

'I'm not sure I can do that,' he hears himself say.

She selects a stick of charcoal, 'I'm sure you'll be fine.'

She is observing him. Not looking at him, but observing him, he thinks. She hasn't even considered the possibility that remaining still may cause him discomfort

He watches as she draws bold black lines. His jaw, his shoulder, he wonders, or his nose, long and thin with a square end; like a comic book hero, he'd always thought.

After what feels to him like hours, she breaks the silence, 'What do you like to do in your spare time?'

He moves his hand up to his chin.

'Ah, you moved.'

'Sorry, I forgot.'

'It's my fault for talking to you. Just concentrate on not moving. You can still talk.'

'Is it all right to move my jaw?'

'At this stage, yes, but only slightly.'

He smiles.

'Ah! Smiling is out.'

'Breathing?'

She laughs, 'Seriously, though, just relax. It'll take you several sittings before you get used to being still, and being stared at.'

'And me not even at the starting line,' he mutters.

She cocks her head to one side, 'I don't get you.'

'Usually people look at me and then quickly look away, embarrassed in case I catch them staring.'

Angela frowns. 'I don't understand.'

'I see it in their faces.'

'What?'

'My disability.'

'I think your disability is part of who you are.'

'Do you think having a disability is like the colour of one's hair or something?' He feels his body stiffen, 'What a glib statement.'

She puts her board down on her lap, frowning. 'I'm not sure I know what you mean.'

'Are you saying I chose to be like this?'

He looks up, not caring if he moves. She is looking down at her board, biting her bottom lip. She looks close to tears. For a brief second he feels ashamed, but then, she stares straight at him.

'It can't be changed, can it?'

He finds himself challenged by her directness, 'Thank you for pointing that out.'

'What I meant was that I see you as a person with a disability, not as a disabled person. Does that make sense? First and foremost, you are a person.'

'Was it the person you wanted to draw?' He wonders how will she get out of this one. She is a strange girl; one minute cavalier, the next, vulnerable, 'The truth is that you can never understand what it's like to be me.'

'Edward, please, just tell me how it feels to be like you. I'm not trying to cause offence here. I really want to know.'

'What, exactly?'

'Well.' He sees her considering her words carefully. 'How it feels to be inside your body.'

He closes his eyes. 'It feels, like…' he opens them again, '… as if I carry a huge burden, a heavy weight that very few have to carry.' He waits for a response but she is silent, waiting for him to continue.

'I remember, as a child, dancing in the rain with a lightness of heart that I know I can never again recapture. I loved the rain, especially thunder storms, I still do, come to that. But I now know that people stare at me with a mixture of curiosity and pity, as if what has happened to me could never happen to them or their kin.'

He watches her face, waiting again for a response. The door clicks open, fracturing the silence. They turn to see a head poke through the gap, cigarette in mouth, fringe flopping over one eye, hair shading from black to grey.

'Just thought I'd see how you were getting on.' The man walks over to the window and stares briefly out into the courtyard before turning and scrutinising the room, and then Edward. Angela picks up her board and holds it to her chest.

'Aren't you going to introduce us then?' The man nods toward Edward.

'Alex, Edward. Edward, Alex.'

Edward notes her sullen tone.

'I'm her tutor. Though you'd not think it with her attitude, would you?' Alex laughs, 'Mind you, they're all the same these days. No respect.'

Edward takes an instant dislike to this man with his dismissive attitude and his handmade moccasin shoes that slip from his heels as he walks.

'So, you're going to model for Ange are you?'

She interrupts, 'No. Edward just popped in to tell me that his niece, who was going to model for me, couldn't make it today.'

Why is she lying? Edward watches her turn away. Niece! What is she talking about?

'Who were you going to use? Anyone I know?'

'No,' Angela stands up, 'Now if you don't mind…'

Alex tosses his head, catches sight of the paper clipped to her board, flicks his hair out of his eyes, 'But I thought you weren't drawing…' he raises his eyebrows, 'Edward.'

'I'm not,' she says through gritted teeth, 'We were just talking. I was doodling, that's all.'

Alex moves away from the window and takes a final drag on his cigarette. Edward sees that he is looking for somewhere to stub it out.

Angela frowns as Alex makes a hurried exit, 'What was that about?'

Edward tries to laugh, but he doesn't feel like laughing, 'Cigarette burning his fingers.'

'He gets right on my nerves.'

'I thought he was your tutor?'

She doesn't notice the sharpness in his voice.

'And doesn't he know it.' She gets up and goes over to the window. 'All he's interested in is showing himself in a good light. He wants his students to do something really modern, *'Why don't you do a short film?'* she mimics, *'Use other media. Drawing's old hat.* And yet,' she muses, 'I've noticed it doesn't stop him drawing.'

'Why did you lie to him about me?' Edward blurts out.

'I'm sorry.' She tilts her head sideways, 'I just don't want him sticking his neb in.'

'Yes, but why did you say niece? What were you thinking of?'

She shrugs, 'Dunno, Just trying to throw him off the scent.'

'Niece! Would he not be able to comprehend that you wanted to draw an old cripple like me?' He waits for a reaction.

'Look, how can I explain this? You know those snow domes that you shake and it looks as if it's snowing?'

He wonders where she is going with this line of thought.

'Well, did you ever try to open one to get the snow out?'

'No,' he says, 'Why would I?'

'I did, my gran was furious with me.'

'And the analogy is?'

'Well, once I'd broken it, I'd destroyed the whole concept, hadn't I? Do you see what I'm saying?'

He laughs to himself. What a strange girl.

'If I tell Alex, if I tell the world what I am trying to achieve here, then I'll have broken the dome, spoiled the magic.'

'So, let me get this right,' he pauses, 'You want to keep me in the dome?'

'Yes, exactly, I want to be able to keep shaking the snow and watching it fall.'

He is so charmed by her analogy that he forgives her.

'So, what do you want to do? You still haven't told me.'

She grins, 'I want to do a series of drawings of you in charcoal.' She adds, 'If you'll agree.'

'But, why me?'

She leans her back against the window, 'Oh God, how do I answer that? I've got a really good feeling about this. I think I could create something really special.'

'You still haven't answered my question,' he persists.

'Why do I want to draw you?' She puts her hand up to her chin, 'Because you're different.'

'Not good enough.'

'Well, let's put it like this,' she says slowly. He watches her searching for the words. 'If I wanted to draw trees, I wouldn't just go out and find the straightest, tallest tree, would I? I'd look for something different.'

'Old and gnarled?'

'Well, yeah.' The colour rises up her neck, 'You like making me feel uncomfortable don't you?'

He smiles, 'I want to know.'

'But why, just because someone is not considered normal, should they not be beautiful?'

He cannot resist, 'So you consider me beautiful, do you?'

'Yes, actually, I do. And there we finally have the answer. That is why I want to draw you.'

'You have a strange concept of beauty,' he mutters. Suddenly he feels shy. An emotion he has not felt for a long time. 'Can I move if you're not going to continue drawing?'

'Sorry, yes of course you can. I think...' she looks at her watch, 'We'll call it a day. Don't want to tire you out on your first session, do we?'

He presses down on his stick and heaves himself out of the chair. 'I don't remember saying I'd agreed?' He walks over to the window to join her

'Please?'

He turns his head to look at her, she seems really anxious about this. He feels suddenly overcome, a welling up inside his own sense of kindness. 'How can I refuse?'

'Thank you,' she says quietly.

They stare out into the courtyard for a moment, in silence.

'I went to see your mother on Wednesday,' Angela says, watching his reflection in the glass, 'I took the portrait.'

'It's of my Granddad, I do believe.'

'I like your mother, you know? In spite of her prickliness.'

'I suppose that, superficially, she's quite acceptable.'

She frowns, 'I don't get you two at all.'

He draws in breath, looks at his watch, 'I suppose I'd better be going.'

'She mentioned you had lent her a book on Schiele, I didn't realise you were interested in art.'

'I bet she complained about it too, didn't she?'

'Edward?'

He turns; she is staring straight at him. He notices the dark circles under her eyes.

She moves to look away, but then looks directly at him again. 'You do realise what this entails, don't you? I want you to model without clothes.'

The words bounce around the inside of his head. He leans on his stick for support, 'What are you saying?' He hears his voice rise to a wail. 'You can't possibly ask me to do that. Get me a chair. I have to sit down.'

She brings a chair, the comfortable chair. 'Do you want a drink of water?'

'No,' he whispers.

'I'm sorry.' She bends forward, trying to see into his face, 'I thought you realised.'

'I should have, shouldn't I? What a naïve old man you must think me.'

He is overcome by a sudden wave of terrible disappointment. He realises how much he had been looking forward to working with her. Could he still do it? She has a nerve even asking.

'So this is what you had in mind all along, was it? Thought you'd lull me into it gently.'

She kneels down on the floor in front of him. 'You look really pale.'

'I'm not surprised.' He breathes out suddenly, 'What a shock.'

She tilts her head, looks up into his face, 'I just didn't know how to broach the subject.'

'I could model clothed?'

'It might be difficult at first, but then,' she shrugs, 'Most people find it really natural once they've got over their initial shyness.'

'Have you done it?'

'No, but I would, if anyone wanted to draw me.'

'But you don't look like me do you?'

'I told you, didn't I? What I thought. Why I wanted to draw you.' The colour is rising up her cheeks again. 'Come next week. Please?' she begs. 'I'll have a think about it. Maybe we can work something out.'

'Like what?'

'I'm not sure, let's talk about it next week, shall we?'

'Maybe I could just remove certain articles of clothing?'

'Maybe.'

He turns towards her, shading his eyes against the bright light from the window, 'I think I need a strong coffee. Would you like to go for one?'

He sees her hesitate. 'I'd love to,' she says. 'But I'm sorry, I can't.'

He twirls the nub of his stick around on the carpet. He feels suddenly rather let down. It must have shown in his body language because Angela stammers,

'I've spent up, except for my bus fare.'

He smiles. 'Surely you'll let me buy you a coffee?'

She shakes her head, 'I thought I'd stay behind, see if I can get on with some work.'

As he makes his way along the corridor Edward hears the front door clang shut in the distance the sound reverberating back down the corridor towards him, a hollow building he thinks.

Once outside he feels curiously restless and wanders round onto the main street, a street of takeaway outlets. He flicks away a brown paper bag with his stick and notices that the underside of the bag is stained yellow with curry. He enters a charity shop and scans the bookshelves for interesting titles. Looking up, he sees Angela hurrying along the street with a five-pound note clasped in her hand. She enters a newsagent. He waits, and sees her re-emerge carrying two chocolate bars and a packet of cigarettes. He wonders if the cigarettes are for her tutor. She could run an errand for him, and yet she didn't have time to come for a coffee, put him at his ease, talk to him about her outrageous request. '*Maybe we can work something out*'. Fat chance!

He waits for a bus, pulls up his collar to protect him against the wind, and remembers that blustery day when he'd first met her, and that first smile, a secret smile, behind his mother's back.

CHAPTER TEN

Edward sees his mother admiring the blooms outside the flower shop. He watches as she bends forward to catch the scent of the long-stemmed lilies. Today, she is dressed in pale lilac. A light, knife-pleated skirt and a short, boxed jacket. The breeze catches at her skirt, fanning the pleats.

He remembers the heady smell of lilac from his great-uncle's farm, and how the tree would bend and nose its heavy flower in through his bedroom window, just like the cows coming into milk would bend their heads in at the kitchen window, where he would stand to watch, safe from getting trampled. He loved their razor-like haunches, their warm pink udders and their long, sad faces.

'Mother?'

Rachel turns. Under her jacket she is wearing a plain white blouse, and around her neck, her pewter pearls are warming to pink in the sunlight,

'Hello, Edward. I was just admiring these flowers. Aren't they lovely? Look how nature creates such intricate patterns.' She pulls back a petal to reveal the delicate brush strokes of pink fading to white. 'Who could imagine it possible?'

The florist comes to the door and hovers, anticipating a sale.

'We were just admiring the lilies.' Rachel says.

'Would you like some, Mother?' He asks. The florist moves forward.

'No, thank you,' says Rachel. 'I just bought a bunch of early daffs yesterday.'

Edward turns and mutters, 'Mother.'

The florist stares stony-faced. Rachel nods and smiles sweetly, 'Good morning, to you.'

Edward edges her away along the pavement, 'Mother? Why couldn't you just have said yes?'

At the restaurant, they wait by the cash desk to be seated. On the counter is a basket of smooth round mints. Rachel takes one and rolls it in the palm of her hand before popping it into her mouth.

The waiter sees her and laughs, 'I think perhaps Madam is hungry. Will you follow me please?'

The waiter leads them to a small round table by a window. The window is partially obscured by a heavily-draped curtain. He pulls out a cushioned chair for Rachel and, as she sits down, Edward observes how she reaches out to feel the fabric of the curtain.

Edward finds his own chair uncomfortable, he frowns and rubs his forehead, wondering if this was such a good idea, then smiles inwardly to himself, recalling that every time he meets his mother for lunch he has the same thought; Why do I feel the need to continue this relationship?

There is a pungent odour, like burnt rubber. They should have gone somewhere else he thinks, the restaurant seems too busy. 'I don't know that this was such a good idea.'

Rachel smiles and pulls her chair closer, 'Why not? I think it's wonderful.' She glances around. 'Why have you never suggested this place before. Are you all right Edward? You look rather jaded.'

'Pearls, Mother?'

'What?'

'You're wearing your pearl necklace, not your white jade.'

She puts up her hand to grasp the necklace, and laughs at his attempt at humour. 'So I am, but you haven't answered my question.'

I wonder, thinks Edward, where they came from, 'They suit you well, Mother.'

She smiles and nods, 'Thank you.'

'Did Father give them to you?'

She shakes her head and looks scornful, 'No, of course he didn't.'

No, maybe not. Father was not a man to have given a string of pearls. He would have had to accept gratitude, although he was sure his mother would have made it as limited as possible. He was the sort of man who emptied the bin when it was full and put the milk bottles out before anyone else was up; little jobs that didn't warrant gratitude.

'So, Mother. What of the funeral? A strange bunch of people weren't they.'

Rachel beckons the waiter.

'Madam?'

'We need your advice on what to choose. This is our first time in your restaurant.'

'Madam, then we are indeed honoured. Now let me see how can I make it simple for you? We have pasta dishes such as spaghetti and lasagne, or we have meat dishes such as chicken or steak, or fish. We have fresh tuna, or of course we have pizza. There is also calzone, which is like a pizza but folded over like, how do you say, a pasty.'

Rachel scratches her neck, 'Well, they all sound delicious. I think I'll be adventurous and try the last one, the pasty.'

'A wise choice, Madam.'

'Yes.' Edward says, running his eye up and down the menu, 'I think I'll have the same. And can we have a glass of medium white wine and a tonic water with ice and lemon, please.'

Edward looks under the table, 'Mother, did you bring the books back? You didn't, did you?'

Rachel shakes her head, 'I'm sorry. I put them in a bag by the door and then the cat distracted me. Do you want me to bring them to the Library?'

'No.' Edward shakes his head. 'It's all right. I'll just have to remember to renew them. Mind you, I think we have had a request in for the Egon Schiele book.'

'They're welcome to it,' Rachel mutters.

'You didn't like it then?'

'You knew I wouldn't. I told that girl. Grotesque I call it.'

'What girl?'

'Oh, I was looking at it on the bus on my way home. I told her, this girl sitting next to me, why can't he draw beautiful people instead of these grotesque creatures.'

Always, he thinks, she has to have her secrets. Why is he here with her, being lied to as usual, when all he wants to do is sit somewhere quiet and calm his thoughts?

'Sometimes, Mother,' he pauses, 'We have to confront our prejudices.'

As usual, she does not rise to the bait. Instead she picks up a tiny glass vase from the centre of the table and inhales the scent of the flowers – Lily of the Valley.

He gives up, follows her train of thought. 'Do you remember those large round soaps and the foil-wrapped bath cubes I used to buy you for your birthday? Sandalwood? I often wondered how they got a scent from a wood – and French Fern, that was another one.'

'And Lily of the Valley,' she smiles, putting the vase back. 'Don't forget Lily of the Valley. Soap like that was treasured back then.'

'Yes, I remember. Father and I, we were never allowed to use your special soap.'

Edward sees the waiter making his way towards them with their drinks.

'I see Madam is admiring our flowers. My mother grows them in our garden in Italy. She sends me a whole box of them to remind me and my customers of spring.'

'I hope she keeps them in check. They can take over your whole garden.'

'But, Madame,' the waiter bows, 'should you check a thing of such beauty?'

She picks up the vase again, sniffing at the tiny bell-like flowers, 'You know,' she says, smiling at him, 'I think maybe you're right.'

Rachel saws her calzone into bite size pieces but, as she lifts it to her mouth, the cheese stretches like chewing gum and she has to put her fork back on the plate and saw again until, she hopes, it is all untangled.

'This tastes very nice but it's difficult to eat.'

Edward fishes in his jacket pocket, brings out a small brown book. He places it in front of his mother. She puts her knife and fork down at either side of her plate.

'*The Observer Book of Birds Eggs.*' She studies him over her glasses, flicks through the pages, 'What a strange choice.'

'I picked it up in a charity shop,' he says. 'Thought it might be better than getting you another book from the Library. I was looking through it and I thought how exquisite some of the egg markings were.' He shrugs, 'I don't know, I just thought you might like it.'

She looks up, frowning, 'Thank you.'

'You know what struck me?' He smiles. 'The markings and colours of the eggs don't have any logic.'

'Why?' she laughs, 'Would you expect a Robin's egg to be brown and red?'

'Well, yes, something like that. I wonder how a cuckoo changes its egg so that it suits the foster nest?' He shakes his head. 'I'm curious.'

Rachel takes a sip of her wine, tipping back her head as she savours it. Edward stares at her throat and the shadow under her chin. It is dusted with a bright yellow powder. He wants to lean over and with his napkin gently brush it away. But the gesture would be too intimate. He can't ever remember being that intimate with his mother. It has also marked the neck of her white blouse. He leans forward. 'Mother, you've got a yellow neck.'

She puts down her knife and fork and, picking up her handbag, takes out her compact and snaps it open. Lifting her chin she surveys her neck. 'You're right, I have.' She rubs at it with her serviette. 'However did I do that? I know. It was those lilies.' She laughs. 'The florist getting her revenge.'

'And serve you right.'

Rachel snaps her compact shut, 'Well, how strange!' She looks perplexed.

'What is it?' he asks.

'The very same thing happened at Claudette's funeral. The solicitor gave me some lilies to take home, do you remember? Said they were going to waste and when I got home my neck and blouse, the same one,' she says looking down, 'were stained with yellow. How very strange.'

Rachel clutches her new book in one hand and with the other holds the seat rail as the bus hurtles around the roundabout. She does wish the drivers would go slower. The bus comes to an abrupt stop outside the park and sits waiting, engine growling. If he had just gone at a steady pace, she thinks to herself, he wouldn't now have to wait here.

Down in the park the boats have all gone from the lake. A solitary duck disturbs the glass surface of the water, an arrow-like ripple following behind as it makes its way across the lake. She looks closer; a Mallard drake. She could look in her book, see what colour egg the female laid, if only she dare let go of the rail, or she could get off the bus and go and sit on a bench next to the lake. She pings the bell just as the driver has decided to lurch off again. He waits impatiently as she totters down the bus.

Pale green or olive white, what an earth is olive white? *Between eight and fourteen eggs in a nest of grass, vegetation or down, the duck usually covers the eggs with down before leaving the nest.* The original eiderdown.

She smiles to herself and, closing her eyes against the sun, listens to the sounds of traffic on the road above and the children screeching in the play-area. When she opens her eyes, she considers a blackbird in the tree, and wonders what colour egg it has. She consults the book: *greenish-blue, finely speckled with warm brown.* First olive white and now warm brown. She turns the page – Ringed Ousel eggs; *blue-green blotched with rufous.* What a man of strange and fancy words the author must be. And yet, for the Robin he has put... she flicks back through the pages...*white speckled with red,* not: *white blotched with rufous.* She flicks again. Now fascinated, she chuckles at the thought that Edward has got her going. She hadn't told him about the girl visiting. She hadn't wanted to. A white wagtail: *eggs four to seven white or bluish-white thickly freckled with grey or grey-brown.* 'Grey freckles?' When did anyone have grey freckles? And yet for the pied wagtail he has put *whitish covered all over with grey speckles,* the same egg, but a different description.

Pied wagtails. How long is it since she saw a pied wagtail dancing, flicking through the dust and the puddles on the road that led up to her uncle's farm; the dainty little speed run and then the hop and away out of danger from the farm cats. They were always there, even when she had gone to her uncle's funeral they were still there, dancing, waiting, and would they be there now?

She remembers the barn next to the generator, where her uncle kept his guns. He would come back there to skin his rabbits, as deft as any fish-monger. She would watch him by the light from the kerosene lamp. Their secrets. Would they still be hidden there? Or would the walls have been plastered and scrubbed, the past hidden away?

She flicks the pages again. Chaffinch: eggs: *grey tinged with pink and brown blotches*. That's better, more logical. She must tell Edward when next she writes.

Rachel watches a blackbird in the lilac tree. She holds the little brown book in her hand. Thank you, Edward, she thinks. Sometimes I realise you are my son, and not the cuckoo I often supposed.

CHAPTER ELEVEN

It had felt so good being asked to go to the studio, to become a part of something rather than always being on the periphery. How stupid of him. How naïve not to realise that she would expect more than he had ever considered.

He props the wardrobe door open with a chair. The door has always swung closed for as long as he can remember, but it has never bothered him before. He undoes the belt of his dressing gown, a present from his Uncle Ruben; paisley silk in mauves and blues, the paisley teardrop etched in gold, a spattering in the centre. It catches the light from the window, highlighting the many hues and shades like the smooth cut of an opal.

He studies himself in the mirror. His contorted chest, his thin legs, his genitals. He cups them in his hand, lifting them upwards. Redundant, except for that one dismal attempt and yet, as he lets them drop and surveys his reflection, if he were a normal man he would be proud of his manhood. He wouldn't mind anyone seeing him naked. He could strut, shoulders back, his whole body on display like a cock bird. He stands feet apart, watching in the mirror as his genitals swing free.

Why should he be embarrassed about showing them? They are no different from any other mans. He tries to study his back in the mirror but he cannot turn his neck far enough to see. He'd been surprised by Angela asking him to model but, well, maybe he should take it as a compliment. Maybe it had never entered her head that he would be so outraged; that he wouldn't just assume that she would expect him to model naked. For how many years had he longed to be a part of life and now, here was this strange girl – he thinks of her snow dome analogy and smiles – wanting to include him.

How different his life could have been. He could have explored the side of life that he had purposely shut down. He could have followed his dreams, with Uncle Ruben's help, and become an archaeologist. He could have spent his days with like-minded people, delving into the secrets of past generations. He could have bought his own house, instead of ending up lodging in this one room. He sees now how his life has become dusty, hollow; a life fit to mirror his job in the library. He pulls his robe around him and goes to stand by the window. A bus, its engine running, is standing at the bus stop. The driver is reading a paper, a hot drink steaming the window in front of where he sits. A cup of tea, one sugar, he decides. He hates Sunday afternoons.

He couldn't do it, not in a million years. He bangs his clenched fists on the windowsill, not in a million years. But an old echo still resonates: *'You should always face up to your fears. You cannot realise who you are unless you do.'* Oh, how glibly Uncle Ruben had given his advice. How could he know what Edward had to endure? What his fears were? Life, that was Edward's fear. But that was not strictly true. He had tried to face up to life, but it had always hit back. If he had been a bird he would have been pushed out of the nest, a scrawny fledgling eaten by a cat. Sometimes nature made sense, but could a mother bird push her chick from the nest if it were her fault that his bones were twisted and crooked?

She couldn't even bring herself to tell him that Angela had been to visit. That she now had the portrait. Why in God's name did she have to hoard secrets like a squirrel hoards nuts?

He shudders. How had Angela the gall to ask him? Always, in life, just as he thought he saw a door of opportunity opening, it slammed shut in his face.

'If I wanted to draw a tree I wouldn't find the straightest tallest one would I?' It was a good analogy, or so he had thought at the time. But what did it mean, how did she see him. What was a normal tree, an uninteresting tree? Did she see him as interesting, or a freak of nature? Anyway, whatever she thought, it was irrelevant. How could she possibly expect him to model naked? She had no comprehension of what she was asking. None! He had looked into her eyes. No fear, just a frankness, an honesty that he had never encountered before. She was very puzzling. He grasps the lapels of his dressing gown and pulls them together, imagining himself standing there before her naked in the studio, her with a drawing

board in her hand. Would she look, then recoil and turn away? Is that why he is so afraid of standing naked in front of this girl?

'After the initial shyness, you'll find it really natural.'

He shakes his head; she was so young, so thoughtless, so lovely. Could he do it? Let her hold all that power? Stand there in all his vulnerability, her noting his every intimacy? Though week by week, as she built her portfolio, she would become more and more dependent upon him. It could take weeks, months, several months, she'd said. Sitting with her in the sunlit studio every Saturday afternoon for months was so tempting, and yet he couldn't, he didn't have that kind of courage. He so wished he had, but he just didn't, and what would his mother say? But then, he would have his own secret. One that his mother, even in her wildest dreams, could not imagine. He smiles suddenly, in spite of himself. She would be furious.

'You young people, why do you revere the grotesque?'

CHAPTER TWELVE

The yellow of the wild primrose and the trumpet of the daffodil were just showing. Rachel, aged eleven, was staying with her uncle and aunt on their farm. Her mother was nearing her confinement and had wanted Rachel out of the way.

Her aunt had needed to go shopping to the local town, six miles away, and Rachel thought she would be left behind to take charge of Robert, her four-year old cousin and their only child. But her aunt, who had never shown that much interest in her before, decided to take Rachel with her. 'She has a good eye for clothes, even at her age. It must be the Jewish blood that flows in her veins. She can help me select some cloth for my new summer frock.' They hurried off to catch the train.

Chapman's Drapers was a shop as grand as a country house. Rachel was mesmerised by a gilt-framed picture of cherubs floating on clouds that hung on the wall above the stairs.

'Choose some fabrics that take your fancy and I'll roll them out for you so you can get a better look,' the woman with the tape around her neck suggested.

Her aunt chose a cloth patterned with large bunches of poppies. Rachel chose one with a white background, speckled with little sprays of cornflowers. The woman thumped the rolls out onto the counter.

'Which one do you think?' Rachel's aunt asked the assistant.

'I think you should go for the cornflowers – a bit classier.'

'There, I said you had a good eye,' her aunt exclaimed, patting Rachel on the shoulder. 'Jewish blood, shame the family won't accept my Robert has Jewish blood.'

Years later, when they were clearing the house after her uncle's funeral, Rachel found that cloth, still wrapped in the same white paper bag.

When they'd returned from shopping, Uncle Jack was milking the cows. Robert was nowhere to be found. Uncle Jack told them not to fuss, that he would be around somewhere, probably poking a stick into the drain to torment the wild cats.

As evening began to draw in and Robert had still not appeared, Uncle Jack sought the help of his neighbours. They searched until dark and then went out again with Tilley lamps. From her bedroom window Rachel saw them bobbing up and down in the field, filtering the orchard, until finally gathering around the pond.

The edge of the pond was one of Rachel's favourite places. She'd loved to perch on the bank, hidden from the farm. She could still hear all the farmyard noises from there, the smell of diesel that leaked from the fuel tank and the lemon mint that grew around it. Built into the wall from where the water flowed into the pond, was a secret well. Rachel liked to think that she was the only one who knew of its existence. The water was icy cold, clear to the bottom and contained by a single slab of slate. Around the upper arch, moss and pennywort grew.

Rachel heard her aunt let out a scream, and knew that Robert was found.

Next morning, the postman cycled up with a letter from Rachel's father. She had a baby brother – Ruben. Her uncle was in the cowshed milking, his face buried into the haunch of a cow, his shoulders heaving. Rachel went upstairs and packed her bag. She could hear her aunt's sobs coming from the parlour.

She left a note and asked a neighbour to take her to the station. She caught the next train back to Leeds, returning to the back-to-back terrace that was her home, and her new brother.

On her next visit to the farm she'd found the pond turned into a waterlogged ditch. They had drained it whilst looking for Robert's body. Uncle Jack had broken the wall that contained it. The water had swollen the stream that ran through the pig field. The rush of water must have disturbed the layers of mud because Rachel could now see the stones at the bottom.

The ditch remained, becoming overgrown with bulrushes and irises, flowering in clumps of yellow and purple. Rachel would pick some for her aunt, waggling the tough stems back and forth until they broke. The picked irises didn't last long. They would crisp, curl and fade to grey. The timbers of the dinghy which her uncle used to row lay rotting, its paint peeled away. The oars still perched ready for the rower.

CHAPTER THIRTEEN

In the sculpture room, a young girl is chipping away at the head of a stone bust. She looks up and smiles as Edward enters. He hesitates, was this such a good idea? He could still leave. He glances over at the girl, she has returned to her task, her face inscrutable. All these artists, he thinks, they're all the same. Totally oblivious of others, totally involved in their work, but, wasn't he glad of this? Angela would never have had the courage to ask him otherwise. She would have seen how inappropriate it was. She would have seen him as other people did, treated him with kid gloves.

He heads off down the corridor, bonging the rubber end of his stick on the black tiles; saving the white ones for his return. He slows as he nears the studio door, listens for any sounds from within and, hearing none, places his hand on the door handle.

Angela looks up and smiles. She is sitting cross-legged on the floor,

'Hi,' she scrambles to her feet. 'Am I glad to see you.'

'Why?' He comes into the room, walks over to the window. Outside in the courtyard it has begun to rain, 'Did you want to continue our interesting conversation from last week?'

He hears her laugh, nervously.

'Or were you thinking about the pursuance of your art,' he asks.

'That's a big word. I like it: Pursuance.' She rolls it around her tongue.

'So, what have you decided?' He says, still looking out of the window. 'Do you still want to draw me if I keep my clothes on?'

He turns. She is standing in the middle of the room; her shoulders pulled back, her hands grasped behind her back. She grimaces, 'Not sure.'

'Why do you want me to be naked?'

'Good question.' She brings her hands round to the front, interweaving her fingers, 'I suppose the text book answer would be that true beauty lies in the naked form. Dunno – I just know it feels so much more truthful, honest, real.'

'You think you would find true beauty in my naked form?' He queries. 'Wouldn't you draw me like one of Schiele's figures, ugly and twisted?'

'I like his work, but that's not how I want to portray you. You have a different quality, and anyway,' she smiles. 'I don't think you're thin enough.'

'You may find it a laughing matter, but I don't.'

She sighs, 'This is just so difficult for me to put across. Once I get going I'll be able to show you what I mean.'

He notices the light from the skylight is catching in her hair, showing up the places where the black dye is growing away from her crown.

'If it wasn't so important do you think I'd ask?' She pauses, 'Do you think I can't see how difficult this is for you?'

'You mean you'd find someone less cantankerous?'

She smiles, 'I don't really think you are cant... whatever you call it. Underneath all that bluster I think you are actually rather nice.'

'Buttering me up won't work.'

'Shame,' she smiles.

'So, where do we go from here,' he counters. She lowers her head. She is so very young, he thinks, and today for some reason, almost vulnerable. He so rarely sees that in another person. He scratches at some loose putty around the windowpane. He waits to see what she will say next, enjoying her discomfort.

She says nothing.

'I'm going to do it.' He blurts it out. 'I've given it a lot of thought and,' he turns to face her, 'I'm going to do it. I've decided.'

She is astonished, unbelieving, 'You're not kidding, are you?'

'I've never been more serious in my life.'

Her eyes brighten with excitement, 'Thank you, thank you, thank you. I could hug you.'

'Well don't. Let's get on with it before I change my mind.'

'You mean, you want to start today?'

'If I don't, I may not have the courage next week.'

She points to the back wall. 'There's a screen there if you want to undress. I'll just unfold it, then I'll go and get us both a coffee.'

He walks with her across the room, 'So you knew I'd say yes, did you?' he says, nodding at the screen.

'The screen's always been here.'

He looks at her, unsure, 'It wasn't here last week.'

'It was, honest.'

Between them they unfold the screen and stand it in a zigzag position.

'After I left here last week,' he says, straightening the screen, 'I went into the charity shop on the front.'

'I always mean to go in there. Is it good?'

'I saw you coming out of the newsagents.'

She looks up, puzzled, then, 'Oh yeah.' She frowns. 'I remember now. Alex said if I went and got him some fags and choccy he'd let me have a coffee out of his thermos.'

'I got the impression you didn't like him.'

'I went upstairs to get a drink of water and he was just getting his thermos out.' She grins. 'Looked like too good an opportunity to pass up.'

She has her head down, he cannot see into her face to see if she is lying.

'It sounds to me as if you would have had time to come for a coffee. Mind you, I suppose you know where your priorities lie. I suppose it's much more important to keep in with your tutor than with a mere model.'

'It wasn't like that at all,' she retaliates. 'I didn't intend any of that to happen.'

She's never entirely contrite, he realises. 'Did you not think it would have helped me to discuss further what you threw at me last week?'

'I'm sorry, okay?' She looks into his face. 'You're right. I should have come for a coffee. But to be honest, I really didn't know what to say.'

'You were avoiding the issue?'

'Yes.'

He doesn't know whether to believe her or not.

The centre panels of the screen are lined with a thin muslin. He presses the fabric with the tips of his fingers, 'Bit thin this, isn't it?'

'Right. I'm going to go and see if the vending machine's working,' she says, ignoring his last remark. 'How do you want your coffee?'

'White, one sugar please.'

She picks up her purse and makes towards the door.

'Angela?'

'Yes?' She pauses, her hand on the door handle.

'Lock the door on your way out, will you? We don't want your nosy friend coming in, do we?'

He hears the click of the lock. He must do this quickly before he loses courage. No chair behind the screen. How thoughtless. He drags the chair with the metal legs over, noticing there are two chairs with metal legs today. They definitely weren't there last week.

First his tie, always his tie, then his jacket. He pauses at this point and looks at his watch. Two o'clock. What would he normally be doing at this time on a Saturday afternoon? Sitting in his room reading. He thinks back to what had led him to where he is now, here in this room, disrobing for this young woman. He must be crazy. Fear churns in the pit of his stomach and yet, there is a certain power in his chest. It has been entirely his decision. He has lived too long in the comfort zone, his whole life droning on in the same dull fashion. I could have been gentler on myself though, he thinks, taken a less drastic path. He sighs, thinking back to the previous Sunday afternoon, studying his body in the full length mirror, wondering what Angela would make of it. And the promise of endless Saturday afternoons in her company, is that what has lifted him out of his dull world?

He is just undoing the buttons on his shirt when he hears the click of the door.

'It's only me,' she says.

'You're back quick.'

'I thought I'd taken ages. I'll put your coffee on the windowsill until you're ready.'

'It takes me a long time to undress.'

He hears her sit back down on the floor. 'Right. I'll drink my coffee then.'

He sits on the chair behind the screen, still with his trousers on. His knees feel suddenly weak. Come on, Edward, come on. You promised yourself you could do this. He grits his teeth and bends forward to undo his shoes.

He stands behind the screen for two, three, maybe four minutes, leaning on his stick, shivering. She is patient, he will give her that.

'Right, I'm ready,' he says quietly from behind the screen. 'I want you to go and stand looking out of the window while I get myself seated.'

Angela stands up and crosses to the window, 'I'll just close the blind.' She starts to fiddle with the cord. He walks across the room and lowers himself into the chair.

'Can I move yet?' she asks.

'Wait,' he whispers. 'Just give me a moment.' His breathing is shallow. He tries to breathe more deeply but it hurts.

She picks up the coffee on the windowsill and takes a sip, 'Whoops. Sorry, Edward, I've just taken a sip of your coffee.'

'Leave it there for now, will you? I want you to come and sit in your chair, but don't look until I say I'm ready.'

She picks up her drawing board and seats herself, careful to keep her eyes lowered. She selects a stick of charcoal and scratches in the corner of her paper.

'Right,' His voice is a faint whisper. 'Shall we begin?'

As she raises her eyes to look at him over her board, he feels his resolve crumble; his whole being stripped to the bone.

Her voice falters at the look of distress upon his face. 'I'm sorry, I should never have asked you. What have I done?'

Her discomfort gives him strength. 'You forget. It was my decision.'

'Why did you?' She asks.

'I wanted to see if you would be repulsed.' He looks over at her. She is staring down at her board. A slight flicker crosses her face. 'Can I get started please?' Her voice is unusually contrite.

'What about my coffee?'

'Sorry.' She gets up and returns with his coffee, her head still lowered. He takes a sip and then places it on the floor next to his chair. Angela selects a different piece of charcoal and looks over at him.

'Can you lean slightly forward, and rest on your stick? Yes, that's perfect.'

He looks down at the floor, and presses his legs tightly together, hiding his genitals.

She works in silence for five minutes, then. 'Would you like to change position?'

He sits back in the chair, quickly crosses his legs and puts his stick to the side, grasping it with both hands.

She pauses, studying him, the neck foreshortened, shoulders slightly hunched. Only part of his back is visible; the flat side. She can see the protruding part slightly raised above his other shoulder. She feels a slight sense of revulsion, yet an undeniable fascination to look closer.

The tension between them is draining her energy. She wishes she could pack up and go, leave him here frozen in time until next week. She is unsure why she feels like this. She had only half expected him to turn up today and, after his outburst last week, she'd never dreamed he'd agree to be fully undressed. She'd spent all week trying to think through how she could make it work.

She looks down at his crossed legs, at the calf-flesh that is plumped around to the front, pushed forward by the leg behind; the skin pulled taut, catching the light.

She draws until the sun has moved over the vaulted skylight and the room is in shadow. She yawns, and puts down her charcoal. 'Thanks. I think we'll call it a day. You must be tired.'

She stands up, arches her back to release the stiffness and walks over to the window. She pushes her fingers between the vertical blinds and peers out into the courtyard. Behind her, she hears him pull himself out of the chair and stump his stick across the carpet to the screen. She still can't believe he's agreed to it. She wishes she'd been able to accomplish more than she has.

After he is dressed, he asks to see what she has drawn. Reluctantly, she flicks open her pad and shows him the drawings of his lower leg and foot.

'Is that all you've drawn?'

'Yes.'

'I had to get undressed and sit there for an hour so that you could draw my foot?'

'And your leg,' she adds.

'Do you know what it cost me to sit there like that? Do you? Do you know? No. You wouldn't. It would be nothing to you.'

She sees that he is shaking with rage, 'Please Edward, don't be angry. I have to work my way into this. It's uncomfortable for me as well, you know?'

'That's rich,' he explodes.

'It's true. I feel as if…' she pauses, 'well, like shy I suppose.'

'Ha! I'll give you shy. So, next week, you'll be naked as well, will you?'

'What?'

'Have you ever modelled for anyone?'

'No.'

'You don't know the meaning of the word shy.'

'Oh God,' she grasps her hands together. 'I just wish I could make you understand. I felt really awkward. I don't know why. I'm sorry. Okay?'

'I can make you understand how awkward I felt if next week you get undressed.'

'What would be the point of that?'

'Why not? Let you see how it feels.'

She rubs her charcoal stained hands down the front of her jeans, 'Well, where would I wipe my hands for a start?'

He moves toward the door, 'I don't know why I ever agreed to this.'

'Edward? Please don't go like this. Let's at least go for a coffee or something.'

'Oh, you want to go for a coffee this week do you? Won't you be embarrassed to be seen out with an old cripple?'

'Why do you say that?' She uses the back of her hand to wipe her eye.

'I wanted to go for a coffee last week,' he says.

'I'm sorry, but I needed to get some work finished.'

'In pursuance of your art. Seems to me this art is a pretty ruthless bedfellow. Or was it because you had a prior appointment with Alex?'

'I'll see you next week? Please, Edward?'

'And,' he looks at her enquiringly, 'You'll get undressed as well, will you?'

'But, you don't understand.'

'I understand very well.' The door shuts behind him with a sharp crack of wood against wood.

CHAPTER FOURTEEN

Angela is alone in the house. Her three house mates have gone home for the weekend. She should have gone to see her gran today. She ought to have known Edward wouldn't turn up. She had waited in the studio for two hours, doodling, listening for his footsteps, the tap of his stick coming down the corridor. What is she going to do now? Scour the streets for an Edward look-a-like? What made him think he was so special? She could find someone else.

Gran would be sitting there now in her chair beside the fire, watching TV. She could try ringing but she knows she won't answer, not at this time of night. Last time she rang and her gran didn't answer, Angela had gone over just to check she was still alive. She looks at her watch. She could still catch the last train. But no, she feels too fed up. She can still see the doubtful expression on Gran's face in the late evening light.

'Gran? I tried phoning to say I was coming. Where were you?'

'Come in, child.'

Gran had not hugged her in her usual way, but had shaken her head from side to side, tut-tutting under her breath.

'Child, child, what are you doing to an old woman?'

'What, Gran?'

'For one awful minute there, I thought you were your mother.'

'Has she been pestering you again?' Angela asked anxiously.

'Every so often the phone rings in the middle of the night,' she shrugs, 'but nothing else. She doesn't even know her father's dead.'

She sits down on her bed and wonders what to do. She could give Dan a ring, he hasn't been around for ages, see if he'll take her for a pint and a cheap curry but no, she doesn't want to go back to his place afterwards. Grey sheets. She wrinkles her nose. She'd thought sex with him would have been good, him being that bit older. She'd been flattered that he was interested; he mostly ignored the others in her year. She knew that he'd got a girlfriend somewhere down south but that hadn't bothered her. She thought she'd just use him for sex, but it had left her cold. She's not even sure she's that bothered about him anymore, and she doesn't like the way he always snipes about her work either, saying that she is Alex's pet.

Angela opens the sketchpad that earlier she'd thrown on the bed and casually flicks through it. Edward's face stares back at her from the page; drawings she'd done from memory after the first sitting. She is pleased at how she has captured the intelligence and humour in his eyes. She thinks back to the portrait of Richard Appleyard. The eyes are not the same but she has captured a similarity in their character, a family likeness. The next page is a simple quick sketch of Edward. Again, she is impressed by how she has portrayed him. What is she going to do? She must persuade him somehow to continue. She flicks through the pages and, like an omen, his face stares up at her again. She has never felt this much excitement about her work. She has to continue. Shivering, she imagines herself naked, seated there on the orange plastic chair. She could never do it. Or could she? Does he think that she would be embarrassed? Why should she be? She could give the silly old bugger a run for his money, call his bluff, see if he had the guts to go through with it.

Unable to stand the emptiness of her room, she lets it drive her out into the fading light. She walks aimlessly along the quiet pavements, peering into lighted windows; the same television program repeated in nearly every house. Outside the pub a few people are seated around wooden tables, drinking and laughing. She hesitates and then enters. Inside there are fewer people still. With relief, she sees Alex standing at the bar, one eye shut against the smoke of his cigarette.

'Evening' he says, looking up. 'Like a drink?'

She hesitates, 'I'll have a pint of Guinness, please.'

'Sure you don't want a packet of crisps as well?' He empties his loose change out on to the bar. 'Bankrupt me, why don't you?'

'Okay then, salt and vinegar please.'

He laughs.

'Well,' she shrugs. 'You did ask, and I'm starving.'

'How's the work going?'

'Okay, I suppose. I was just going through my folder earlier.'

'And?' He hands the barman the correct change.

'Well, I really like what I've done so far, but my model has decided to throw a wobbler so I might be back to square one.'

'Is she experienced?'

'No, unfortunately.'

He shakes his head, 'Not easy you know if they're not experienced. You have to know how to put them at ease.'

'I tried but,' she pauses, 'she got annoyed because I only drew her feet.'

He places her pint in front of her. 'You don't fancy doing a spot of modelling do you? Me and Felicity, you know her don't you, we're looking for a model.'

She takes a sip of her froth, 'How do you mean?'

'It's a commission from a gallery in London. I've got an idea for a series of drawings and you would be just perfect. I want to use oils and pastels and maybe a combination of other media. I'm really excited.'

'Well, congratulations.'

'Thanks. I'd pay of course.'

'I'm sorry, I can't. I've got too much on.'

'Surely you could fit in a couple of hours, here and there?'

She shakes her head.

'Twenty pounds an hour?'

'Listen,' she says, raising her voice. 'I don't want to. Okay?'

He grins sheepishly, 'There's no need to get aerated.'

She wishes she had the courage to strut out of the pub and leave her nearly full pint of Guinness untouched. He is so out of order. For God's sake, he's her tutor. She picks up her pint and her packet of crisps and without another word goes to sit over by the empty fire grate where he can't see her. Her heart is pounding. Why couldn't she have just said 'no' and left it at that? He had to push the matter, the creep. Although, she thinks, it would give me the perfect opportunity to experience modelling, the chance to practise so that I could beard the lion in his den, so to speak. Edward would never think in a million years that she would agree to his stupid demands.

And another thing, she thinks, taking a sip of her Guinness, Alex has the cheek to go on about me not being adventurous with my work, and there he is getting his knickers wet about life drawing.

She finishes her drink, gets up and goes over to the table where Alex is sitting,

'I'm sorry I got huffy with you. It's just, well, obviously I felt a bit awkward about it.'

He is sitting at a table with a pale woman; skin, hair, clothes, melting into one as if all the colour has washed out of her. The woman looks up, knowing, not knowing, sizing her up. Angela notices pale blue milky eyes.

Alex stubs out a cigarette, blowing the smoke upwards in rings. 'Never had you down as the shy type.'

'I'm not,' She grits her teeth. 'But don't you think it's a bit inappropriate.'

'Your model's thrown a wobbler. Isn't that what you said?'

Angela nods, wondering where this is leading.

'Which is why I suggested you model for me, or for anyone for that matter. You'd be much more in control of the situation if you understood how your model felt.'

She grimaces, 'I don't see why.'

'Then,' he shrugs. 'I suggest that you find yourself an experienced model.'

She stands, arms folded, not sure what to say. I can't change models, she thinks to herself. I have to get Edward back.

'So,' He taps the end of a new cigarette on the table. 'Will you model for me?'

'Why?'

'Because you are perfect. You have exactly the look I need.'

Angela shakes her head. She wants to wipe that smug look off his face. 'No, but thanks,' she adds.

The look of smugness changes to irritation, 'Never mind, some other time maybe. When you've grown up.'

She screws up her face. 'Go to hell!'

She stops on her way home to buy a bag of chips, forgetting the crisps still unopened in her pocket. In her anger, the chips stick in her throat. She throws them into a privet hedge. How dare he talk to her like that? And why had she told him to go to hell when she meant to take him up on his offer? And why had she forgotten to bring up about it being alright for him to do life drawing and not her.

CHAPTER FIFTEEN

'Can I get you anything, Sir?'

Edward had not seen the waitress approaching. He wants to ask her, 'Does Angela still work here on a Thursday?' But instead he orders a coffee.

What would he have said to her if she'd suddenly appeared to take his order? Every Saturday afternoon for the rest of the year, please, and I promise not to lose my temper again?

He's missed two Saturdays now, and he'd only been going for two Saturdays before that, for Christ's sake. It unnerves him to think how quickly she's made a difference to his life. He misses sitting there with her in the studio. The waitress approaches with his coffee. I'll ask her this time, he promises himself. She puts the coffee down and is just walking away.

'Excuse me, Miss?'

She turns, 'Sorry, did you want to order food?'

'Ah, yes. I'll have tuna mayonnaise on brown bread, please.'

'Well done, Edward,' he thinks, as she walks away. Never mind, I can ask her when she brings my sandwich. Outside, the sky is clear. He watches people on their lunch break sauntering past, enjoying the warmth of the winter sun.

She had written him a letter. Not one that Mrs Ingram could examine closely, this one arrived at work. Someone had placed the envelope on his desk; addressed to him, care of the library, scribbled in untidy handwriting.

Edward,

Please don't give up on me. What can I say? I'm sorry. I'm not sure how I could have avoided upsetting you, unless of course I'd not asked you in the first place. If I was insensitive, I am sincerely sorry. I would never intentionally hurt you. To be honest, I was so fed up when you stormed out I just wanted to throw the whole thing out the window but, on reflection, and looking through the sketches, (one of which I enclose) I can't give up on you. We have to carry on. Don't ask me why. I just feel that between us we could produce something really unique. Please Edward, come on Saturday.

Yours,
Angela.

He had read the letter over and over not caring who saw him and then had looked in the envelope for the sketch. It was of himself, standing, leaning on his stick for support. She must have drawn it at their first session while he still had the dignity of his clothes. He'd held it at arm's length. It was really good. No, it was more than that. She had actually captured him. He was there on the paper. He'd tilted his office chair and leaned into it, suddenly feeling so raw. Why was that? It wasn't the girl. He liked her, but that was all. He wasn't in love with her or anything, though she did seem to have pushed open doors that for so long he had managed to keep shut; doors beyond which there was pain, and feelings he didn't wish to confront.

He decided, as he folded the letter and put it carefully back in his breast pocket, that he would go and see her at Henry's that lunchtime before his courage failed him.

He takes a sip of his coffee and looks at the time: 12.30. He rubs the pad of his thumb over the glass of the watch; such a pleasing face, he thinks, a white background, with black roman numerals of almost filigree fineness. The watch had been a birthday present: his first watch. The brown leather strap had worn through after five years but luckily, when it broke, it dropped into his drawer at work. He was always careful after that to check the strap for signs of wear. The watch was irreplaceable. It was one of his few links to the past; to happier times when his father was still alive and he and his mother still had some semblance of a relationship.

He knows the inside of the watch intimately. When he first got it, Uncle Ruben had taken the back off, prising it open with his thumbnail. It flipped open with a ping, like the lid off the shoe-polish.

'I want you to have a look in the back of the watch, my boy,' his uncle had said. 'See all the intricate workings. Then you can really appreciate what the family have bought for your 21st.'

The rubies. It was the rubies that he remembers most, pale as pomegranate seeds.

'Why do they use rubies?' he asked his uncle.

'They don't wear. They'll last you a lifetime.'

And up to now, they had, and he knew that there, behind the face, were the pomegranate seeds, little pinpricks of rubies, making his watch special.

Half way through his sandwich he sees Angela rush past the window. He doesn't recognise her at first. Her face is set hard, making her look older than her years. And she looks somewhat bedraggled. Her clothes are crumpled, her hair uncombed. She is obviously late. He beckons over the waitress,

'Can I have the bill, please? I have to go.' He hands her the correct change and fishes into the breast pocket of his jacket. Just as she turns away he calls her back and hands her the folded sketch. 'Would you be very kind and make sure Angela O'Donnell gets this please.'

She looks at him, curiously. 'You can give it to her yourself if you like, she's just walked in. I think she's out in the back.'

He looks at his watch, 'I'm running late. I'll catch her another time. You will make sure she gets it won't you?'

CHAPTER SIXTEEN

Felicity smiles when she learns that Angela has never modelled before and puts her immediately at ease, 'Take your clothes off and walk up and down a bit.'

Angela looks back at the door. 'What if he walks in?'

'Who? Alex? Oh, don't worry about him. Remember whose body it is.'

Angela likes Felicity, admires her work greatly. She'd bumped into her in the corridor, asked her if it was true that she was looking for a model. She'd let Felicity persuade her into agreeing to model, allowed her to make all the arrangements. Angela didn't want Alex taking any satisfaction from the fact that she'd changed her mind. She starts to peel off her clothes. She feels okay until she gets down to her underwear and then she is suddenly self-conscious and cold. She shivers, wondering what to do next. Felicity is watching her with interest, 'Go on, take the plunge.'

Angela turns away, unhooks her bra from behind, lets it fall down her arms to the floor. She takes a deep breath and, with one slick motion, flicks off her knickers. Crouching, she gathers all her clothes to her and stands up. She turns and stares defiantly at Felicity, daring her to stare back.

Felicity laughs, 'Go on, strut up and down a bit. Loosen up. Get into your skin. Feel comfortable with yourself. You'll soon feel empowered by your nakedness.'

She is right. Angela feels like a ballerina, walking with precision up and down the room and, when Alex arrives, she is already seated and being drawn by Felicity. He doesn't say a word, but sets up his easel and works in silence, studying her from different angles. Angela has to constantly remember to keep still. The very fact of having to stay motionless makes her whole body long to move. Alex had been right, damn him! She'd given little thought to how it would feel to sit still for so long and although she subconsciously knew how defenceless Edward felt, she hadn't really empathised. Oddly though, she doesn't feel vulnerable herself, in fact she feels a sense of freedom, of power almost.

She watches the hands on the clock move slowly around. After an hour, just as the light is beginning to fade, Felicity begins to gather up her things.

'Are you carrying on, Alex?' she asks.

He looks up, irritated at being disturbed. 'Why do you ask?'

'I was just checking. Making sure Angela was okay to keep going, seeing it's her first time.' She glances over at Angela who gives a small nod of her head.

After Felicity leaves, Alex begins to speak to her occasionally, but only to ask her to change position,

'Can you stand, please? Hands behind your back.'

She watches the windows darken further and tries to look at the clock. But she can't see it without moving her head.

'Okay, we'll call it a day.' He looks up and smiles, as if acknowledging her for the first time.

Angela picks up the gown that Felicity had provided. Slipping it on, she walks across the room to the window. The grey pewter of the day is darkening to black. Under the streetlight is a small mound of russet coloured leaves left over from autumn. She can just make out the lines of ink-drawn trees on the horizon, a single-decker bus making its way up the hill on the opposite side of the valley. A magpie squawks on the lawn. Angela searches for the other one.

One for sorrow
Two for joy
Three for a girl
Four for a boy

Alex stands up and crosses the room to join her. She continues to stare out of the window, suddenly very aware that all she has on is the gown.

'It's wonderful up here isn't it?' He says, looking out across the city.

Angela walks back across the room and picks up her dress. She hadn't had time for a shower that morning and as she pulls her dress over her head she can smell the musky odour of her armpits.

She knows that she should feel scared here, alone with this man, but she doesn't. If anything, she feels a strange sense of power.

He watches as she buttons up her dress. She walks over to where he has put his work on the bench, looks down at herself looking up.

'What do you reckon?' he asks.

'I like them.'

'Good. Glad to have your approval.' He takes his coat from the back of the chair.

She's not sure if he is taking the Mick.

'I'm going outside for a fag. I'll walk you home when you're ready.'

'I think I deserve a drink, don't you?' she asks, pulling on her boots.

'You most certainly do. You were sensational.'

She feels her face grow hot, 'What do you mean?'

'You're a natural, girl. A natural.'

Alex buys two pints. Angela sits down at the table next to the open fire. They are the only two in the pub.

Alex draws on his cigarette. 'He was an interesting old bloke you had in the studio the other day, shame everything's got so politically correct.'

'What do you mean?'

'I just thought, oh forget it, it was a stupid idea.'

She breathes a sigh of relief. He'd nearly come up with her idea.

He changes the subject, 'Well, in spite of your reservations, did you enjoy being a model?'

Angela runs her finger round the rim of her glass and sucks off the foam, 'I did, actually. I learnt a lot.'

'I don't know why you were so reticent. Did you think I had another agenda or something?'

Angela can feel herself beginning to blush, 'And don't you?'

'It's about time you decided if you're an artist or not. It's a totally different issue.'

'Always? It didn't stop those Pre-Raphaelites did it?'

'Different era, and the models weren't their pupils, were they?'

'And on that note I think I'll go,' she says and drains her pint.

'Can you manage the same time next week?'

'I don't remember saying I'd sit more than once.'

'Come on Ange, don't let me down, I need you to do this. This is a really important commission for me.' He fishes in his wallet and pulls out forty pounds, 'Here.'

'That's too much,' she protests.

He shoves it across the table towards her, 'No, it isn't.'

'That good, was I?' She smirks in spite of herself.

'See! You're starting it again,' he admonishes, 'Don't dish out what you can't take young lady.'

She stands up. 'How long will it take?'

He takes a sip of his drink, 'I don't honestly know at the moment. My mother's really ill and she's taken herself off to Cornwall with her sister so, instead of having to go to Nottingham to visit her, I now have to go all the way down there.'

'What's she gone down there for?'

'I'm not sure. I think it's got something to do with my Aunt Hilda. The silly old cow's into complementary medicine. I think she's convinced my mother she can find a cure down there.'

'Talking of old ladies,' Angela sits back down again. 'Do you remember an old lady called Rachel who used to model, about three years ago?'

'Who? Rachel Anderson? Yes, I remember her. Why?'

'I met her at a funeral a couple of months ago and I knew I'd seen her before, but for ages I couldn't figure out where. I think she knew, but she wasn't saying.'

'She wouldn't. She's a wily old bird, that one.'

'Does she still model?'

'No, I think she stopped around the time you mentioned. Not sure why. She had a good body.'

'Fancied her, did you?'

'No, but there were some that did.'

'And?'

'I'm not sure. She played her cards very close to her chest, that one.'

CHAPTER SEVENTEEN

Edward stands on the Library steps and wonders what to do with the rest of his lunch hour. It has been a busy morning; it must be the rain, he thinks, bringing people into the shelter of the library. He looks over the tops of the buildings to where the sky is beginning to clear, and then descends the rain-washed steps. He needs a walk to clear his head. Tomorrow is Saturday and he intends to go back to the studio to see Angela. He sighs at the thought and stops to gaze into a shop window, taking little note of the contents. He doesn't have to go back. With the end of his stick he flicks water out of a puddle. This girl has given him a new courage. When she looks straight into his eyes she lends him an inner strength, as if they are both following a predestined course.

It had been different with Tessa. He shakes his head while watching his reflection in the shop window. He'd felt powerless then. He'd been unable to tell her he didn't want a relationship with her. But with Angela, if anything, he feels a new strength. As if they are moving forward together.

He had very nearly married Tessa. Poor, clumpy Tessa! He'd met her on an archaeology holiday. Unfortunately, she'd an aunt who lived in Sheffield. Tessa had suddenly taken to visiting this aunt on a regular basis. He remembered how he finally got the strength to break it off. Ironically, it was his mother who'd helped. She'd written to him and suggested they meet at the Claremont; for some reason they hadn't seen each other for several months. He was already engaged to Tessa by then and, knowing he would have to tell Rachel at some point, had informed her by letter.

They were waiting to be seated for lunch. Edward had ordered Rachel a glass of white wine and she was holding it up to the light coming through the window behind her,

'What is it, Edward?' she'd asked.

'What?' He shook his head.

She looked straight at him then, 'You seem, well... dejected.'

'I don't know what to do.'

'Is it this Tessa woman?'

'Yes,' he said, surprised by his mother's perception.

'Don't you love her?'

'No. No, I don't,' he said, realising for the first time that he had never considered this.

'Then why have you got engaged to her?'

'It's what she wanted.'

'Does it make you happy?'

'No, Mother, it doesn't.'

'Then you'll have to tell her.'

'But I can't. I haven't got the courage. I've tried several times to break it off, but it's like my head thinks one thing, and then I hear myself saying something totally different.'

'Write her a letter then.'

'But that's the coward's way out.'

'Maybe. But it is a way out.'

Edward looked up at his mother who was still peering into her wine glass. He noticed the flap of putty coloured skin that hung from her underarm.

'Write to her. Tell her you don't love her. She'll not bother you again. A woman has no defence against such honesty.'

He had written. And then... silence. Wonderful, blissful, silence that filled all the voids in his life that she had tried so hard to fill.

Edward is just climbing the library steps when the rain begins. He must write to his mother, he thinks, and arrange another lunchtime meeting. He stands in the doorway and watches the precipitation. He loves the rain. Sometimes he wishes it would always rain. Then he could just get on with his everyday life and never have to think whether he should be out in the fresh air or not. He could just sit reading. All day, every day.

When he was a child, his father made him go out to play whenever it was fine. It irritated him to see his son reading a book. The worst days were those when it had been raining all day and then, at about four o'clock, just as he was really settling down with a book, out would come the sun and he would be thrown into the street to be savaged by Paul O'Grady and Andrew Winters. Edward felt it would have been better if he'd gone out to play when it was raining. At least then he would have enjoyed the rain coursing down his neck, splashing in the puddles and, best of all, the excitement of the thunderstorm and the strange, green, tension in the air. Andrew Winters use to call him a wimp, but Edward never saw him playing out when there was a thunderstorm.

Edward sees him sometimes. He doesn't think that Andrew recognises him, or at least he doesn't acknowledge him if he does. He works for the council, digging holes in roads. Edward can't begin to imagine the misery of such a job, the mind numbing noise of the drill, the cold in winter, the heat in summer, limping from one tea break to the next and that fusty taste of thermos tea. He's felt like that himself sometimes, like a drone, especially when he was with Tessa. There had been no part of his life that he'd felt was his own.

Edward often wondered why Tessa had chosen him. Did she think he would be grateful? That there would be no risk of him refusing her proposal? By now she'd probably latched on to someone else.

One night she had come to his lodgings, determined, as he found out later, to have sex. It was the only time. She must have planned it earlier. He didn't know how she knew Mrs Ingram would be out. She went to the toilet and when she came back she was stark naked.

Edward was so shocked he just stared. He'd never seen a naked woman in the flesh before. Her breasts were quite beautiful; her nipples like the rubber ends of pencils; the area around them a darkened pink. But her skin was mottled and blotchy, and two rings of overlapping fat encircled her belly. He'd wondered why there were two rolls and not just one large one.

She'd seated herself next to him on the sofa, taken his hand and then tried to kiss him on the mouth. It all felt very strange. He'd noticed that there were cat hairs on Mrs Ingram's chair.

'Shall we go upstairs?' She'd said. 'I'm getting cold down here. Don't worry, I've brought some Durex.'

He wanted to say, 'But what if Mrs Ingram comes back?' But he hadn't. He'd just followed her upstairs and allowed her to remove his trousers like he was still a little boy. There had been a space, an absence of intimacy between them, which made it feel like he was at the doctors, especially when she tried to give him an erection.

It hadn't worked and they went back downstairs, thankfully before Mrs Ingram returned from bingo. He shuddered to think of the mileage she would have got out of that. Hanky-panky! That's what she'd have called it. Little did she know.

He shakes his head to clear the cobwebs, and makes his way back down into the archives.

CHAPTER EIGHTEEN

Angela turns over in bed. She wishes now that she had not opened the window in the middle of the night. The noise of the traffic is disturbing her. It is raining and the water splashing off the tyres makes a low swishing noise. She is replaying in her head the conversation she had with Jenny, another waitress at the restaurant.

When she'd come on duty that day, Jenny had handed her the sketch of Edward. Angela had been puzzled as to how Jenny should have come by it.

'An ol' bloke asked me to give it to you. He'd got sort of a hunched back and he walked with a stick.'

'That's a bit rude, calling him a hunchback.' Angela had felt suddenly defensive of Edward. 'He is a human being you know.'

'Sor-ry. For Christ's sake, I was only trying to help.' She'd turned away. 'Take your own messages in future.'

Angela grabbed her arm. 'Look, I'm sorry. Just tell me what happened, please. Was he angry?'

'No.' Jenny looked at her strangely. 'Why should he be? He was fine, pleasant as pie. He came in, had a coffee and a sandwich, then he asked me to give you that.'

She nodded at the sketch that Angela had refolded, 'I told him you'd just arrived but he said he couldn't wait.'

Throughout her shift, Angela puzzled over the return of the sketch. She examined the paper to see if he'd written a note, nothing. Did it mean he wanted to carry on or not?

She leans out of bed, eyes still closed, and picks up the clock from the floor. It is 12:30. She is supposed to meet him at 1 p.m.

'Shit, shit, shit! I was going to be early today in case he turned up. Jesus!' She sits on the edge of her bed and drags her hair to the top of her head, drawing it back from her forehead. She observes herself in the mirror. The black dye is fading. She'll have to give it another rinse... when she's got time.

She picks up an ethnic-style skirt from the floor and steps into it. On the back of the chair is a woolly jumper, with a tee shirt still inside. She slips it over her head and quickly peruses herself in the mirror. The jumper, which she got from Oxfam, has become matted and all the colours have blurred together. The sleeves have also shrunk. She tugs at them but to no avail. She grabs her bag and slips her feet into her unlaced boots.

Angela has just missed her bus. She knows what her gran would say if she could see her now. '*If you'd done those laces up properly, you could have run for the bus.*'

She grits her teeth. Why do bus drivers have to be so nasty? He'd seen her, waited until the last minute and then driven off.

A blind man at the bus stop moves forward. He can hear a bus and sure enough, around the corner comes a green one. When they reach the next set of traffic lights, one car has run into another. The car behind has only slightly dented the bumper of the car in front but the drivers are arguing in the middle of the road as if it's a major incident. The bus driver leans his elbows on the steering wheel and watches the performance. Should she get off and walk? She is not going to mess it up this time. She will do whatever he wants: be naked, bring him a box of chocolates every week, anything to keep him sweet.

Angela can hear her gran's voice again,

'*If you had water in your head, there'd be steam coming out your ears.*'

Why does everything go wrong when she's in a hurry? She gets off the bus and runs as fast as she can in her unlaced boots, still gritting her teeth.

Her watch says 1:10 p.m. 'Please Edward, be there.' She comes round the corner. He is not waiting outside the door. She slows down. Shit! What if she's missed him, but what if he never intended to come? She leans against the door trying to get her breath. It's then that she sees him, thank God. He is standing in the middle of the small curved footbridge that crosses the river and he is looking down into the water.

She walks over and stands by his side. 'I'm really sorry I'm late.'

He looks up and, to her surprise, she sees his face soften.

Angela groans and puts her head in her hands, 'I've no excuse. I slept in. Woke up at 12.30. Jumped out of bed, threw some clothes on and came straight here. And of course, I had to miss a bus, and when I did get one, there was a traffic jam. So that's why I'm so bloody late.' She stops for breath.

'Yes, you do look a little dishevelled.' He looks her up and down. 'Tell me, what are you late for?'

'What do you mean?'

'I didn't know we'd arranged to meet today.'

He is looking down into the water, but she can see just the corner of his mouth twitching.

'Good job I interpreted your weird message correctly then, eh?'

He looks up and laughs, 'I don't know what you're getting at.'

'Yes, you do.' Angela bows her head and realises how at ease she feels with this man, 'Thanks for waiting.'

'For what?'

'Oh, shut up.' She nudges his shoulder, and they stand looking down into the water. Under the road-bridge further up, some ducks are feeding on chunks of white bread.

'Do you still want me to,' Angela pauses, 'I mean, get undressed too?'

He searches her face and then shrugs, 'What do you think?'

'That's right,' she laughs. 'Play it back into my court. Well if that's what it takes, then I'll go along with it.'

He nods. 'It really means that much, me modelling for you?'

'Christ, how many times do I have to tell you? And besides,' she bites the inside of her cheek. 'Bastard-features said something to me the other day that got me thinking.'

'Who?'

'Alex. He said, or words to the effect, that if you really want to draw someone well, you also have to learn to be a model. Not that I don't think he's got ulterior motives,' she mutters.

'And me? Do you think I've got ulterior motives?'

'No, of course not. Why should you?'

He laughs, as though in disbelief, 'I suppose it's escaped your notice that I also happen to be a man.'

'You know what I mean,' she says crossly, 'You're not a creep like him.'

'So, on that note, shall we go in and get started, or shall we see if we can get a coffee on the front and discuss the matter further?'

CHAPTER NINETEEN

The house was quiet. Rachel's aunt had gone to bed. Her uncle was still out rabbiting. Picking up the enamel candleholder, Rachel tiptoed along the polished floorboards of the landing and up the stairs to the attic. The moonlight shone in through the skylight. Under the eaves she could see the black form of the trunk, her treasure trunk. She put her fingertips on the edge of the lid and tried to lift it. It didn't move. She placed the candleholder on the floor and used both hands to tug at the lid. Still it would not open. She picked up the candle. A padlock had been secured around the latch.

She sat down on the floor, pulled her knees up to her chest and shivered, rocking gently back and forth. What was she to do? Her head said one thing, her heart another. For the necklace, she would go to meet her uncle in the barn, let him 'service her', as he called it. But it was not only for the necklace. She wanted again to feel the sensations she'd felt that afternoon, to see if the feelings became stronger, more intense; an unbearable electric current feeding through every nerve end.

Rachel put her hands inside her nightdress and held her breasts in the same way her uncle had. They were surprisingly heavy, the flesh yielding to the shape of her hand. All these years, and she never once thought, until now at nineteen, to hold them that way. She moved her hands down and pressed hard with her knuckles into her belly, rocking back and forth. Opening her legs, she fondled for the first time in her life what her mother called her 'secret place'. She tugged at the slippery flesh, trying to ease away the strange, aching sensation.

Rachel took an old paisley dressing gown from the hook at the back of her bedroom door and blowing out her candle went quietly down the uncarpeted stairs. The slate of the kitchen floor was cold on her feet. The mother cat lay asleep on her aunt's chair by the Rayburn. The moonlight caught the cutlery laid out on the table for breakfast. At the back door, she slipped her feet into her aunt's Wellington boots. As she walked across the yard, the rims scratched against her bare calves.

'You came, then.' He didn't lift his head. He was bent over a kerosene lamp, his dog sitting patiently by his feet.

'What are you doing?' she asked.

He held up a limp rabbit. Rachel watched as he laid it on the bench, its white belly slashed from head to toe. He peeled back the fur, paring with his sharp knife. The flesh was a pale pink, little blood, mostly just flesh sculpted around delicate bones.

'Why no blood?' she enquired.

'I hang 'em up to drain first. It's just the carcass left now.'

He picked up an old rag, wiped his hands and turned, catching at her hand as he did so. He nodded towards the straw in the corner. The collie bitch whimpered.

'My! You're a fine sight in your wellies and night-dress.'

'Uncle?'

'Shush, sit down.'

He pulled off her Wellington boots, first one and then the other.

Rachel's aunt put her head round the bedroom door, 'Come on Rachel, get up, what a sleepyhead you are this morning.'

Rachel awoke with a start. 'Coming,' she mumbled.

She stretched, clawing her toes round the metal bedstead. She placed her feet on the pink linoleum, stood up and lifted her nightdress over her head, stretching full length as she did so. She caught sight of her small, slightly rounded belly in the dressing table mirror and, breathing in, pressed her hands hard against it. She bent over and peeled herself apart; looked over her shoulder, staring, fascinated, for the first time at her raw pink flesh. The hair around it was encrusted with blood.

'Rachel!' Her aunt shouted from the bottom of the stairs.

Her uncle was seated at the breakfast table; half a fried egg lifted to his lips.

He put it into his mouth and nodded.

'Morning, Uncle.'

Her aunt was placing a bowl in the Rayburn. 'Rachel, you are a slow coach this morning. Have you forgotten it's washday? Now hurry up. I want you to set up the mangle.'

'Let the girl eat her breakfast in peace, for God's sake.'

'There's a letter for you,' said her aunt, fishing into her apron pocket. 'Think it's from your mother.'

Rachel used her clean knife to slit the pale blue envelope

23 Green Mount St,
Leeds,
May 27th 1943
Dear Rachel,

Just a short note to say that we expect you home on Friday the 3rd. Catch the 10 o'clock train. I want you to help spring clean before you go back to work on the Monday. Your father is very busy making outfits in time for Whitsuntide.

I hope you have been a good girl and helping your aunt, and not had your nose buried in a book at every opportunity.

Give my best wishes to your aunt and uncle. I hope they are in good health.

Love,
Mother

Rachel waited for the train. The brightly coloured posters in the waiting room showed happy smiling families off to the coast, the children with bucket and spade. The colours were so bright they gave the scenes a strangely nostalgic feel. Like a mid-day August sun that gives little shadow.

The door opened. It was her uncle. He took off his cap. 'Here lass, I've brought you these. Take good care of them now and keep them from your mother's prying eyes.'

Rachel removed her hat and shook out her black hair. She took the pouch from her uncle's hands and pulled open the drawstring neck.

Inside, coiled like a snake, were the pewter pearls.

He winked, and was gone.

CHAPTER TWENTY

Edward goes behind the screen and hooks his stick over the frame. Angela begins to undo the pearlised buttons on her black cardigan. She swallows hard, and wonders why, last week, standing on the bridge over the river, she had agreed to this bizarre arrangement. She peels off her clingy trousers and hesitates, thinking for a moment to keep her knickers on, then slips them off and hides them under her trousers. She sits down quickly before Edward comes out from behind the screen. She'd thought the session with Felicity and Alex would have made her feel more relaxed, but this feels different. She waits, remembering what he had said last time about taking a long time to get undressed. He must be nearly finished. She tries to detect his shadow behind the screen. He seems to be seated, 'Are you okay behind there?'

She hears the chair scraping back, him standing up, his voice: 'Are you ready?'

She shakes her head in disbelief. He is checking to see if she has kept her part of the bargain. 'Yes. I've been ready ages.'

He makes his way, eyes lowered to the floor, to where he thinks the chair is. To raise his head and look around is always a conscious decision, she notices. He will pause like an animal suddenly smelling danger, then lift his head and swivel it from side to side.

He comes to a standstill under the skylight, looks around for the chair. He is doing his best not to stare directly at her. The fact that she has also removed her clothes seems to have unnerved him even further. Good. She is glad. Sensing that he will not look up unless she asks him to, she observes him without trepidation

It is as if a sculptor, modelling him in clay, has bunched his ribs to one side and moulded them into a peak to form the distortion to one side of his back. She sees how he wields his stick like a cloak, hiding behind it; scrunching his body around the familiar.

'Edward, could you put down your stick?' She was also going to say, 'and rest your hands on the back of the chair,' but hesitates. For him to do that, she will have to get up and move the chair into position.

Startled, he lets the stick clatter to the floor. To steady himself he has to put his legs slightly further apart, allowing his genitalia to hang free. She sees a look of anger flicker across his face, but he does not speak.

She begins to sketch his profile. His jaw line is still firm but the tension in his cheek seems to have slackened. The mouth, she notes, is quite full for a man of such lean features. She studies his back, thinking how she would love to mould her hands into the gnarled and woven shape of his bones.

After five minutes she hears him quietly say, 'Have you nearly finished? I can't keep this position much longer.'

She is just drawing his shoulder line, trying to weigh up the uneven perspective, the one shoulder higher than the other. If he can keep still a bit longer, 'Whatever you do, don't move yet. I'm at a really crucial point.'

'I need a chair, NOW!'

She looks at him, he has moved position. 'For Christ's sake,' she says it under her breath. 'Can't you keep still for just a second longer?' She looks down to the drawing. Damn!

'My stick,' he gestures towards the stick on the floor.

She stands up and, holding her board in front of her, retrieves his stick.

'Chair,' he says, rudely.

As she walks over to the window to get his chair, she knows his eyes are on her. Suddenly she feels self conscious, even more so when she hears him say, 'A body of perfect curves.'

She sits quickly back down, trying to hide the lower part of her body behind her board, and laughs nervously, 'I'm supposed to be the observer here.' She half covers her breasts with her arms wondering how long it will take her to feel less inhibited.

'I'm sorry. You didn't mind me saying that did you? I meant it purely as a compliment, as a fellow observer of the human body.'

She cocks her head nervously, uncertain of his remarks, unsure how to play it. She goads him, 'Okay then, tell me what you see?'

'Your skin is like milk, as the saying goes, but milk is not really the right word. Perfect as a button mushroom.'

He seems pleased with himself, though she had thought to disconcert him. 'Good, go on.' I sound like a teacher, she thinks to herself.

'The bones in your neck and your collar-bones are carved and honed out of a seasoned piece of cherry wood and,' he pauses, 'your breasts are perfect.'

'That's not a description.' She instinctively wants to bring her board up to cover her front.

'No, I know. Let me think. I never knew that a body could have so many exquisite shapes. Like dough plumped and rising. Sorry, I can't think of a better metaphor.'

She can feel herself beginning to blush. He's good at description, she'll give him that. 'You make it sound as if perfection is the only true beauty.'

'Isn't it?'

'No. I think perfection can be rather boring.'

'Would you rather have a body like mine, then?'

She pulls her face into a wry smile. Whatever she does, she mustn't upset him this week.

'You haven't answered my question,' he says.

She wishes he was a dummy that she could just put into whatever position she wanted and leave him, and not have to listen to him banging on.

'Of course I wouldn't,' she says, 'but I'd rather draw your body than mine. Now can I get on?'

'That's a bit of a cop-out isn't it?'

She puts down her charcoal and stares at him. She wishes she could bite her tongue, but she can't. 'Would you like me to be dishonest? Would you like me to say: Oh, it must be so interesting having a body like yours?'

'Now you're being patronising.'

'I'm not. I'm being truthful.'

'Are you?'

'Look. I surrender. Okay? I don't know what to say.' She sighs, 'Now can we get on?'

'How would you like me to sit?'

She narrows her eyes, studies him long and hard. 'In the most uncomfortable position I can think of.' She smiles then, 'But unlike you, I think I'll take pity, just this once. Adopt whatever position you want.'

'Miss, you're so considerate.' He takes a mock bow.

She laughs and shakes her head, 'And here was me thinking you would be so meek and mild.'

'Like a cripple should be.'

'For Christ's sake!'

He puts his hand up to his mouth, 'I'm sorry, it's my favourite occupation, making people feel uncomfortable.'

'Well, you've certainly had plenty of practise.'

'I've got an awful feeling I may have met my match.'

She shakes her head, 'Now, do you think you could adopt a position – and shut up?'

He pulls his feet in under the chair and places his hands in his lap, covering his genitals.

She looks at the position he's adopted and smiles, 'Shy, are we?'

'Don't get me started again.'

'Sorry, sorry.'

'While you're drawing me, describe how you see my body.'

She wishes he would just be quiet but she'd better humour him, this week anyway. 'Mmm, let me think.' She narrows her eyes. 'I know this may sound slightly odd but your body has a foetal shape about it, as if you are still all curled-in trying to protect the centre. Your skin has a slightly yellow, slightly gingerish tinge to it; maybe that's the freckles. The way your bones have formed on your back gives you,' she hesitates. 'I don't know really. I just want to smooth it, make it look less vulnerable.'

'Now who isn't giving a proper description?' He says quietly.

'It's very difficult, there aren't any ready-made words to describe it, so let me think. Like, like the middle of a pie, you know, where the china bird is put to support the pastry, but the pastry still pulls downwards.'

He laughs, 'What sort of pie is it?'

'Best steak, of course, with plenty of gravy.'

'Do you like it?'

'What?'

'My china bird.'

Is she, she wonders, getting into dangerous territory again?

'You do ask some very demanding questions.' She wrinkles her nose, 'Do I like your china bird? Yes, I suppose I do, but it's a bit like asking if I like your face. It's just another part of your body.'

'Thank you, thank you for that.' he says, quietly.

She sees that, for once, she has said the right thing. 'Do you want me to go on with my description?'

He nods.

'Your limbs,' she frowns, 'are a bit thin, the flesh is slightly wasted, I think you're lacking a bit in muscle tone.' She looks up and sees that he is amused by her awkwardness. 'Doesn't it upset you, me saying these things about your body?'

'No. It's such a novelty to have someone actually looking at me.'

'You have good hands,' she continues. 'Strong, clean, elegant hands. Strange how even your body hair is tinged with ginger.'

He looks directly at her, 'Why do you dye your hair?'

'Don't you like it?'

'What colour is it, really?'

'A sort of mousey blonde.'

'I think your natural colour would suit you better.'

'I don't know why I dye it, really.'

They fall into silence. The charcoal scratches across the textured paper, drawing the squareness of the shoulder line, the short neck jutting forward, the upper arms. She is really pleased at how her work is developing.

Four sketches later, she puts down her charcoal. Her automatic response is to stretch but, she smiles to herself, today she feels inhibited by her lack of clothes, 'Okay,' she says. 'Shall we call it a day?'

Angela doesn't leave with Edward. She had intended to, but at the last minute realised that she had forgotten to spray her work with fixative. She unzips her portfolio case and lifts out the charcoal sketches she has done that day. She props them up against the window and rattles the can. At last she is getting somewhere. She can feel the whole thing beginning to build into something tangible. She studies his face, his chin cupped in his hand. He has discovered that if he does this, and speaks through closed teeth, he can hold a conversation without getting told off.

It is a nice face, a clever face. She is surprised. She has never thought of Edward's whole face in any context before now. It is the eyes, and that dry mischievous humour that she trips over time and time again. It's almost sexual, she thinks. But no, she shakes her head; don't be stupid, he's an old man. She'd imagined that the sessions with Edward would be long and arduous but instead, apart from when he's being annoying, they have become afternoons of unrelenting banter.

CHAPTER TWENTY-ONE

Claudette's house was a cottage, not a semi like the other houses that her Gran cleaned, or a brick terrace like the one she lived in with her grandparents, but a real cottage, built of stone in a little village caught between the city and the moors where, if you stood at the front gate and looked into the distance, you could just make out the motorway that snaked across the Pennines.

They caught two buses to get there. As Angela grew older she would sometimes wonder why her Gran went to all that effort twice a week, when she could have easily got another cleaning job locally. She loved going there too, but she hated the journey. She'd asked her gran once, while they stood waiting in the cold for the second bus,

'Gran, do we have to go today.'

She'd put her arm round Angela's shoulder and hugged her into the warmth of her old grey coat with its smell of cabbage and fried food.

'What questions you ask, child.'

Angela asked again, once they were safely seated on the bus, 'Do you like going to see her, Gran?'

'Yes, I do. She's very special, our Claudette. She's not like the others; she treats me like a person.'

Her gran had been visiting Claudette since long before Angela was born. She didn't take Angela with her until she was nearly five. Before that, she left Angela with Mrs. Ramsbottom who had lived next door. Angela hated going there and begged her gran to take her with her to Claudette's. Eventually, she relented. At least she wouldn't have to owe Mrs Ramsbottom any more favours. The first time she went to Claudette's, Angela skipped down the road past Mrs. Ramsbottom's house. She was free at last of old dog smells, patterns, the wallpaper, carpets, curtains, even the woman herself. Once she broke a vase and there were harsh words.

Afterwards Mrs Ramsbottom tried to engage her in conversation, but Angela remained silent; it was her only armour against this woman and her ridicule.

'What's the matter, cat got your tongue?' She would pinch Angela's cheek hard and laugh.

Her gran would have been horrified if it had ever occurred to her that by taking Angela to Claudette's house, she was leading her grand-daughter down the same path as her mother and into a world of images and colour.

At first Angela was frightened of the old French lady, who must have been of similar age to her gran. There was a peculiar musty smell about her, like the scent of damp cellars. She always wore black; even her stockings were black. Wisps of wiry hair protruded from her chin and when she spoke, Angela at first found her difficult to understand and could only nod in answer to her questions. While her gran cleaned, the old woman followed her from room to room, engaging her in her low, heavily-accented voice. Angela would be seated in a worn armchair, with her crayons and pad, trying to avoid the horsehair that poked through the bald patches and scratched at her bare legs. She remembers vividly the first time she went. She sat the whole time copying a picture hung on the wall. It was of a man with a funny hat. Claudette had come to stand behind her, and then she had called her gran.

'Elsie? Come here quickly. Have you seen this?' She took the pad from Angela and showed it to her gran. 'You never told me she could draw.'

Her gran had shrugged it off, 'Oh, she's always drawing.'

Claudette asked her if she could keep the drawing. Angela thought it strange as she already had the original, but she gave it to her. The next time she went it was framed and hanging on the wall beside its bigger brother. It was the first drawing she ever had on show.

The cottage was over three hundred years old so the walls were very thick. Next to the chair where Angela sat, a small window was tunnelled out of the stone. A fish tank containing hundreds of tiny, silver-bellied guppies filtered the light from the window. The flash of their bellies captured that light and illuminated the whole space. It made Angela feel that she herself was inside the tank. She drew many pictures of it over the years. When she was about ten, Claudette asked if she could keep the fish drawing she had done that day. Without telling her, Claudette entered it in a National Competition. It won first prize. She could have gone to London to collect it but instead she received a certificate through the post and a cheque for twenty pounds.

One day when they visited there was a book on the chair arm and, as Angela sat down, she accidentally knocked it onto her lap. She opened the book carefully and started to turn the pages from back to front. It was an art book. All the drawings were in fierce, black, charcoal lines. Gypsy people; old men with hooked noses and rings in their ears, laughing women with large calves and thick forearms, urchin children with bare feet and shaven heads.

The next time Angela visited, she plucked up the courage to ask Claudette, 'May I please look at the book of Gypsy people?'

The old woman had seemed surprised, and then slightly irritated.

Her Gran scolded, 'Don't go pestering Madame Mason, Angela. What have I told you about behaving yourself.'

Claudette pulled the book from the shelf. 'No, no, no. Perhaps it is good she is interested.'

Whenever Angela visited after that, she waited until her Gran and Claudette had left the room and then she would pull the book out herself. Occasionally, Claudette would catch her with it, but she would only smile conspiratorially and shake her head. One day, while Angela was looking at the photo of the artist, a man with thick, black-rimmed spectacles and white sprouting hair, she noticed that under the photo was some writing, most of which she couldn't make out except for the name - Claudette.

'Excuse me, Madame Mason. What does this say?'

Claudette took the book from her and put it back in the shelf. She pulled out a bigger book of coloured drawings.

'I think it is time you look at a different book, don't you?'

'Excuse me, Madame. Is this by the same artist?'

Claudette laughed, 'No, child. This artist is called Degas. When you get tired of this book I shall choose another for you.'

Over the years, Angela studied all the art books on Claudette's shelves, but always the book of Gypsy people was her favourite. When she began to study art seriously, she found she had a penchant for charcoal, smudging life into her models with the hard, brittle stick and the soft pad of her finger.

CHAPTER TWENTY-TWO

Angela has placed the chair sideways and asked Edward if he could manage to sit on it cowboy-style, with his arms resting on the back of the chair. She can now see only one shoulder and one side of his back. The profile jutting up like a folded elbow.

'Edward, how did it happen?'

'What, my back you mean?'

'Have you always had it?'

'I just woke up one morning and there it was, like I'd started to grow wings, or a wing at least.'

She looks up, startled for a minute, and then laughs. 'Is that why you are such a wise old bird?'

'Am I allowed to laugh?'

She is drawing his neck, the shadow under his jaw reflecting onto his shoulder like the smooth curve of a pebble.

'As long as you don't move and as long as you tell the truth.'

'Have I always had it? It seems like it. I can't look at pale green without thinking of hospitals. All my childhood pulled first one way and then another, trussed and bound so I had to walk like the Tin Man.'

'So, what caused it?'

'I know this may sound strange, but I'm not quite sure. My mother says it was polio, but I think I've always had a problem with my back. It suits her better to think it was polio, then she doesn't have to take the responsibility for producing something like me.

Angela shakes her head in disbelief. Whatever had his mother done to him to make him hate her so much? 'Jesus! Edward. Why are you so hard on your poor mother? You must know whether you had polio or not?'

'Yes. I did. I caught it when we went to Mablethorpe for our holidays when I was six. I remember being in a hospital room all on my own, and my parents looking at me through a glass window.

When I returned to school I felt like a leper. For a long time no one would talk to me or even sit next to me – which is probably why I became a loner. I wasn't really trussed and bound, but if I had been I might not be like this now. My back started to go when I was in my early teens.'

She stands up and moves round behind him, studying his body, trying to find what it is that draws her instinctively to the deformity. Then she has it.

'It's balance, you know,' she says out loud, without meaning to. 'That's what draws the eye.'

'How do you mean?' he asks.

'Well, we're used to seeing two halves of a body that are almost a mirror image of each other. So if they're not, we find it shocking or slightly disturbing, depending on how severe the difference is.'

'So you're saying that if I had a matching hump it would be acceptable?'

'I wonder, we could try it. Stuff some towels up your jumper.'

'Don't you think I'd look like a camel?' The side of his mouth is twitching.

She starts to laugh, 'Maybe more like wearing a rucksack.'

'I think I'd prefer the camel.'

'Okay, camel it is.' She is surprised at how relaxed she feels this week; last week seems to have broken the ice. 'You know, Edward, don't take this as an insult, but you're really comfortable to be around. There aren't many men, or women, who I could sit naked in the same room with and still feel comfortable.'

'That's because I'm a cripple.'

'Sometimes you can be so cruel, you know?'

'Yes, I know. I enjoy it. It's one of the few ways I can have power over other people. I don't do it often though, do I?'

She looks at him, 'No, just all the time.'

She is circling him, looking for a new angle. She sketches quickly the line of his neck, the way his ear lobe joins his head, the top of his hair, the way it spreads, ginger-tinted, slicked across his scalp where it thins at the crown, the little gnarl right at the centre. Like a small boy.

'What are you doing now?'

'Quick sketches of different angles.'

'What? On the same sheet of paper?'

'Yes, it creates a good effect.'

'I feel like a rabbit with a bird of prey hovering,' he says.

She sits down, puts her drawing board on her lap and smoothes her hand across the paper. She concentrates on her work, does not respond.

Edward stares at her in wonder, sitting in front of him, entirely naked yet so at ease. But then, remarkably, so is he. After the first session, when he'd been frozen with fear and cold, he'd begun to relax. When she first removed her clothes he'd felt an initial shyness, but also a certain feeling of power at being able to observe her. Admittedly, not in quite the same way as she had been able to observe him. At first he had been careful to glance only fleetingly. Her body had seemed so unexpectedly human. So vulnerable, like his own. She is still staring down at her drawings, as if in a trance.

'Are you pleased with them,' he asks.

She stands up and tilts herself and the board forward, displaying to Edward her charcoal sketches. He notices the under-flesh of her breasts pressed plump against the board; voluptuous, the word comes into his head. He is filled with a sense of delicious mischief. He is so tempted to put out his hand and lift her right breast from the board, where he is entranced to see it touches against a drawing of the side of his neck.

Angela lowers the board, 'I might even be tempted to give these a colour wash, if I can manage to get enough done that is. I'm not really feeling in the mood today.' She puts her hand to her belly, 'God, I'm hungry.'

"Haven't you had any lunch?'

'No. Nor breakfast. Woke up late.'

'You're good at doing that, aren't you?'

She laughs. 'Yes, but I have a good excuse. I wasn't out partying last night, I was working.' She moves round behind him.

'What at? This?'

'Yes, it's really coming on. Still loads more to do, like, but it's building up nicely.'

He is not really listening to her. He is trying to quell his thoughts, trying to stop imagining how it would feel if in fact her breast was caressing the side of his neck.

He hears her sigh. She moves from behind him and bends

forward, placing her board on the chair. He can see faint wisps of hair and a pinkness, the colour like the inside of one's cheeks. She seems unaware of him; she is looking through sketches, deep in thought. He is suddenly angry; she just sees him as some old man without any feelings.

Without a word he fetches his clothes and begins to get dressed. She dresses quickly. He notices she has on her jeans with the rip in the knee. She picks up her can of fixative and begins rattling it. She glances over at him,

'You look fed up.'

'Do I?' At last she's noticed. 'I didn't realise you knew I had feelings.'

He stands, pulling his trousers up and fastening them at the waist.

'Where did that come from?'

'So when I say I have to sit down, like last week, you automatically think of my discomfort do you? Or are we more interested in pursuing one's art?'

'Am I that bad?' She frowns. 'You haven't stood or been uncomfortable today though, have you?'

'Last week's still rankling.'

'How about, to show my gratitude, I get you a burger. After I've been to the cash machine, that is.'

'No thanks, my tea will be waiting for me when I get home.'

'A coffee then? They do good coffee.'

They sit down at a plastic table covered in grains of salt. She is right. The coffee is good, but the polystyrene cup is awful.

'Are you sure you don't want a burger?'

The ketchup is running out of the burger and down her chin.

He laughs, 'No thanks. I'm a well brought up boy. My mother taught me never to eat things that have been ground up. Like she says, why go to the bother of grinding them up if it's not to hide something.'

'So you've never had a burger?'

'Nope. Never been in one of these places before either. Mind you, I can see why now, they're nearly as dreadful as I thought.'

'And the coffee?'

'I must admit it's not bad, but the cup's awful.'

'What would your mother say?'

'You'd think I'd enjoy it, wouldn't you? The thought that

she'd disapprove.' He looks across the table at her, 'You never did tell me why you thought she would model for you if I decided against it.'

She gulps and wipes her mouth with a napkin, 'I'm not sure I should really tell you.' She looks at him and screws up her eyes, 'You might find it a bit shocking.'

He remains silent, polishing his nails with the pad of his thumb. Little does she know that there is nothing about his mother that he could find shocking.

'Oh, all right then.' She takes a sip of her coke. 'But don't tell her I told you. She used to be a life model up at the college. You remember at the funeral when I was so sure I'd seen her somewhere before. Well, she was the first model I ever drew.'

'Wait a minute, what are you saying?' He finds this hard to take in. He puts his coffee down on the table and stares at her, 'You're not serious? In front of a whole class?'

She nods.

'I don't believe you. Not my mother.'

'Why not?'

He clicks his tongue, 'Are you sure?'

Angela nods again, 'Positive.'

'I wonder how long she was doing it for? Well, I never, I suppose, thinking about it, it's not really surprising. It fits in with some of her other behaviour patterns that she thinks I don't know about.'

'I don't know how long she did it for, I only saw her the once. Alex said she stopped shortly after I started college.'

'You've been discussing my mother with him?'

'I was just checking,' she pauses, licking at a blob of ketchup at the side of her mouth, 'that I wasn't imagining the whole thing. Are you shocked?'

'I'm not sure what I feel. I've always known my mother was vain. But, well, I don't know what to say.'

'I shouldn't have told you.'

'No, I'm glad you did. She has so many secrets it's good to find out something new about her.'

'What makes you think that vanity made her do it? It could have been for the money, or for the pleasure of doing it.'

'I assure you, in my mother's case it is. The world always did revolve around her.'

'I think you're wrong.'

'So, you know my mother better than me, do you?'

'So you're saying, are you, that you are modelling for me out of vanity.'

'No, of course not.'

'What, then?' She takes another bite of her burger.

'God knows, for all the gratitude I get.'

'You're dodging the question.'

He is amazed at her resilience. 'You know, you once told me that if you got a good degree you could go on to fulfil your dreams; get a scholarship, do an MA in London. I got a good degree. I wanted to become an archaeologist, but no one was there to help me. Does that answer your question?'

'I don't know what to say.'

'Well, there's a first. A simple 'thank you' will do.'

She leans across the table and lightly touches his hand. Her hand is cold to the touch. 'Thank you.'

He takes a sip of his coffee.

'You still haven't answered my question, though.'

He looks up, 'What?'

'Why you think you're mother did it out of vanity.'

'Oh God, I don't know. Shall we just say she has always been a woman in pursuit of beauty. She wouldn't have taken her clothes off if she'd looked like me, that is a fact.'

'Yes, you may have a point there. I'd never thought of it like that. She did rather like preening herself, always wore a grey pearl necklace.'

'My point exactly, I don't know what her obsession is with her bloody necklaces. She's always worn them.'

'Edward?' He looks up. 'I can't get my head around why you're so hard on her. What ever has she done to you?'

'Are you saying I am hard-hearted?' He watches her studying his face to see if he is joking.

She smiles, the ketchup is still marking her chin. 'It's just, sometimes, like you say, you can be very cruel.'

'And do you think cruelty makes one hard-hearted?'

'I'm not sure.' She twists her face, the ketchup blob twisting with her. 'I don't think you're actually cruel. I think you just like sounding cruel.'

'What's the difference?'

'I think you can be very cruel with words, but I don't think you'd ever carry out a cruel act or, I dunno, it just feels like some anger inside you trying to get out.'

'A regular little psychiatrist, aren't we?'

'Very patronising, aren't we?'

He laughs. 'By the way, you've got ketchup on your chin.'

She wipes it off with her napkin. Some still sits at the corner of her mouth,

'I know you don't want me to be serious, but actually I think that the barbed jibes are a way of trying to keep people at arms length, but I, My Lord,' she makes a mock bow, 'have to look at the evidence presented to me. I don't know many other people who would have given up their Saturday afternoons without pay to do what you're doing for me.'

'Even worth being seen walking down the road and sitting in a burger joint with an old cretin like me, is it?'

'See. You're at it again. I pay you a compliment and there you are fishing in your box for another barb. Do you think I give a damn what anyone thinks?'

'Then you must be one remarkable young lady.'

'Has it taken you all this time to suss that?'

He laughs, 'There's just one slight improvement you could make.'

'What?'

'Wipe the ketchup off your chin.'

CHAPTER TWENTY-THREE

His father had been a keen fisherman. Edward would hear him downstairs early on a Sunday morning packing up his lunch for the day. In winter, Edward would snuggle further down the bed and wonder why his father would voluntarily get up and venture out into the cold dark morning to sit all day in the rain.

One summer morning, when Edward was eight, he awoke to the sun shining in through the gap in his curtains. It felt like a journey to the seaside sort of morning. He got out of bed and crept quietly downstairs. His father was seated at the kitchen table eating toast and studying a crossword. At first he didn't notice Edward but then, sensing a presence, he turned. Edward saw a fleeting look of irritation cross his face.

'You're an early bird.'

'I couldn't sleep, the sun woke me up.'

'It's a grand morning. A grand day for fishing.'

'Can I come with you?' Edward asked.

'You want to come?' His father looked at his watch, 'Aye, I suppose so. Why not? You'd better get your skates on though, we have to leave in ten minutes. Go and wash your face and get dressed while I make you some toast. You may have to eat it on the way to the bus stop.'

They left his mother a note propped against the milk jug on the table.

Mother, gone with dad,
Love, Edward

At the bus stop, men with big square baskets slung over one shoulder scraped, rubbed and jostled against each other. As they climbed on board the bus it filled with their laughter. Edward now understood why his father ventured out in all weathers to go fishing.

They settled down on the bank and early, too early, had eaten all his father's cheese and Marmite sandwiches.

'I never knew you liked cheese and Marmite, Dad. Mother always gives you fish paste or ham.'

'Aye, I know lad, women are strange like that; always give you what they think you ought to have. I don't think your mother has ever actually asked me what I would prefer.'

Something fell into place in Edward's head. Every Monday morning, when mother was making him his sandwiches, she would always complain,

'I don't know what happens to this cheese I get. The mice must eat it.'

Crumbly Cheshire. Edward picked a bit off his father's chin and popped it into his own mouth. 'Mmm, my favourite.'

His father ruffled his hair. 'I'm glad you came with me, lad. We'll have a good days fishing. Here, I'll show you how to hold the rod.'

For a while Edward was content to sit and watch the sun speckle through the leaves above. The river was brown, stained with peat but clear, and if he caught the light just right he could see below into the polished depths. As the day progressed he began to feel restless. Holding the rod hurt his back and besides, the fish weren't biting. Behind them, further up the hill, Edward could see a ruined castle. The sun shone directly on to it, soaking into the sandstone, lighting it up, Edward thought, like a magic place.

'Dad, can we go and look at those ruins?'

His father shook his head, 'Lad, I've come for a days fishing. I can't just leave all my tackle and go sauntering up there.'

Edward sat delving into the depths, looking for the fish that weren't coming out to play. With the sunlight now directly above them it was difficult to see below the surface. Edward sighed and his father relented,

'If you like, as long as you're not above an hour, you can go on your own.'

Edward expected that he would be the only one visiting the ruins, that maybe he would enter a secret kingdom and be put under the spell of the master magician. He entered the castle and was rather disheartened to find it busy with people. In several places the pristine turf had been rolled back like his mother's hearthrug. Holes resembling wide, shallow graves had been dug out of the fine dry soil. Lines of binder twine, marking out boundaries, were held taut between pegs.

Edward approached a group of people huddled at one corner who were looking into a deep pit. Something in their voices told Edward that they were excited.

He sidled up, cautiously hoping that no one would see him, still invisible in his imaginary kingdom, but then a young man in his early twenties turned and smiled, displaying a mouth full of crowded teeth, like a cluster of snowdrops. When he spoke he had an accent like Edward had only heard on his mother's radio.

'Come here,' he said, 'Come and see what we've found.'

In the pit was the skeleton of a young child, the hands clasped together across the chest and, Edward noticed, on the index finger of the uppermost hand was a gold ring that fell loose against the bone.

'Who...?' He had asked, shyly.

'A boy,' The man looked Edward up and down, 'probably about your age, he could've have been the son of a lord. Look at the ring he has on his finger.'

'What was his name?'

The young man laughed. 'I wish we knew. I wish we could have a magic lamp to take us back into the past, but we are only humble archaeologists. We can only guess and surmise at people's lives by looking at their bones and the everyday objects they left scattered about them.'

On that day, Edward decided he was going to become an archaeologist, but it was to be another four years before his father would relent and take him to see a dig.

It was the Easter holidays and his Mother was making plans, as she usually did at that time of the year, for her and Edward to go on a two-week break to his uncle's farm. Edward loved everything about the farm: the farm dogs, and being brave enough to slide his hand under the warm, soft hens, the excitement when he felt the smooth roundness of the egg, collecting them carefully in a wicker basket and best of all, boiling one for his breakfast. His great-uncle Jack teased him, but it was in a gentle way, and when his mother took him to the local town he would slide a shiny sixpence into Edward's palm, and on their last day when they stood waiting for the train to take them home, his uncle would always say, and always at the last minute, 'Shake hands like a man then, lad,' and in the palm of his hand would be a half-crown. He would curl Edward's fingers around it and whisper, 'Don't tell yer mam.'

His great aunt Rosemary was different again. She regarded him with a coldness that, even as a very young child, he'd sensed. His mother told him not to mind his aunt, she'd had a great sadness in her life and didn't intend to be unkind. But that year, when he was twelve, Edward refused point blank to go to the farm.

His mother tried everything that she could to persuade him. It was the first real confrontation they'd ever had. He heard her telling his father that his defiance must be the start of adolescence. She wouldn't let the matter rest. The day before they were meant to go she packed his suitcase and put it by the back door. When he came in from school he carried it straight upstairs and promptly unpacked it.

At the dinner table that night she said to his father, 'George, have a word with him will you?' But much to Edward's relief his father sided with him.

'Just leave the lad. If he doesn't want to go, he doesn't want to go. I'm due some time off work. I might take him to York. We could pay a visit to my aunt. Would you like that, son?' He placed his arm around Edward's shoulders, 'We could even go and look at one of those digs that you keep nattering on about. There's usually one going on around the city walls somewhere.'

CHAPTER TWENTY-FOUR

Angela is standing, half-dressed, looking through the work she's done the week before. She has on a pair of faded jeans and a white lacy bra that has turned to grey.

'Sorry I'm late, although I see you're not ready either.' Edward closes the door.

She looks up and smiles, 'I was just thinking how pleased I am with these.'

Edward stands beside her. 34B, the label sticks up from the fastening on the back of her bra.

'What does that mean, 34B?'

'What?'

'The label on the back of your bra, it says 34B.'

Angela groans, 'Oh please, don't look at my bra. It's disgusting.'

'Why?'

'A, because, I can never be bothered to wash them by hand and B, because I can never afford to buy a new one. This one must be five years old.' She plucks at the strap and worms of elastic wriggle away from the lace.

'Why don't you buy a black one?'

'Good idea, but you know what, I always get seduced by the white ones.'

Edward sits down and begins to take off his shoes. He half wishes that Angela will forget the rest of her clothes and stay half dressed. He has been perturbed by the emotions he'd experienced at their last sitting. All week he has tried desperately to blank them from his mind.

He notices that in the centre of the floor under the skylight there is a piece of A1 size paper. It is grey-blue in colour, the colour of paper towels,

'Why the sheet of paper?'

'I'm going to draw around your feet and then superglue you to the spot, so you can't move.' She smiles.

'If I'm going to be a statue, I'd rather be placed somewhere a bit more salubrious than in this old building.'

'Where, then?' She asks.

He loops his tie over his head. 'A railway station, I think.'

'Just think of all the people that would see you. They'd place their rucksacks at your feet, stare up at you and wonder who you were. Who would you be?'

'Edward Anderson, born of this city 19...' he tails off. 'I don't know about the rest. What do you think?'

Angela shrugs her shoulders. Edward notices that when she does this, two small, triangular-shaped pits appear either side of her neck.

'Can I ask you a question?'

He looks up from unbuttoning his shirt, 'What?'

'Would you want to stand there as you are, or well,' she pauses, 'able-bodied?'

'You know,' he looks up. 'At one time I would have said elegant and poised, but now I think I'd like to stay the way I am, so that I could study the raw curiosity on people's faces.'

'Do you think people would look at you with pity?'

He looks over at her. 'Is that how you view me? With pity?'

She is standing beside an untidy pile of clothes on the floor. He glances down at his own tidy pile placed neatly on a chair. His question has startled her. She moves towards him. He can see the clear grey of her eyes, the black rim encircling the iris.

'Pity?' She says the word as if she is trying it out for size, 'I don't think it ever occurred to me. Would you like me to pity you?'

He chuckles, amazed at how little she is fazed by him. 'Occasionally, maybe.'

'What, you want even more breaks?'

He laughs, 'Some chance. Seriously though, how do you think people in general view me?'

'Dunno, never really thought about it.' She smiles. 'They probably think you're a bit weird though.' She wrinkles her nose, 'They wouldn't be entirely wrong there.'

He smiles, 'That's really reassuring, thank you. I shall think of you next time someone's gawking at me.'

She doesn't take the bait, 'Do you have your own I'm-feeling-sorry-for-myself corner at work, maybe?' She raises her eyebrows.

He sees she is trying not to laugh. 'I'll know not to come to you if I'm looking for sympathy.' He pauses, 'At work, I'm just Edward in Archives. Every place has to have its obligatory oddity.'

He stands up, using the chair to balance himself.

'I'm sure you fill the role admirably,' she laughs.

'I really don't know why I put up with it,' he says, more to himself than her, 'Now tell me how you want me to stand before I change my mind and go home.'

'Will you need your stick?'

'Yes.'

She passes him his stick. 'OK, I want you to stand one leg in front of the other on this paper... let's try both hands resting on the stick.' She fetches a splinter of charcoal.

'Don't go dirtying my feet with that,' he says, looking down. 'Wouldn't it be easier to use a pencil?'

'I'll be careful, don't worry.' She draws around his walking stick and then, placing her hand over the top of his foot, draws round his toes. He glances down and cringes at the sight of his toenails; thickened and yellowing. He looks away, down at the rope of her spine, the sweet curve of it, sighs deeply.

She looks up, 'Something the matter?'

'No, no. It's just wonderful to feel your touch.' He sees that she is uncertain as to how to take his remark, 'The touch of another human being.'

She gives him a half smile, 'I'll leave my hand here then, shall I?'

'I suppose you think I'm a strange old man?'

She stands and clips a sheet of paper to her easel, 'I think you're very strange, Edward, very strange.'

He looks down at his hands, one placed over the other, resting on his stick, the roundness of his knuckles catching the light, the veins on the back of his hands.

'I want to spend quite a bit of time on this stance.'

'Don't forget, joking aside, I need regular breaks. I can't stand for long'.

She turns her easel sideways and pushes her chair against the wall. He isn't sure she's heard him. 'At least every ten minutes.'

'Okay,' she says, staring intently at the blank paper on her easel.

'Oh good, you're standing as well,' he says.

'Yeah, I can move easier if I stand. It makes for more fluid arm movements. Drawing you in a standing pose means there are more unbroken lines.'

'I didn't realise I would get to learn so much about art just by modelling for you.'

She doesn't reply, he sees she has gone into work mode. It is almost trance like. Today he can observe her as she works, he can even see what she is drawing. She draws the line from his neck to the crown of his back and then takes a sideways skew and down again to the base of his spine and, from there, out again, for the line of his buttocks.

He loves to watch her, her face so serious, so concentrated, the light gleaming behind her, the sun catching the fine downy hair at the nape of her neck, the pale brown patch of her pubic hair and how, as she lifts her arm, her breasts rise and fall against her rib cage. He wants to put out his hand and touch her skin, to trace with his fingers along each rib. His whole body tingles, as if a small current of electricity is passing through every nerve. He must think of something else. He closes his eyes, leans into his stick and listens to the sounds around him; the faint hum of traffic on the road at the front, the scratching of charcoal on paper, a lathe being worked somewhere else in the building.

The smoothness of his stick is pressing into his right palm. He tries to picture it in his mind. He can recall every detail. The stick had been his father's. Other than that, it is a very ordinary stick made of polished wood. Willow, or is it hazel? The handle is curved like a shepherd's crook. The colour reminds him of the trays of toffee his mother used to make.

On the end of the stick is a green ferrule. He suspects that it was one of his father's adaptations, or something that he had poked his stick into by accident one day and found that it fitted. Was it lying grubby on a pavement? Or did he find it on the polished floor of the community centre or was it the end of a chair leg maybe; a now rocky chair? His father would have secretly delighted in this act of mischief. Edward didn't like the green ferrule much; it gave a dull thud on wooden floors and an almost noiseless bong on tarmac pavements. He would have much preferred the stark tap, tap, tap, of the wooden end, like the blind man in Treasure Island, but the green ferrule reminded him so much of his father that, most of the time, he left it in place, only occasionally wrenching it off and slipping it in his pocket; his own act of mischief.

He grasps the handle, feels the place where both his and his father's hands have worn a pressure groove.

He lets out a loud groan, a pain that started earlier between his shoulder blades is now radiating in waves across his back.

'I need to sit down.' He looks up. She is totally absorbed in her work. He looks across at the clock. He has held this pose for nearly twenty minutes. 'Did you hear me?' She gives him a flicker of a smile, a slight acknowledgement.

'It's my size.'

'What?'

'34B.'

'Oh.'

'I thought you would have known that, with all your tailoring experience.'

'Didn't you hear me? I need to sit down.'

'34' is the measurement all the way round under my breast and the 'A' denotes the cup size.' She is gabbling now, trying to keep him distracted so that she can finish. 'A woman could measure 34 if she had a really broad back and small tits or if she had really big tits and a narrow back. So you can be A, B, C, D or even F cup. I don't know if they go any bigger.'

He is intrigued, despite the pain stitching down his back. 'So 'A' is a small breast?'

'Yes.'

'You haven't got small breasts though.' He has spoken before he realises what he's said. He looks across. She hasn't heard. She has gone back to her work.

'I'm going to move.'

'Edward, please, just two more minutes.'

He closes his eyes, 'God… you're merciless.'

'I won't be a second. I've just got to finish this outline.'

He watches the second hand on the clock for another minute, gritting his teeth against the pain.

'That's it. I can't go on any longer.'

She pulls a face.

'You'll have to help me sit down.'

He groans in agony. She takes his elbow in the palm of her hand and guides him gently to the knitting chair.

'Are you all right? You look really pale.' He notes the sudden concern in her face.

'What do you expect? I'm in agony.'

'I'm sorry, I didn't realise.'

'When I say I need to sit down, do you think I'm just being awkward?'

'Shall I get you a coffee?'

'Could you look in my jacket pocket? There should be a foil card of Paracetamol.'

He watches as she pulls out a neatly folded hankie with the initials EA embroidered in pale blue, a Yale key and some loose change. 'They're not in this pocket.'

'Look in the other one, will you?'

She pulls out a rabbit's foot. 'Never had you down as superstitious, Edward.'

For once he is glad of the pain. He doesn't care that she has found his lucky charm. The little white foot that he found on the seat of the railway carriage the last ever time he went to the farm as a child. His mother hadn't seen it. He didn't tell her, she might have made him give it in at lost property. He doesn't think anyone has ever seen it before.

She is examining it, 'It's weird.'

'Put it back please.'

She looks at him curiously and delves back into the pocket; some receipts, neatly folded, a bus ticket and a penknife. 'Not in here either.'

'Oh God, I must have forgotten them.'

'I'll pop round to the paper shop and get some?'

'Take some of that change in my pocket.'

He watches her pulling on her jeans, the flesh of her bottom riding up as she pulls them to her waist. She slips her arms first into the sleeves of her jumper and then pushes her head through the neck.

'Why aren't you putting on your underwear?'

'Haven't finished yet, have we?'

'That's what you think.'

'You'll be all right if you're sitting down, won't you?'

'We'll see.'

She picks up her bag and pauses at the door, 'Is there anything else you want?'

'Get some chocolate?'

She counts the change in her hand and grins, 'Do you think I deserve any?'

'No, but I want to fatten you up for the oven.'

Her face dissolves into a childlike softness. 'That was one of my favourite stories, Hansel and Gretel. I loved the thought of a house made of gingerbread, with window frames of barley sugar and a chocolate door.'

'What about the old witch?'

'Yes, but somehow because she's got such a lovely house, you never quite believe she's that bad. I had a lovely book of fairy stories: Hansel and Gretel, Tom Thumb, Puss in Boots, the Wild Swans....'

Edward raises his eyebrows at her, 'Tablets?'

'Sorry, sorry.'

She pokes her head back around the door, 'You should have said you were in so much pain you know.'

'I did.'

She pulls a face. 'Sorry... is it any better now?'

'Go.'

He closes his eyes and waits. He can hear again the murmur of traffic out on the main road and the gentle creaking of the heating pipes. He can feel the sun on the top of his head. He stares down at his outstretched feet and thinks it's time he went to the chiropodist. The silly man, why didn't he ever suggest another appointment? That way would have seemed much less effort than having to wait until he looked like a donkey in need of hoofing. Of course, if he wasn't so cantankerous, he smiles to himself, he could get Mrs. Ingram's mobile chiropodist to do it, but he couldn't cope with her hovering around, underlining the fact they were sharing. God forbid, the same chiropodist! Why does he find it so hard to accept her kindnesses?

He watches the concentration on her face as Angela pops the pills out of the foil into the small circle of his palm.

'I need some water.'

'No probs,' Angela fishes in her rucksack and hands him a plastic bottle of water.

'Don't you mind me sharing your water?'

'Why should I?'

He smiles, 'No matter.'

CHAPTER TWENTY-FIVE

There is a note in Angela's pigeonhole: *My office. This morning. Alex.*

She screws it up, throws it over her shoulder and goes to the canteen for a coffee. He wants to see her work. She doesn't want to show him. Not yet, it's not ready, she's not ready. If she were to show him now it might break what has been created between herself and Edward; like a secret child. For God's sake, Angela, she smiles to herself. How could she and Edward ever create a child? She chuckles at the idea of her and Edward having some kind of torrid affair; an old man, with yellowing toenails.

'Ange?' Alex shouts across from the door of the canteen. She remains seated. He lets go of the door and walks over. 'I've been watching you through the window, smiling away to yourself. What's so funny?'

She shrugs, doesn't reply.

'Didn't you get my note?'

Angela nods her head. He sits down opposite her.

She folds her arms, leans back in the chair, 'What did you want?'

'It must be three weeks since I asked you to let me see your work in progress, and the other thing is...,' he pauses, 'I need to know when you're going to model for me again.'

She doesn't want to sit for him again. There seems to be a tension building between them that makes her feel uneasy. 'How many more sessions will it take? I've already done three. Isn't that enough?'

'It's going to take me another two or three sessions at least.'

'Do I have to? I could do with concentrating on my own work.'

He flicks his fringe away from his eyes, 'Don't be stupid. I don't want to start with another model, not now. You of all people should know that.'

'I'll think about it, okay?'

'What's happened with your work?'

'I'm well on with it.'

He narrows his eyes, leans back in his chair and takes out a cigarette.

'Honest, I am,' her voice rises in pitch.

'So. Where is it?' He lights his cigarette.

'You can't smoke in here.'

'Oh, for fuck's sake,' he pinches the end with his finger. 'You haven't answered my question.'

'What?'

'Where's your work in progress?'

'Can I ask you a favour?'

'Go on then,' he leans forward staring at her intently.

She crosses her legs, turns her body sideways. 'I don't know if you can understand this, but I need to complete the work before I show it to you. It's going so well I don't want anything to spoil it.'

'Are you taking the piss?'

'No, honest I'm not. I've been working on it for weeks.'

'So, how are you approaching it?' he asks. She notes his suspicious tone.

'I'm doing a series of life studies.'

'Back on the same old nugget.'

'It's what I do.'

'It's what I do,' he mimics. 'What makes you so bloody cocky? You're good, I'll give you that, but where do you get this supreme confidence from that you can pull it off. All the others in your year are pestering me night and day. What if you really mess up? You won't have time to do anything else.'

Out of the corner of her eye she has seen Dan enter the canteen. He has a stupid smirk on his face, just because Alex is sitting with her. She wishes he wouldn't wear his dreadlocks in that stupid hair band; it doesn't suit him at all.

'Please Alex, just trust me. I'm not going to mess up. Okay?'

He bends across the table towards her. 'I'll go along with you on one condition.'

'What?' She is weary of him now, weary of the whole subject. She wishes he would just go away. Dan is sitting down, still smirking. When Alex gets up to go, she'll go with him. That'll really piss him off. Wipe the smirk off his face.

'You keep on modelling for me.'

She crosses her arms and scowls across at him, 'That's not fair. I need to be working on my own stuff now.'

'For Christ's sake, it's only a few hours. Cut down on your waitressing job. I'm sure they don't pay you as well as I do.'

'No, but I enjoy working there.'

He glances at his watch and stands up. 'It's not all in charcoal is it? That's not why you're hiding it from me?'

'What?' She is exasperated. Can't this man just leave her in peace?

'Your work.'

'No, of course not.'

'Right. I'll go and see the dwarf man. Now there was a man who knew how to use colour: Toulouse-Lautrec.'

'Is there an exhibition on? God! I'd love to see his work.'

'No, an old film,' he checks his watch again, 'in thirty minutes. Flick wanted to come but now she can't. I hate going to the cinema on my own.'

'Just leave your raincoat at home and you'll be okay,' she laughs.

'And there was me going to ask if you wanted Flick's ticket.'

It would be a good idea to go, she thinks. After all, it was the photos of Toulouse-Lautrec that had inspired her in the first place, given her the courage to pursue Edward. It seems like a lifetime ago, that day in the library. She should go. It might give her another angle. 'How long's it on for?'

He gets out a cigarette and taps it on the box. 'It finishes today.'

'Flick's not going to the flicks, eh?' She smiles at her own joke. 'Would I have to sit with you?'

He looks down his nose at her, 'I'll take that as a 'no' then.'

After the cinema, Alex gives her a lift back to her house. He leans forward, encasing the steering wheel with his arms, 'Now this would be a good opportunity for me to come in and look at your work.'

'I thought we had a deal.'

'You're going to sit for me then?'

She opens the car door, 'I'm going.'

'Thanks for the film, Alex,' he mimics, 'very enjoyable, that.'

'It was, thanks.' She starts to shut the door.

'Ange!'

At first she is tempted to close it and pretend she hasn't heard. 'What?'

'Give me your number then I can ring you about the modelling.'

She rattles off the number and closes the door, watches his car lights tracing the terrace opposite. She takes out her key and then, changing her mind, wanders down the road looking in other people's windows.

They had discussed the film over a pint of Guinness in the foyer bar. She had been fascinated by Alex's depth of knowledge, his passion for the man's work.

At first she'd been disappointed in the film. She thought it would be a film of Toulouse-Lautrec's work, and it was, partly, but mostly it showed the man and his life and his desperate pursuit of love, even if it meant losing his dignity and degrading himself. Her stomach twists as she remembers him, pitiful in his deformity, begging for each small crumb of human comfort. Was it his deformity that made her pity him? Or was it his utter loneliness. If she had known him, how would she have treated him? Would she have pitied him? But how could she, if she admired his work so much? She thinks of Edward. She wonders, would she pity him if one day he begged her to love him. But that would never happen. Edward, unlike Toulouse-Lautrec, had dignity.

CHAPTER TWENTY-SIX

'34B.' has been ringing in his head all weekend. He tries a mix of other numbers and letters '38C', '36F', but none of them have the same ring about them as '34B'. He imagines standing outside an old house converted into flats, an illuminated plaque saying '34B', Miss A. O'Donnell', and him pressing the button at the side of her name, hearing the bell echo up the stairwell. The opening of an internal door. Expectant footsteps thundering down the stairs. A key turning… and she would be there, looking out into the darkness… but his courage would have failed him once again.

He shakes his head and closes the book he has open on his desk. Is he going daft? At lunchtime he will have to get out for some fresh air. He looks out of the window and wonders if the weather will hold. He will walk along Surrey Street, cross over onto Pinstone Street and wander up to Barker's Pool and his mother's favourite department store. He has never studied ladies underwear before.

He will get the lift to the top floor, he thinks, as he passes in through the automatic doors. He will then work his way down through the store on the escalator to see if he can spot the ladies underwear section. He passes through the perfume section. The women behind the counters don't accost him. They don't see him as a man who would buy perfume for his lady. Just a bra, he smiles to himself.

Top floor: electrical equipment, a wall of televisions all with the same faces, the same people talking. Next floor: carpets, sumptuous rugs and then, the ladies-wear section. To the right he sees the underwear section: matching knickers and bras on individual hangers, negligees as flimsy as candyfloss. He hesitates on the wooden walkway that will take him there. There is an aura about the whole section like a mist of secrecy. He turns and puts his foot on the down escalator.

He rides it to the basement, and the men's section. It is a long time since he has been down here. He studies the jackets. A young man approaches him.

'Would Sir like to try anything on?'

'And how, Sir, do you propose to get one of these jackets to fit me?'

The young man reddens and turns away.

A vest, maybe he will buy a vest. It is along time since he wore a vest and he remembers that there is something pleasing about a vest; the comfort of cotton next to skin, and something extra for Mrs Ingram to wash. He can hear her now '*I see you've decided to start wearing a vest, Mr Anderson?*' expecting an explanation. Ha! She wouldn't get one.

The vests are all in packs of two. He asks the lady behind the counter if he could buy just one.

'No, duck, sorry, I can't split a pack.'

'Couldn't I just take one and you charge me half?'

'No duck, sorry.'

'Well, could I just take one and pay for two?'

She shakes her head and rings a bell under the counter, 'I'll get the manager, Sir.'

'Now Sir, how can I help you?' It is the young man again.

Edward turns, sees the embarrassment still in the young man's face. 'I want to buy one vest.'

'We only sell them in pairs, Sir'

'Like socks?'

The young man, confused, shakes his head, tries to clarify his thoughts, 'Ah, well, no sir, not like socks.'

'I only want one vest. I've only got one body.'

'But sir, these are very good value, if you were only buying one it wouldn't cost much less.'

'Well, can I just pay for one then?'

'Sorry, sir, it's head office policy. I can't split a pack. It would mess up our stock levels.'

'And would that be a problem?'

'Yes Sir, because everybody, except you, Sir, wants to buy two vests.'

'So I'm an awkward customer?'

'I didn't say that, Sir.'

'How do you know that everyone else wants to buy two

vests?'

'I'm sorry, Sir,' the young man clasps his hands together. 'I'm only doing my job.'

Edward finally takes pity on him but the irritation stays with him all afternoon. Irritation that he has let such a trivial matter as buying a vest get to him, and that he hadn't had the courage to even look in the ladies section.

He leaves work early, sits in the window of the Blue Moon café drinking a coffee that is much too strong and eating a wholemeal scone that he knows he should find delicious but doesn't. The baking powder in the scone coats his teeth and he runs his tongue over the roughness, trying to smooth it away.

He looks at his watch. What shall he do? He doesn't want to arrive home early. Home! Whenever had it been his home? He had never looked forward to going there, however dreary his day at work had been. Every year he promises himself that the next year he will move, but he never does. It's like being trapped in a time warp. But life is changing, he can feel it. Maybe next year he will move. But why leave it until then. He could buy a paper tonight and see what is available. He wanders back up the street. He supposes he could go back to work. He stops and looks over the railings into the shelter of the church courtyard, a place for reflection; a rare place in the heart of town. Edward has often thought to go and sit there and study the small brass statues, but the bench is usually occupied by a drunk. Today it is empty.

The bench is wet. Before sitting down, Edward takes a handkerchief from his top pocket and flicks the water from the wooden slats. He sits down and rubs the embroidered corner of his handkerchief between his thumb and forefinger; EA, good initials, almost as pleasing as '34B'. He laughs to himself. Is he going mad?

Every year at Christmas his mother buys him a box of handkerchiefs. To expect something, he thinks, is actually a luxury. At least he can look forward to receiving them; the see-through lid, the handkerchiefs placed in triangles with the initials uppermost. He appreciates the trouble she goes to of having his initials embroidered in pale blue. But why always blue? Why not one year red, the next green, so that he could note the passing of the years? Janice at work always teases him about his hankies. '*I thought it was only married men that had proper hankies, Edward. You must really appreciate what a treasure you have in Mrs Ingram*'. If only! Every week without fail she complains about them. '*Why you want these sort of handkerchiefs Mr Anderson, I'll never know. Why, I have to boil them up 'specially in my dishcloth pan. Kleenex is so much better for you. They don't make your nose sore, or spread germs.*'

He folds up his wet handkerchief into a padded square. It brought him such comfort to put his hand inside his pocket and feel the softness of the cotton. He looks up at the church clock. He could go back to the department store and replace the white hankies that Mrs Ingram has managed to turn grey only, this time, order his initials in red.

He gets in the lift and presses the down button. The lift takes him up. The doors open onto nightdresses, and petticoats hanging on flimsy satin straps. He pauses, taps his stick three times and walks out of the lift. There are bras on hangers: crimson, black, white, patterned, plain. A woman with a huge cleavage smiles down at him from a cardboard cut out. There is something so beautifully engineered about the bras, as if tailors, like his uncle, have moulded them using steam and a damp cloth.

'Can I help you, love?'

Edward feels his face turning hot. He leans on his stick and swivels round.

The woman tilts her head and smiles at him. 'Do you know what size she is?

'34B.'

'Our most popular size. Do you like this one?' She picks out a deep crimson one with scalloped lace edges.

'Er, yes.'

'Do you think she would like this colour, or white.'

Edward hesitates. The woman hooks the crimson one off the rack. He remembers Angela's words: '*I am always seduced by the white ones.*'

'Can I take the crimson one please?'

'Yes, certainly. Would Sir like it gift-wrapped?'

Edward watches as the woman wraps the bra in tissue paper and then places it carefully in a buff-coloured box. She ties a pale pink ribbon loosely and then with scissors and a flick of the wrist, curls the ends of the ribbons.

He walks back along Surrey Street, stops and looks down for a moment at the Yorkshire flagstones and the black circles of discarded chewing gum. Damn, he forgot the hankies! He bangs the bag containing his new purchase against his leg. A full week's keep on a bra. But if he moved, he reminds himself, it could be double that. That was the one good thing about lodging at Mrs Ingram's. It was cheap. What would she say? He smiles smugly to himself. Well, she won't ever find out. He's going to lock his secret in his drawer at work, along with Uncle Ruben's letters.

CHAPTER TWENTY-SEVEN

Edward arrives at the studio's front door just as it is swinging shut. He puts out his stick and catches the door ajar. It is strange to be walking alone down the empty corridor. Would Angela be there, in the studio, waiting for him to ring the door bell? His stomach churns. Why on earth had he brought her the bra? He will have to give it to her now or, he could go and chuck it in the river and then come back. He hears voices coming down the stairs at the end of the corridor and recognises Angela's laugh. He sees her legs first and, alongside them, Alex's moccasined feet. He hurries past and waits outside their door. She arrives shortly afterwards with two cups of coffee.

'Are those for you and Alex?' he blurts out.

She pulls a face. 'No. Why, should they be? Get the door, will you?'

He presses down on the handle. The light of the room spills out into the corridor. He loves the brightness of their room. 'It's just, I heard you coming down the stairs with him.'

'Thought I'd get us a coffee in, for a change. Does that seem so impossible?'

'No, but what was he doing up there?'

'He really gets up your nose doesn't he? While the art school's being refurbed, quite a few of us have to work down here. Him as well, unfortunately.'

'You're right, I don't like the man. I find it hard to understand how such a superficial person can be an artist.'

She considers his statement. 'You've only met him the once. I can see what you mean, though. But I'm not sure; I think there may be another layer to him. His work's really good.'

He is surprised at her defence of Alex. 'How do you define good? I presume you mean technically.'

'No,' she purses her lips. 'I don't think I do, although that goes without saying. There is a great sensitivity about it, a tenderness. Yes, it's surprising.'

Her words really rankle with him, 'You sound as if you admire him.'

'Only his work.' She passes him his coffee. 'The man's a prat!'

'How can you distinguish the two?' He sits down on the comfortable chair, watches her tilt her head to one side, as if she has to do this to think.

'Odd, isn't it.'

He puts down his coffee and begins to loosen his tie.

'Edward, I have to go early today.'

His head lifts in surprise.

'So I thought it'd be a good idea if I did some studies of you dressed.'

Thank God, what a relief. He nearly hadn't come today. He hasn't been sleeping well. His head is in too much of a turmoil. Out of the blue he keeps being overtaken by an irrepressible longing, but for what he is not sure.

He takes off his tie and lays it across his knee. The sheen of the fabric catches the sun. He has placed the bag behind the screen out of sight. He could tell her about it now, say that he'd been looking for a present for his mother, remembered their conversation from the week before and on impulse had bought her the bra.

Angela draws the 'V' that Edward's unbuttoned shirt collar makes, the Adam's apple protruding slightly from the opening, and the buttons down the front of his shirt which are of equal distance apart, a perfect line, one under the other. A brown leather belt with a small gold buckle sits on top of the bunched up waistband of his trousers. She draws in the square of the buckle.

'So, where have you got to go this afternoon that's so urgent?' he asks.

She pauses in her drawing, stares at him. 'I bet you're relieved it's only a short sitting after what I put you through last week aren't you?'

'Ambivalent is the word, I think. I'm tired today. I've not been sleeping well.'

She looks up at his face, and yes, he does look tired.

'You didn't say,' he persists.

'What?' She wishes he would shut up.

'Where you're going.'

She has a good mind to tell him not to be so bloody nosy. Why is he so insistent. She is just going to tell him that she has to see Alex about some work, but she thinks better of it. 'I stupidly said I'd help a fellow student with his work.'

She looks up and sees he has moved his hand up to his throat.

She clucks her tongue, 'Hey, you moved.'

'Who is he? Is his work more important than yours?'

He is seriously getting on her nerves now, 'Dan. He's a lad in my year, a friend. Okay?'

He knows she is lying. 'I thought you were going to say you had to see Alex.'

'I will have to at some point.'

'Why?'

'He's my tutor isn't he? I don't have a lot of choice in the matter.'

'Have you told him yet that I'm modelling for you?'

She looks up. 'He keeps asking to see my work. I'm supposed to show him the work in progress, but up to now I've managed to ward him off.'

'Are you ashamed of me or something?'

She puts her board down on her lap. 'What's up with you today? You're like a bear with a sore head.'

'So? Are you ashamed?'

'For Christ's sake,' she looks down at the drawing. 'If you must know, it's the opposite. I think I've got something really special here.' She looks up again. 'Thanks to you. So if you don't mind, I'd like to get on.'

'I'm not sure I want him looking at drawings of me.'

She has had enough of this, she doesn't care anymore whether he storms out or not. 'Edward, make up your mind will you? One minute you're asking if I'm ashamed of you, and the next minute you don't want me to show Alex the drawings. You can't say that. Not after all the work I've done. Surely you didn't think I was just going to lock you away in a cupboard for Christ's sake!'

He puts his hands to his collar and refastens his shirt button.

'Oh God! I'm sorry. I don't know which way to turn. If you knew how important this whole thing is to me.'

'That's why you treat your model with so much disrespect is

it? Do you think I come here every week just so you can be rude to me?'

She feels a lump rising in her throat, she has always hated conflict. A single tear courses down her cheek, plops onto her paper. She remains silent, unable to speak. She hears him say, softly, 'It really means that much to you?'

His face is filled with consternation.

She looks up and nods, 'Don't you realise that art is my whole life? I'm not like the other students. I don't go out drinking every night. This work I'm doing with you, I feel it's my best work yet.'

'Really?' He suddenly seems impressed. 'Why?'

'I was thinking about that the other night. There's a certain…' she pauses, searching for an appropriate word, '…frisson, I think the word is, about you.'

He seems pleased with the description, even while he tries to hide it.

'I'm still annoyed about you cutting the session short, though. I mean, it's a nice afternoon, I could have planned to do something else if I'd known.'

She can't resist, 'I thought you said you were tired.' She sees his jaw stiffen, and realises she's goading him again. Why does she do it? 'Look it was really stupid of me to make other arrangements,' she says, hastily. 'Will you forgive me? Pleeease? I promise never to do it again.'

He sighs and undoes his collar button.

She draws in the shape of the shirt collar, the line of the shoulder, the way the jacket falls open at the front. She shades in the area around the throat shadowed by his neck; studies him on the paper, hands down by his side, bottom slightly forward, sitting back in his chair.

He sighs, 'I don't know what I thought. I suppose I could become a modern Dorian Grey. You could hide me away in your attic.'

What is he on about now? 'Sorry, I don't understand.'

He laughs at his own joke. 'The drawings you are doing of me. You could put them away in an attic so I remain young and beautiful.'

She should really broach the subject with him, tell him he may, if she's lucky, end up hanging on a gallery wall. She could even sell him, she laughs to herself, into slavery, that would shut him up.

'A nice sunny attic with a skylight, like in here, eh?' She peers up to the light above her head. He chuckles. She breathes a sigh of relief, returns to her drawing. The skewed line of his shoulder, the tension in his neck, tendons taut above his shirt collar, the well-tailored collar of his jacket that fits snugly around his neck, are all etched sharply by the light; the raised crown of the sleeve, slightly above the line of the shoulder, crimped like the edge of a pie, the slight fullness of the cloth, perfect in their displacement. The sun is shining directly down on him. She notices that there are beads of sweat on his top lip.

'Have you nearly finished this pose? I need to move.'

'Are you getting too hot?'

'I'm boiling. I need to move out of the sun.'

'Right, have a rest then. I'm just popping to the loo. Would you like another coffee fetching?'

'I'm okay, thanks. Two in one day, that would be spoiling me.'

When she re-enters the room Edward is standing at the window with his back to her. She notices something strange about his jacket where it hangs over the back of the chair. She observes with interest that the tiny orange speck in the tweed is almost an exact match with the orange of the chair, but there is something else.

She walks behind the chair and surveys the jacket. 'There's something odd about your jacket. Why doesn't it drape over the chair properly? It's all askew.'

Edward turns. 'It's moulded to the shape of my back. Not the chair.'

'Doesn't it just go like that with time?'

'No, no.' He walks over to the chair and pokes his stick up the inside of the jacket, accentuating the nub that has been moulded to fit his shape. 'I have my very own pattern. Good, isn't it?'

'I'm not quite sure I understand.'

He lowers himself back down into his chair. 'I'll explain while you're drawing. How would you like me to sit?'

God, he's keen now, she thinks, her words must have hit home. 'Can you sit sideways on the chair?'

'Like this?' He turns his body and drapes an arm over the

back of the chair.

She nods, 'And would you roll your sleeves up a bit?'

'Getting a bit carried away, aren't we?'

She smiles. He begins to roll the shirt cuff up his arm, creating a fat sausage of white fabric just above the elbow. She studies his back. His shirt, unlike his jacket, is pulled in several directions, the yoke cutting across the slope of the hump.

Angela draws his head, thrust forward, the shortened neck, and then the line of the shoulder. 'It's really difficult trying to make out how the bones sit under your shirt.' She draws the profile of his back, 'There, I think that's right. Do you have a special pattern for your shirts as well?'

'No, I'm afraid I can't quite run to that expense. Have I got on a shirt with a yoke across the back?'

'If a yoke is where you have a separate piece of fabric that runs across about a third of the way down your back, then yes.'

'I meant to put on a different one. I have some that drop straight from the shoulder. They're better, but they're a bit hard to get hold of these days.'

He closes his eyes, rests his chin on the back of the chair and listens to the faint scratching of charcoal on paper. It sounds like a mouse behind a skirting board. He remembers the bag propped against the wall, over in the corner. Will he have the courage to give it to her today? He must. But he is weary now, perhaps too weary to find the courage.

He opens his eyes. 'I was going to tell you about my jacket, wasn't I? It's custom made, just for me, you know? My Uncle Ruben was a tailor, and he could craft me a jacket so that it fitted like a glove. My back wasn't always like this. It became gradually worse over time so poor Uncle Ruben, as well as supplying me with a couple of new jackets every year, had to redraft the pattern every time. I would go to his factory and he would measure me this way and that, clucking away to himself, comparing my measurements to the previous year. Luckily, since he left, my shape hasn't altered much, so when I want a new jacket I just take the special pattern that I keep hidden under my mattress along to the tailor.'

'What happened to Uncle Ruben?'

'He left, went to America.'

'And have you never thought to visit him?'

'Why should I?'

'Well, you speak so fondly of him.'

'You know, the strangest thing is, he used to love doing my jackets. He said it was the only time he got to use all his skills. This is one of his.' He fingers the cuff of his jacket. 'I dread to think how old it is.'

'I love the colours. You have one with a mauve tinge in don't you? It makes me think of the moors with speckles of moss and heather.'

He nods, 'Harris Tweed. Have you never heard of Harris Tweed?'

She shakes her head and he continues, 'Originally, it was made by crofters on hand looms, in their own homes. Uncle Ruben used to hate Harris Tweed. Said the fabric was much narrower than normal, owing to it being made on a handloom. Instead of just being able to lay out his pattern pieces quickly, he used to have to plot the new layout to get the maximum fabric usage. Very expensive fabric you see. Aren't I boring you with all this?'

'No, I'm fascinated. I can really visualise what you're saying. It'll help me, I think. I want to know how he got the jacket to fit your back.'

'I'm just coming to that. As far as I can remember, to take measurements for a jacket, they use a certain formula. With a hunched back you have to first work out what the proportions would be without the hump, and then again with the hump, so that the area and size of the hump can be allowed for in the fitting. I think what the tailor does is put the fullness into the right area, like you would do for a breast dart on a woman, except they incorporate the fullness into the seam. Then there are other considerations, like the different width and height of the shoulders, and the shortness of the neck. Most of the change occurs in the pattern and then a bit of manipulation is required in the making process.'

'What do you mean?'

'Steaming, mostly. He had a specially shaped pad, similar to the shape of my back, that he would drape the back of the jacket over and steam-in the shape. You can mould wool into almost any shape, did you know? I always had to have pure wool and there were certain rules about fabric design as well. My uncle would never let me have a check or a stripe fabric, or something with a definite pattern. As he said, it would only accentuate my deformity. I had to have plain cloth, or something like a tweed.'

She looks at her watch, 'I'll be a tailor by the time you've finished with me.'

He is feeling better, he wants to sit here with her all afternoon until the light begins to fade. She takes a container of fixative out of her bag and shakes it. 'I'm going to have to go.' The tin rattles like a penny in a can.

'May I just take a quick look?'

Angela stops rattling the tin. Edward sees she has captured something of him that he likes. His own face stares back at him, carved out in bold black lines that somehow manage to be him. The second drawing, with his face resting in his hand, is softer, smudged, less defined, yet in the eyes there is humour. Does she see humour in his eyes?

Edward walks back along the corridor. He takes a sideways swipe at the heating pipes, and listens as the sound clangs and bongs back down the corridor. Again he can hear Alex's voice coming from upstairs. He remembers Angela's words. '*He really gets up your nose doesn't he?*' She was right there. He opens the front door.

Next week. Next week, he will give her the bra. He bangs the box against his leg. He will have to remember to take it to work with him on Monday so that Mrs Ingram doesn't find it.

CHAPTER TWENTY-EIGHT

'Where are you taking me today?' Rachel says, by way of a greeting.

'The Blue Moon.'

'I've never heard of it.'

'It's on Norfolk Street.'

The sun is hot and glints off the steel street furniture on Fargate. The grey cobbles of Italian granite press up through Rachel's soles, displacing her thin heels. They turn off down Norfolk Street. Outside a café, people are seated at white metal tables.

'Why did you choose here, Edward?'

He looks at her, shading his eyes from the sun, 'Why? Don't you like it?'

She peers in through the doorway, 'Not quite up to your usual standard.'

'I thought you might like a change, somewhere a bit more casual.'

'Why?' she says. 'I like going to nice places.'

Edward pulls out a chair and nods towards the café, 'Shall we give it a try?'

Reluctantly, she sits down. 'I'm not sure it's quite warm enough to sit outside yet.'

'I think,' Edward says, 'that the menu is written on the chalk-board inside.'

He asks the girl behind the counter to bring the board out to their table. Rachel chooses a Stilton and Broccoli quiche, with salad and new potatoes. He has a leek and mushroom bake in a round earthenware dish.

'You said in your letter, Mother, that you went to Leeds.'

She nods, her mouth still full.

'Did you go to the art gallery? If I remember rightly, there are some very fine Grimshaws there. Do you remember that time you took me?'

'I never took you, Edward.'

'I'm sure you did, or was it Father?'

'Your father wouldn't take you either. Wasn't his sort of thing.'

'He did take me. I remember now. You'd gone to visit your mother in the Infirmary. We arranged to meet you at the station and it was raining and Father couldn't make up his mind whether to catch the bus out to the museum at Kirkstall or to take me in the Art Gallery. Then suddenly he said: *'Let's go in the art gallery, lad. I haven't been in there for years. I used to love going in there as a kid'.'*

'Well, he never told me about it.' Rachel says.

'Maybe it was his little secret.'

'He probably went on a school visit once.'

Edward shakes his head in disbelief. 'You'd never allow the poor man any graces, would you? Or allow me the illusion of him having had any.'

'Your father always said he was a simple man, with simple pleasures. And he was.'

'And does that not include art?'

'Can you ever remember any other instances where he was interested in art, reading, or anything else cultural? I'm not trying to discredit him. I'm simply telling the truth.'

'Why did you marry him if you had so little in common?'

Rachel examines Edward's face. There is something strange about him today, he seems agitated. What can she say to him? She shrugs, 'Why does anyone get married?'

'For love?'

'Very rarely, I fear. We got married because we met and there was no one else, and it just sort of happened.'

'Do you think he loved you?'

Where has this line of questioning come from? She wonders. After all these years why does he want to dig all this up? 'Yes, I think he did in his own way.'

'But his love wasn't good enough.'

'I'm surprised you don't think it was me that wasn't good enough for him.' She is gratified to see him redden slightly. He changes the subject, 'How's your lunch?'

'Contrary to all expectations, it's very nice. Just a shame about the lack of ambience.'

'What more could you want, Mother? The sun is out, you have a clear blue sky, and my company.'

'More comfortable chairs.'

'There, I have to agree with you.'

She raises her fork daintily to her lips and chews slowly whilst busying herself in preparation for the next mouthful. 'By the way, did I tell you that girl, Angela, came to see me? She brought me that portrait.'

'The one of your father?'

Rachel nods.

'Are you going to tell me, Mother, how you are related to that French woman?'

'Oh, you do go on. My father's mother was French. All right?'

'Why don't you ever want to talk about these things?'

'What's the point? They're all in the past.'

'Yes, but don't you see,' Edward says, gesturing with his hands, 'that's why I want to talk about them.'

'She seems a nice enough girl. Interested, almost passionate, about art.'

'I presume we're talking about Angela, now.'

'Yes,' she smiles. 'Someone in the present.'

'She asked me to model for her.'

Rachel thinks she has misheard. 'What did you say?'

'She's asked me to model for her.'

Rachel feels her face stiffen. 'What a nerve. What did you say?'

'I've been going to her studio for about a month now.'

He sounds very pleased with himself.

She ponders for a moment, 'Not… nude?'

'Yes, of course.'

'Are you crazy?' She shakes her head. 'Why on earth would she want to draw you?'

'Maybe, unlike you and most other people, she doesn't find me grotesque.'

'She's using you, more like. How dare she?'

'I am a grown man,' he says quietly. 'Perfectly capable of looking after myself.'

'Edward, you mustn't let her do this. It's wrong, very wrong.'

His voice rises in pitch, 'Why, for God's sake?'

'What do you think she is going to do with the drawings when she's finished? Put them in a drawer and forget about them? No. She's going to display them. Tell me you feel comfortable having your naked body paraded before the world.'

'You mean, like a freak show?'

She notices the tone of his voice is now lower. 'Always you have to twist what I say. Look at you. You walk through life hoping no-one will notice you and then some girl comes along and flatters your vanity and you end up naked. What if you got your portrait in the newspaper? How would that feel?'

'Don't worry, Mother. I won't tell them I'm Rachel Anderson's son – the woman who surrounds herself with beauty, but didn't quite manage it with her son. Anyway, what about when you did it?''

She searches his face. Surely, she thinks, he doesn't know, couldn't know. How could he?

'Did what?' she whispers.

He looks down into his lap and fiddles with the end of his tie.

'Edward? Did what?' Her voice is unsteady.

He looks straight at her. 'When you were an artist's model?'

She finds it difficult to take in what he has just said. He wasn't alluding to Uncle Jack after all, but this. 'How did you find out about that?' She sits back in her chair.

'Angela told me. Were you doing it while Father was still alive? While I was still living at home?'

She can feel all the blood drain from her face. 'I can't remember,' she stammers.

'Well, Mother. Why did you do it?'

'Listen to you.' She sits forward, suddenly angry. She picks up her bag from the table. 'What right do you have to pry into my private life?'

Rachel stands waiting for the bus. She is still shaking with rage. How dare he question her on her private life, and how dare he question the way she had treated his father. He had no idea what she'd had to put up with.

She had met him at a dance in the City Hall. He was a good-looking lad, in an ordinary sort of way. He kissed her on their third date. It was a good, sweet kiss, but nothing else. She wished he had at least attempted something else, like some of the other boys had. Their desire for her had made her want to go further, but with George, there was none of that. Was he too respectful? He obviously liked her. She was puzzled. War broke out and before he went off to the front he asked her to marry him. The war brought with it a sense of possibility, a smell of change, so she said, 'Maybe, maybe not!'

Her mother had been furious with her. 'You silly girl,' she'd said. 'You could be getting and saving his wage, ready for when he comes home.' Rachel hadn't cared. She wanted to see what other hands the cards dealt her and, until they were married, she was still free.

She remembers him coming home on leave in 1944, two days after her twentieth birthday. He seemed different. He had become quieter, stronger and thinner; and Rachel could see the muscles in his face twitch taut. They went to Whitby for their honeymoon. Two days in a boarding house. Rachel wanted to ask him if he'd ever done it before, or if it was just her that he felt no passion for?

Edward must have been conceived in those two days; silent sex in the dark each night before they went to sleep.

Nine months later, Edward was born while George was still in Germany. For reasons of her own she had expected that the baby might come after seven months.

By the time George came back, Edward was already three months old.

CHAPTER TWENTY-NINE

She had started school that Easter, so she must have been nearly five. It was the first time since she'd been a baby that her parents had returned. Her gran didn't tell her it was her mum, but Angela knew that this woman with black toenails and an open sore leaking down the side of her nose was her mother. She never heard what they were talking about that time; her mother never got past the front door and only stayed five minutes. Angela watched from her bedroom window as they loped off down the street without a backward glance. They hadn't come to see her. That much was obvious.

The second time they came, Angela's life changed forever.

She'd been torn between observing the man she thought was her father, who stood across the road nervously picking his nails, and listening to what was going on downstairs. The whining tone of her mother's voice drew her to the top of the stairs. She was pleading for something. The same tone over and over. Her gran wasn't saying anything.

'Please Mum, just to tide us over. Let us try and make a new life for ourselves.'

When her gran spoke, her voice was low and precise, so low that Angela could only just make it out, 'Don't you think I have enough expense bringing up your daughter without one penny from you? Your poor father at sixty-six is still having to work his socks off.'

What her gran said hurt Angela, but what her mother said made her break out in a cold sweat.

'I could take her off you, you know? She only stays here because I let her.'

Angela heard the front door open and her grandmother using the same tone, low and precise,

'Get out! Get out!'

Occasionally over the years they would get a phone call in the night. The phone would ring and ring. Once, she got up to answer it. She knew then why her grandfather stopped her grandmother from answering it. The voice was slurred as if the woman was drunk:

'*Mother?...Is that you? Could you send me some money?*'

She replaced the receiver without a word and went back to bed. She could hear her grandparents arguing; her granddad threatening to get the number changed. It never was. Her gran needed the ring of the phone in the night because, however painful, at least she knew her daughter was still alive, eking out an existence somewhere across the other side of the city.

CHAPTER THIRTY

Edward feels tired, his back aches and he has pins and needles in his right foot. He can hear Angela scratching, rubbing... more scratching.

'You're quiet today,' he says.

'Yes, sorry. I'm concentrating. I think this is the best pose yet.'

He is kneeling as if praying to Allah, his forehead resting on an old piece of blanket that Angela has brought from home. Edward finds the blanket prickly. It is a rough grey army blanket. Its only sense of luxury is a pale blue blanket stitch neatening the edges. He remembers one from his childhood. It was pink and soft and the ribbon had frayed all along one edge and sometimes when he awoke in the morning it was tickling his nose. His mother had eventually mended it, making the ribbon band narrower. Edward, for some perverse reason, had missed the tickle.

He feels slightly disgruntled that she has asked him to take up such an undignified pose. She seems to have taken little account of his disability, or his dignity come to that. He looks between his legs, sees his penis dangling free. There is only one benefit to being in this pose; he can't see her. He wishes now that he had never got her to agree to being undressed. He thinks back to that time. Would he have still gone ahead with the sittings? Yes, probably, and he wouldn't be in the tangle he's in now. But there again, does he not wait all week just to be here, studying the wonder of her? He feels so fragile, as if perched on the edge of a deep ravine, knowing that if he jumps he will feel the exhilaration of flight, but knowing that when he reaches the bottom his whole being will be smashed into a thousand pieces.

'This blanket's scratchy as hell,' he grumbles.

'Would my lord like me to bring a nice soft baby blanket next time?'

'You may mock, but you don't have to have your face pressed into it.'

Angela laughs, 'That's why you sound like you're underwater.'

'Can I rest yet?'

'No. Please, just hang on a bit longer. That was my granddad's army blanket you know?'

He smiles to himself. He knows that she is again trying to distract him away from wanting to move.

'I know what you're saying about it being a bit rough,' she continues, 'but it means so much to me that I wanted to draw it into the picture. I did all that blanket-stitching around the edge, you know? My gran had to show me over and over how to do it. I was really proud of myself once I'd finally mastered it. When my granddad came in from work that night he was so thrilled with what I'd done to his blanket, or he pretended to be. He gave me the whisker treatment. It took me days to finish it, especially since I kept stitching it to my skirt.

'What happened to your parents?' He waits for an answer.

'Nothing,' she says. The quiet tone of her voice warns him off asking any further questions.

He has put the bag with the rope handles inside a nondescript plastic carrier and hidden it under his coat that he has placed in the corner at the back of the room. Today, he grits his teeth. He will give her the bra today. He will do it just before he leaves.

'Are you okay?' she enquires, still drawing.

'I need to move.'

'Just hang on... Bugger... Edward, you moved.'

'Like I said, I need to move.'

'Just try and keep still for a bit longer.'

He'd thought that, over time, she might have learnt to be a bit more considerate. Fat chance! The dust of the old blanket is making him want to sneeze. His face feels hot, flushed where the blood has gathered.

'I won't be a sec, I just need to hatch in these lines to create the indents in the small of your back.' Edward hears her sigh. 'I'm really struggling to get the shape today. The contours, the shadows, all seem to be playing tricks on me. Okay, relax.'

'I've set. Give me a hand.'

'Edward, before you move, can I ask you a question?'

'Make it quick.'

'Can I, would you mind very much… if I wanted to touch your back?'

He laughs, a sharp intake of breath, 'Why?'

'I'm really struggling to get the angles, so I thought, maybe, if I moulded it with my hands it might help.'

'Okay, but not in this position. Sit me up.'

'This position would be better.' She stands over him.

'Well, tough.' He presses his hands into the blanket and raises himself up off his elbows. Angela helps him sit up.

'Right.' he says, 'First, I want a drink of water.'

He feels her place her hands, like a healer, one on top of the other, on the most prominent part of his back. The pressure of her hands, her fingers trying to separate the line of his ribs. He feels her breath on his skin; smells again the faint musky unwashed scent of her, so close. She presses harder into his back. He feels himself drawn back to the edge of the ravine. A shudder runs through him.

'Surely you're not cold. Your skin feels lovely and warm, you're like a little oven. Does that hurt?'

She separates her hands, moulds both of them around his hump.

'No, no. It may look strange but it doesn't hurt to touch. In fact, it feels lovely.' He gives out a deep sigh. 'How does it feel, my china bird? Like you expected?'

'Knobbly, yet smooth and warm and soft. It's like, as if it's how it should feel. I don't know. I'm not making sense am I? Each side feels so different.' She traces her finger down his spine, 'It's curved, like a loop in a river. How can it happen? I don't understand. Is it the spine that contorts the ribs, or the ribs that contort the spine?'

'Imagine that you have a straight spine with a circle of ribs extending from it, like a rounded wicker basket, one of the vertical poles being the spine. Now if you put a twist in the spine, the ribs are still coming off in a circle but it's no longer a round circle, it has a skew in it.'

'Is it operable?'

'In a lot of cases, yes. In fact, you don't even have to operate if it's caught early enough. It can be moulded back into place by using a Plaster of Paris girdle.'

'So why didn't that happen to you?'

'Mine started when I was older.'

'Didn't anyone notice?'

'I did, but I just sort of kept quiet. I was of the age where I'd stopped undressing in front of my parents and they didn't notice until it was too late. Uncle Ruben was the first one to see something was wrong. I went for a jacket fitting and he kept clucking and frowning, then he insisted on coming back on the train with me to see my parents.

'And have you never thought of an operation?'

'No. I just want to be left as I am.'

'But what about the pain? Do you get much pain?'

'Only when some young woman expects me to take up strange positions and stay still for hours on end.'

She laughs, 'All in the pursuance of art, my good man.'

'When I was in my late teens the consultant suggested surgery. Having my back pinned and rodded, my ribs removed and refitted, like re-caning an old chair. I don't think so.'

'But why not? It could've made a huge difference to your life.'

'No, I'm not sure it would. If I'd ended up paralysed, as they said I might, I wouldn't be sitting here with you massaging my back. Don't stop.'

'Is it that good?'

'You have really good hands. Strong but gentle.'

Edward closes his eyes. He is imagining himself watching Angela tracing the lines of his back. He sees her bending forward, whispering his back with the tips of her nipples. He is slipping, falling over the edge of the ravine. Oh God, he must think of something else. The rope handled bag, lurking in the corner. How is he ever going to give her the bra now? He imagines her wearing it; her breasts encased in crimson lace. He quickly opens his eyes.

'Right!' She stands up. 'I think I'll have another go at drawing your back. Can you try and get back into the same position?'

Edward groans, 'I thought we'd finished.'

'Please........'

'I'm not sure I can. I don't feel so good.' He takes a deep breath, trying to slow down the beating of his heart.

'I won't be long, honest,' she pleads, 'If you just give me ten minutes I think I can pull it off now.'

He shakes his head in disbelief. 'What a slave driver,' he says, placing his head back down on the blanket.

'Right, I'll just put a fresh piece of paper on my board.' She comes to stand above him, board in hand.

'Why are you standing so close?'

'Gives me a different perspective, I can now see all of your back and with the sun having moved the light is catching different areas, like sand dunes in the late afternoon. I can see the whole of your spine, follow it right down to its source where it splays out at the base; shadowed as it passes the valley created by your hump.'

'Are you sure you aren't a poet as well as an artist?'

'I wonder how the spine decides which way to curve.'

'I can't remember which way it is but it's more prevalent on one side in boys and vice versa with girls,' he mumbles into the blanket.

'Are you on the side of the boys or the girls?'

'Probably the opposite from what I should be.'

'I think I'd already supposed that.'

Back at his lodgings, Edward realises that he would like nothing more than a hot bath to ease his aching back. His tea, a cold-plated salad, is waiting for him on the side in the kitchen, cling-filmed to perfection. He'd hoped that Mrs Ingram would be out at the bingo, but no, she is there, hovering,

'Late tonight, Mr Anderson? Good job I did you something cold.'

She laughs at her own joke. As if it isn't written in stone that Saturdays are always cold ham salad.

'Would you mind if I had a bath, Mrs Ingram?'

'But it's not Thursday.'

'Yes, I'm aware of that, having seen what's for tea, but I would still like a bath.'

'Well, yes, all right then, but I was about... I was thinking about going to the Bingo.'

'Then go.'

'Yes, but, I don't like leaving you on your own if you're going in the bath, and there's no hot water. It'll take half-an-hour.'

'If we switch on the immersion now and I have my tea meanwhile, then the water will be hot enough, and I promise I won't drown while you're out.'

'My Gus drowned in that bath you know. They said it was a heart attack. It was awful. They had to lift him out of the bath naked.'

Edward holds onto the metal handles and sinks into the warm water. If only he could put enough in so that he could float and not feel the hard surface of the enamel on his back. He still hasn't given her the bra. Next week, definitely. Next week he will give it to her, he promises himself. He closes his eyes and there, floating in the water, is Mr. Ingram. He sits up. Now, every time he takes a bath, he'll know that Mr. Ingram is with him.

CHAPTER THIRTY-ONE

Rachel is seated on a bench in the centre of the main gallery. She is studying a painting of a woman with glossy black hair. The woman is looking out of an open window, leaning her elbows on the stone sill. The pale yellow paint of the house is peeling away to reveal the grey rendering beneath. The woman is smiling invitingly down to the street below.

Her teeth fascinate Rachel; they are slightly crooked but of a perfect size for her face and the artist has caught exactly the glint and translucency.   There are no secrets in the woman's eyes; everything is on display. The picture irritates her, especially since it has temporarily replaced her favourite picture, a bowl of glistening white roses. Rachel closes her eyes and breathes deeply. She feels so restless that even the picture of the white roses would not have calmed her today. She delves into her shopping bag and retrieves a sandwich box and a red thermos flask with a white screw-on cup.

It was today that she had wanted to meet Edward for lunch at Henry's, but for some reason he had put her off until next week. And she had the girl's ballet ticket, not that she deserved it. Fancy manipulating Edward like that. What was she playing at? If she'd seen her at Henry's she could have taken her to task. Is that why Edward had put her off? Had he seen through her little plan? She supposed there was nothing to stop her going to Henry's on her own. She could save her sandwiches for tea.

She thinks back to their last lunch together at the Blue Moon Café. Strange, Edward saying that about his father taking him to the art gallery, and about the Grimshaw paintings. It was as if he knew why she had been to Leeds. She had gone to see if they were still there. The ones her mother used to take her to see as a young child.

She knew instinctively the days when her mother would be taking her to the art gallery. A few days before, a restlessness would come upon her mother, a noticeable anger with her work. The bursts of the sewing machine would be faster, louder, not caring if she annoyed the neighbours on all three sides. Then one morning Rachel would wake very early, sometimes, in winter, before first light, to silence. Rachel knew that day they would be going to the art gallery.

Her mother would pack salt beef sandwiches and a thermos of strong, sweet black coffee into a canvas bag. The coffee was the family's only luxury; coffee beans her father brought home from the market.

They would walk into the city, away from the ugliness of the back-to-back, red brick streets and always they would go to the gallery. It was free and warm and there were their pictures. Her mother would wander round and round. Rachel would try to keep to her mother's pace but often she was too slow and Rachel would dance ahead. Sometimes her mother would sit on the bench in the centre.

'Soaking it all in,' she would say, 'Storing a bit of beauty for later.'

When Rachel's brother Ruben was born their secret visits stopped and her father stopped grumbling about her mother getting behind with work.

Her mother had never told her not to tell anyone where they'd been but Rachel knew, even as a young child, that she didn't want to tell her father or anyone else of her favourite picture: a canal bronzed by the sinking sun, and her mother's favourite, a dimly lit street of winter trees, a carriage waiting, the horse fretting. Her mother told her how it reminded her of her childhood in Russia, and how much she missed her homeland, and how Rachel's granddad had been a furrier, making coats for all the rich ladies, and how she imagined them in the carriage wrapped in the fur coats her father had made for them.'

'Why did you come to Leeds,' Rachel had asked.

'By mistake,' her mother had replied. 'We were going to America but when we got off the boat at Hull my parents thought we had arrived in New York. When grandfather realised his mistake he wanted to go on but your grandmother was already three months pregnant with your Uncle Jack and had been very ill just crossing the North Sea. She begged him to wait until after the baby was born. He agreed as long as they moved to Leeds where he had heard there was plenty of work for furriers and tailors, and that they would stay only until after the birth.

It had felt so delicious sharing these secrets with her mother.

She wonders which of the pictures were Edward's favourites. Why had she never thought to take him as a child? She has a sudden pang of regret and then she remembers his comments about her modelling. How dare he pry into her private life?

No, she won't go to Henry's to see the girl.

Once home, Rachel places her sandwich box and flask on the small table next to her chair. The table had been the largest of a nest of three, and the next size down was now her bedside table. When George was alive, he had made a matching pair of white Formica bedside cabinets. She threw them out the week after he died. Hers had been stacked with books, his empty, except for a few balls of grey fluff, one gardening magazine, and a pink plastic mug containing his top set of teeth. The undertaker asked her for them but she feigned ignorance. The smallest table had been George's. It was charred with black lines around the edge, where he had rested his burning cigarette while reading his paper. She had thrown that table out with the cabinets.

She lowers herself slowly into her chair and exhales, glad to be home. Turning, she twists the top off her flask and pours hot milk into the lid. She places the lunch box on her lap to act as a plate and peels back the lid, picking up one of the small triangular sandwiches. Her lunch and her tea can be as one, she thinks, as she places Edward's unopened letter that she had found lying on the mat, on the table beside her.

The envelope for some reason reminds her of her brother Ruben and, for the first time in years, she yearns to see him again. To see his crooked smile.

A movement against the French window distracts her. She looks up to see the cat pressing its body against the distorted old glass, meowing to be let in. Rachel ignores him and stares up at the one remaining blood red rose. She had not had the heart to cut it back last winter and it had become crystallized by the frost. The branch must have worked its way loose from the trellis, the thorns scratching gently against the glass. She looks down the garden and notes that the few stray bells on the wild fuchsia bush are a softer red than the rose. She hadn't had the strength to cut it back properly and now it is flowering early. In the past she had always been impatient to cut away the dead wood, knowing, as George had taught her, that if she cuts it back before March, then the flowers the following summer would be sparse against the green foliage. Maybe that was the only thing they eventually grew to have in common, the garden. He taught her that she could not have the garden as tidy as the house, that you had to wait, let nature take its course. They would argue about it when, bored with the house, she would start to tidy the garden, cutting back the dishevelled daffodil leaves.

He had shaken his head. 'You'll spoil it for next year, lass,' was all he'd said. She laughed at him, told him not to be so daft, but each spring, her daffodils, that he had so lovingly planted for her one cold October day, became less and less until one year they disappeared altogether. He said nothing, just bought some more bulbs in the market and went out on a cold October day to plant them. She had helped him that year. Edward had stayed inside. She could see his face now, pressed up against the French windows, wondering what his parents were doing out together in the cold, working in silence.

That night, for the first time in years, they'd had sex. She had awoken to find him fumbling up her nightie. Is that what had aroused him, her silent submission with the bulbs? She'd felt for him, pulled him towards her.

'Steady lass, steady.'

He began to slacken in her hand. She turned away and let him continue, after a pause, with his fumblings.

The garden had gradually become hers. That summer he had applied to the council for an allotment. They gave him one, high on the hill, south facing. In the summer, he'd told her, he could see the peaks far in the distance, and in the winter he would watch the weather roll in off the Pennines.

George had been an ordinary man, a very ordinary man. She had not wanted to be ordinary herself but, as his wife, she supposed she had become ordinary by association. He'd died one July, twenty-six years ago. An odd time of the year to die, when all the rest of the world was bursting with life. He had gone to sleep as normal, while she read her book. She had not even said goodnight to him. In the morning when she awoke, he was lying still beside her. He had always been an early riser, even in retirement. She sensed immediately that something was wrong and slowly, very slowly, put her hand out to touch him. His flesh was stone cold. She jumped out of bed and ran from the room.

She found some of her old clothes she'd put out for jumble in the spare bedroom and put them on over her nightie before ringing the doctor. She remembered thinking how quickly the doctor had arrived to see a dead body, as if it had been an emergency. When Rachel stripped the bed later, she wondered, as she threw all the bedding in the bin and turned and scrubbed the mattress, why she had felt so afraid, why she had been so frightened of a body that she had slept next to for all those years. It was still George after all. But the fact that his body was no longer warm seemed to have changed everything.

There were some things about George that she missed; the cabbages from his allotment, the neatly folded hankies in the drawer, his half-done crosswords that she would finish. But gradually, the space that he had occupied filled up, and the house, the cat, and she herself, breathed a single sigh of parting.

She took to visiting the art gallery every day, just for something to do, to get her out of the house. There was a bench in the centre of the main hall where she could gradually shift along the outer edge of the black leather circle, feeling the piping under her fingers, studying the pictures. Sometimes, she would stand up close to a painting to study a detail, a shipwreck; waves high and white, a wicker basket being carried out to sea. She wanted to know what was inside the wicker basket. Some days she imagined it was just a woman's sewing basket, but on others it contained a baby lost at sea, to be washed up, days later, on a strange shore.

CHAPTER THIRTY-TWO

Edward has placed his chair under the skylight and, like a lizard on a rock, is basking in the sun. He lets out a soft moan,

'I love sitting in the sun. I wish I'd been born a cat.'

Angela closes the door. 'A stripy ginger tom?'

'Marmalade. I would like to be called, Marmalade.'

'Thick cut or thin?'

'Just old-fashioned 1864 variety.'

'Are you a connoisseur of marmalade?' Angela tilts her head sideways, 'Yes, I can just see you in the morning, china rack full of toast triangles, white I think, and a newspaper and a pat of butter in a small white dish, the butter indented with a clover leaf shape, of course, and a china bowl with a lid on it and a silver spoon and inside, glowing orange marmalade with thin strips, like little goldfish in jelly. And a china cup and saucer filled with real coffee, with maybe hot milk or cream and, of course, a crisp linen napkin rolled in a silver ring.'

Edward gets up and pulls his tie to one side. 'Oh, I wish, I wish. Mrs Ingram wouldn't know class like that if she fell over it in the street. I have to have the mandatory egg, scrambled or poached, every day. Yes, every day.'

'You're only supposed to eat three eggs a week.'

'And cornflakes.'

'No toast?'

'She can't ever do it without burning it, so I've given up on the toast, and we don't get butter, we have something that 'spreads straight from the fridge'.'

Angela takes off her coat and places it on the back of her chair. She crosses her arms over and, clutching the ribbed border of her jumper, pulls it off over her head.

Edward had expected to see a cotton tee shirt, and then that peeled away too, revealing a bra, but, no, not today – just skin.

She grins at him, 'Easy access.'

He frowns, 'I don't understand.'

'I couldn't be arsed putting it all on to take it all off again.'

He watches her. She is so uninhibited about her body. He stares in amazement at her breasts, so different from Tessa's huge ones bulging with blue veins. These are tender, nubile.

Angela grins. 'Are you observing?'

'Yes.' He looks up into her face. 'Don't take this the wrong way, but I was just thinking, well, how I'd like to cup your breasts in my hands.' The words are out of his mouth before he can stop them.

He whispers, almost to himself. 'Would it be like holding freshly-laid eggs?'

For a split second he sees the shock on her face, her hands automatically moving up to her breasts. He looks down at his shoes. Oh God, what has he done?

'I shouldn't have said that, sorry. It's just that, well, all this,' he gestures with his arms. 'I just don't know what to think anymore. I suppose I look at your body from an artistic point of view now,' he lies.

She lets her hands drop to her sides, 'Okay then.'

'What do you mean?'

'It's only fair, I suppose. You let me touch your back last week.'

His voice sticks in his throat. 'Slightly different, don't you think.'

'Not sure. They're bumps too, aren't they?' She looks straight at him, goading him, daring him to take up the challenge.

He can feel the heat rising up his neck. Damn her. 'Are you making fun of me?' His voice is only just louder than a whisper.

'Listen, Edward. Whoa, a minute. If you don't want to, no hassle,' she shrugs her shoulders. He sees her give a half smile.

He closes his eyes, wishing the floor would open and swallow him up.

'Can I ask you something?'

He notes the curiosity in her voice. He opens his eyes.

'It's a bit personal,' she adds.

He nods, 'What?'

'I just had a thought, have you never touched a woman's breasts before?'

'Of course I have.' She knows he is lying, he can see this in her face.

She stands in front of him, looks straight into his eyes, reaches out and takes his hands, guides them to her breasts and holds them there. He wants to weep with joy, his whole body is singing.

'Tell me how they feel?' she whispers.

He closes his eyes, rubs his thumbs over the curved surface and almost instinctively catches her nipples between his thumb and forefinger. He can feel her warm breath on his shoulder. More than anything he wants to bend and place his lips to them. Instead, he opens his eyes and pulls his hands away, sits down heavily on the comfortable chair. He doesn't want to speak. He wants to sit there with his eyes closed, hold the moment forever, but he feels that he must break the tension. He looks up at her, 'Such a unique sensation. They have a weight all of their own, and such a pleasing shape. And they're warm. For some reason that surprised me. I now know why I thought they'd feel like new-laid eggs. Have you ever put your hand under a sitting hen to collect an egg? That's how it feels.'

She wraps her arms around her body, covering her breasts. 'You have a lovely turn of phrase,' she grins.

He suddenly feels emboldened, nods towards her, indicating her arms,

'Feeling shy are we?'

She laughs, letting her arms fall to her sides, 'I think we'd better get started.'

Oh God. He'd forgotten totally why he was here in the first place. He tries to sound light hearted, 'And how would Madame like me today? Like lamb on lettuce?'

'Not sure how to tell you this, but today I want to draw your manhood.'

'What do you mean?'

'How shall I put it politely, your groin! I want you to sit back in the chair with your legs open.'

This is the last thing he wants to hear. 'And why, may I ask?'

'When I said I wanted to draw your manhood, I wasn't just being polite. The other night I was looking at what I've done so far and I realised I hadn't done much in that area. Been trying to preserve your modesty.' She gives him a little smile.

'Hmm.'

'What I'm trying to say is, part of you may be deformed, but you are a man, and your manhood is also a part of who you are. I'm not doing very well here, am I? Look, I don't just want to draw pictures of your disability. I want to show you as a whole person. Your face, your genitals, all of you. So how about getting undressed?'

'After what you've just told me?'

She laughs. 'There is one advantage, you can talk and move your head around today, Mr. Fidget. Just keep your tackle still.'

'I didn't realise you saw me as a man.' He watches for her reaction.

She gives him another smile, 'I'm full of surprises, aren't I?'

'I think this is a conspiracy. Revenge.'

'Would I do such a thing?'

'Yes.'

He goes behind the screen, deciding it's better to get undressed in privacy. He sits down to undo his shoelaces and wishes he could remain dressed today. Maybe he could say he isn't feeling well.

'Come on, Edward. Don't take all day. I've got loads to do.'

'How about fetching me a coffee then, bossy boots.'

'Oh, all right,' he hears her grumble. 'I'll have to put my top back on though.'

The door clicks shut. He breathes a sigh of relief. He has a few minutes to still his thoughts. He looks down at his penis nestling against his leg. She is going to draw his manhood. Why should he have a problem with that? In a certain way he is glad. He smiles to himself. It is one part of his body he should not be ashamed of. He sits back and waits, listening for her coming back along the corridor, all the while thinking... she had let him hold her breasts. In his wildest dreams he had never expected that. A sudden awful thought occurs to him, it wipes away the joy he had been feeling. Why had she done it? Why had she let an old crippled man touch her beautiful breasts? Out of pity? Of course, there could be no other reason.

Angela is looking at him, one eye closed. She nods. He sees her tentatively start. He wants her to talk. He doesn't want to sit in silence again. He wants her voice to still the thoughts in his head,

'Talk to me while you're drawing. Describe to me what you're doing.'

She gives him a quizzical look, 'Okay, I'll try.'

He sees her bite into her cheek, trying to concentrate.

'Go on then.'

'I'm starting at the indent of your waist, then working downwards along the outer thigh. The muscle there is slightly tensed, it appears rounded where the light catches.' He looks down. Yes, she is right.

'And then the inner thigh,' she continues. 'I'm now working back up, hatching fine shadows along the darker, denser areas, moulding up to the slight, bulbous shape of your testicles.' He sees she is smirking to herself.

'Now your penis, It's similar to your leg in that it catches light on one side, shadows on the other; masses of tiny creased rings down to the head where it forms into a soft flap. And now the navel… an indented shadow… and up to your ribs; one side is placed like evenly splayed fingers, the other side a tangled wreck which distorts your nipple up and away from its twin…God, I'm exhausted.' She sits back.

'Have you finished? Can I have a look?'

He comes and stands behind her, wanting no further permission. He looks down at the drawing of himself, yet it is not quite him. This man has such assurance.

'I look quite a stud, don't I? If it wasn't for that bit of twisted metal there,' he points to his ribs, 'you'd think I was a man in my prime. I think you haven't caught me quite right.'

'Edward, that's exactly how you look. I admit, the languid pose helps. The assurance of the pose says: This is who I am. You may look at me in my entirety.'

He smiles, 'You're very good, you know.'

He feels suddenly awkward, standing naked beside her. He goes behind the screen and gets dressed. Seeing those drawings has given him courage.

'Can I ask you something,' he says, from behind the screen. He hears her still the rattle of her fixative can.

'Yes?'

'I want to know why you allowed me to hold your breasts. Was it out of pity?' There, he has said it. He comes from behind the screen.

'No.' She shakes her head. 'You're strange.'

He looks her in the eye. She is telling the truth.

'I was just wondering you see…' he tails off.

'Let me ask you a question then,' she counters. 'Do you come here to sit for me week after week out of pity?'

'No,' he laughs, 'of course not.'

'Then let me grant you that small request, eh? Out of pure gratitude for all you have done for me. Pity.' She picks up her can and rattles it urgently.

He pauses, his hand on the aluminium door handle. She turns again, smiles,

'You still here?'

'I've got something for you.' He hesitates, 'I wasn't going to give it to you, it's a bit silly really. Sort of, bought it on impulse.'

Angela, who is kneeling on her haunches, stands up slowly, curious, 'What do you mean?' She looks down at the white paper bag with rope handles he is clutching. He places it on the chair between them and backs away towards the door.

'Hang on. Don't go. I don't understand. What's wrong?'

He reddens, 'I just bought you a present and now… and now I'm embarrassed at my silliness. So I'm going before you open it.'

'Please don't. Just think how much more embarrassed you will be next week if you go now.'

He watches. As if in slow motion, she puts her hand inside the bag and pulls out the buff coloured box tied with a pink ribbon. She pulls at the ribbon and in one motion it ripples to the floor. She lifts the lid, tugs at the tissue paper, lifts out a crimson bra. She gasps, letting the box rattle to the floor. He sees, as he backs towards the door, her face and neck blotch with red. He hears the door click shut behind him. His own footsteps as he makes his way down the corridor.

Edward wakes. It is the middle of the night. Something is wrong with his body. Oh God! He thinks of his father and the silent heart attack that had killed him in the night. But there is no pain in his chest. It is his groin. There is something wrong with his groin. He fumbles for the bedside light switch and throws back the sheets, blinking. Has he wet himself? He undoes his pyjama cord. His penis, erect and at right angles to his body, nods out. Edward gasps, reaches down and takes it in his hand. He gasps again, but this time with the pleasure of skin on smooth skin. His stretched penis is silky soft and has its own weight, like Angela's breasts. He stands up, letting his pyjamas drop to the floor. Stepping out of them he drags his chair across to the dresser. He clambers onto the chair and stands looking in amazement at his erection in the mirror. It looks so very strange. He presses it down but it bobs back up again. He must have been fifteen the last time he had an erection. He climbs cautiously down and as he does so the end of his penis touches the edge of the chair. He lets out a little squeal of pleasure. Slowly, he starts to rub his hand along his penis, delighting at how the skin slides up and down. He hears the landing light go on and Mrs Ingram shuffling along the corridor to the bathroom. She stops outside his door. He thinks she is going to knock and ask, 'Is everything is all right, Mr Anderson?', but she passes.

He looks down at his penis.

It is a crumpled shell in his hand.

CHAPTER THIRTY-THREE

For how long had he tried to forget that day in the barn? Snuggled there among the straw, bale upon bale, balanced almost to the rafters? His mother had told him not to go up there. She'd said there were rats, so when he clambered up the bales he always dragged with him his favourite farm cat, black and soft and kind natured, not like the other cats that ran wild. Mouser, they called her. Uncle said she was the best.

He had lain there stroking Mouser, looking up at the rafters, watching the swallows dive in and out, for what seemed an age. He heard someone come into the barn. It was Uncle Jack. He was mending a piece of machinery at his bench, using that grease gun that looked like a squashed metal teapot. He was humming to himself and Edward was just about to call out to him, proud to be king of the castle, when he saw his mother silhouetted against the door. She was wearing a floral summer dress, belted at the waist, that she had made herself the week before they had travelled down. It was yellow with big red poppies. Edward had thought she looked beautiful in it.

His uncle stopped what he was doing and wiped his hands on an old rag and then, to Edward's surprise, he put his arms around his mother's waist. She'd laughed and tried to pull away, but he'd held her, all the time trying to unbuckle his belt. He undid his fly and fumbled inside. Turning her around with one hand, he bent her over the bench. He lifted the hem of her dress, showing her bare white legs, and Edward saw that she wasn't wearing any underwear. And then he was doing something to her, pushing and thrusting into her. She was groaning out loud, head flung back, teeth bared like a horse.

Edward wanted to shout out – Stop it! Stop hurting her! – but it was as if he was frozen in time. He tried to turn away but he couldn't. His mother had her elbows on the bench, her hands around the vice and the thought flashed through his mind that he hoped she wasn't getting oil on her new dress. Suddenly and without warning she screamed out, followed shortly by a loud cry from his uncle. And then silence, except for the faint sound of their breathing as it quietened to nothing. His uncle pulled away from her and Edward saw his penis, pink and slimy. His mother picked up the oily rag from the bench, wiped between her legs and then without another word, turned and walked out of the barn, her yellow dress catching the light as she walked across the yard.

Edward lay there in the straw all afternoon gazing up at the rafters, or watching his uncle working away as if nothing had happened. Had he dreamed it? He clutched his head in his hands and tried to erase image but he couldn't. Later, he heard his mother calling him from the farmhouse. He watched his uncle wipe his hands on the same rag his mother had used, and leave. He waited a few minutes, then followed.

After that he saw his mother and uncle through different eyes. He noticed new things about them, even in the way they laughed. He looked at his aunt, but she was unchanged, unseeing.

A few days later his uncle called in the vet. He said Meg the mare needed seeing to. The vet brought with him a stamping white stallion in a horsebox. Edward swung on the gate and watched. He saw the stallion mount poor Meg and bite viciously into her mane. His eyes were pulled back and wild and he was foaming at the mouth, his lip curled back revealing brown teeth.

His uncle came to stand beside him, 'You shouldn't be watching this, lad. You'll get me in to trouble with your mother.'

'What are they doing? Why are you letting that horrible horse hurt Meg? Why don't you stop it?'

His uncle laughed, 'You city boys. He's servicing her.'

Edward frowned, uncomprehending.

'Giving her a baby,' his uncle continued, 'unless a boy and a girl horse do that, they can't have babies.'

'Do other animals do it?'

'Yes, of course.'

'Do humans?'

His uncle ruffled his hair. 'How do you think you got here?'

'Does my mother want another baby?'

His uncle frowned. 'How on earth should I know that, lad? That's between your mother and father.' He shook his head and walked away.

That week Edward watched his mother closely. He noticed that on the day they were leaving she again sought out her uncle in the barn. Edward crept close and heard again the same animal-like noises.

On the train home Edward sat in the opposite corner to his mother, pretending to read. He hated her. When they arrived at their destination his father was there to meet them and his mother was all smiles. Edward busied himself with the suitcases. He didn't know how he was ever going to look his father in the eye again.

CHAPTER THIRTY-FOUR

Edward pushes the brass bar that slants across the glass door of Henry's Restaurant. It opens without effort.

'Up there, I think.' Rachel says, pointing to a raised area to their right. Edward pulls out a chair for his mother and then walks around the table to take his seat, while at the same time hanging his stick over the railings. He looks down into the bar area and watches the waitresses receiving their instructions for the lunchtime shift. No sign of Angela. He breathes a sigh of relief.

In the area where he and his mother are seated, a cool darkness pervades. Overgrown ferns on high plinths shade the light from the large windows of old-fashioned glass that mist and distort the street and the people hurrying past. He watches a waitress approach and notices how the high ceilings echo the sound of her heels on the plank floor.

He wonders what people must make of him and his mother. He looks across at her; an old lady, dainty as a child, so expectant, her arm held tightly across her body, grasping the flesh of her other arm, anticipating her lunchtime treat. Himself? He glances at his image distorted by the glass, his deformed back, and yet, he looks again, there is a certain style. Are they two actors on a stage for all the world to see, acting out a farce, their relationship pure theatre?

'Mother?'

Rachel is scanning the faces of the waitresses. Edward suspects she is looking for Angela, 'Mother?'

'Sorry?'

'The waitress is here. What would you like to drink?'

Rachel frowns, still scanning the room, 'The usual.'

Edward shakes his head. 'Would you be so kind as to bring us some drinks? A white wine and a coffee?'

'Are you ready to order food?' the waitress asks, pen ready above her pad, 'Only we're quite busy, and if you order now you won't have to wait so long.'

Rachel opens the snap on her handbag and takes out a soft beige spectacle case, places the half-lens glasses carefully on the end of her nose.

Edward smiles apologetically at the waitress, 'I think I'll have the char-grilled chicken, please.'

'What shall I have?' Rachel says, addressing the menu, 'I think I'll have the poached salmon.'

Rachel watches the girl as she moves away. 'How can someone take so little pride in their appearance? What a plain little thing she is.'

'Maybe she doesn't see her appearance as being that important.'

Rachel snorts, 'That's obvious.'

'What about Angela then, wouldn't you put her in the same category? She can be a bit scruffy. Mind you, with her I think it might be lack of finance.'

'She's a completely different affair, she has a delicacy of feature and that wonderful translucent complexion, and she's not lumpy like that girl. Maybe it's down to breeding.' He sees her smile inwardly, she's obviously included herself in that category but he can't deny that class is something his mother has always had.

'I was surprised,' he leans forward, 'that you wanted to meet up again so soon after our little contretemps at the Blue Moon.'

'It was you who suggested it,' she counters.

No it wasn't, he thinks. Always she has to twist things, to lie to suit her purpose. Why does he put up with it?

'I was going to suggest next month, on your birthday,' he says. 'Thought we could have given this month a rest.'

'I like it here.' She rubs a fern between her thumb and forefinger.

He remembers he has something for her, a book, their only common interest. He puts his hand in his jacket pocket and pulls out a brown package, 'Here.' It is a second-hand book bound in leather with gold writing on the spine. She flicks through the leaf-thin pages,

'A poetry book. Thank you. Look. Listen to this. My mother used to read me this poem:

Quinquireme of Nineveh from distant Ophir
Rowing home to haven in sunny Palestine,
With a cargo of ivory,
And apes and peacocks,
Sandalwood, cedar wood, and sweet white wine.'

'*Quinquireme of Nineveh.* Oh my! Doesn't it have an exotic ring to it?'

'Angela and I were looking through the poems the last time I sat for her.'

Rachel's voice is pinched. 'And what did she think of it?'

'Not sure. She seems to like fairy stories best.'

'What, Beauty and the Beast?' Rachel snorts and shakes her head in disbelief.

'Mother, have you heard yourself? Snipe, snipe, snipe. Can't you, just for once in your life, be happy for me?'

'For what?' She looks at him over her glasses. 'For making a fool of yourself?'

He twiddles his teaspoon in the saucer, chinking it against the side of the cup. He looks straight at her, 'I'm not making a fool of myself. Not that it's any of your business.'

The waitress returns up the steps with their food. He watches his mother place her serviette on her lap and sit forward expectantly, her knife delicately splicing the flesh of the salmon, admiring how it separates into gleaming chunks.

'How is it, mother?' he asks, by way of breaking the silence.

She nods and pauses, her fork in mid-air, 'Good. Very good, thank you.' She looks around, 'I thought Angela might have been here today.'

'Did you? Is that why you wanted to come?' He raises his eyebrows, furrowing his forehead.

'Not especially.'

'And what would you have said to her if she had been?'

She pauses and places her knife and fork on her plate. 'I would have told her that I had purchased a ballet ticket for her as a thank you for bringing the portrait, but that since she has been exploiting my son...'

'Who is a grown man...'

'...I'm having second thoughts about giving it to her. By the way, did you say something to her about the ballet tickets? Only I got a card from her thanking me.'

He nods, 'Yes, I mentioned it.'

'Might take you instead. Not sure I want to see that young lady again.'

He places his knife along the char line of the chicken and cuts into it, 'Mother?'

She looks up.

'Can I ask you a question?'

She nods.

'Did you feel exploited when you were a model?'

She gulps down a mouthful. 'No, of course not.'

'Are you sure? All those men ogling you.'

'Don't be stupid, you know it's not like that.'

'What did father think about it?'

'He never knew, did he? I never told him.'

'Surely he had a right to know.'

'No. It was none of his business.'

'You always had areas of your life that you kept fenced off, didn't you?'

'And what is wrong with that?'

He raises an eyebrow, 'Depends what was going on.'

'You said in your last letter that your landlady had ruined your scarf. Why do you continue to live there if she irritates you so much?' she counters.

'I thought you of all people would have known the answer to that, Mother.'

'What an earth do you mean?'

'Well, look at all those years father and I irritated you, yet you never left.'

She pulls a face, 'That was different.'

'Was it?'

'You know it was. You still haven't told me.'

'What?'

'Why you continue to lodge with Mrs Ingram. Is it so that you can have someone to vent your spleen on? After all, life would be very dull for you without Mrs Ingram to complain about, wouldn't it?'

'One day I'll summon up the energy to leave. You'll see.'

She nods knowingly, 'Yes, we'll see.'

'What did it feel like to sit there naked in front of all those people?' He retaliates.

She looks at him boldly, 'I loved it. I felt like the Queen of Sheba up there. It gave me such a sense of my own power.'

'Yes, I think that's it exactly. That's how I feel. It has made such a difference to my life,' he adds shyly.

On his way back to the library he pokes his stick between the cracks in the slabs. He wonders if he should be grateful to his mother. Had what he witnessed saved him from years of confusion and heart ache? Had he been so shocked by the experience that he'd closed down, sexually that is, until now? He wishes that he didn't have to go back to work, that he could go home and be alone.

CHAPTER THIRTY-FIVE

She has arranged to meet Dan. He's late. She's noticed that about him. He's always late. The few times they've actually arranged a date, that is. Usually they just bump into each other somewhere and go on from there. She watches the queue for the popcorn diminish. If he doesn't turn up soon they'll be late for the film. It's then that she sees him circling in the revolving door.

She closes her eyes against the flickering of the screen. She doesn't like these self-indulgent French films. She tires of reading the sub-titles. She drifts, thinking of other things. She has on her new bra. The wires are digging into the sides of her breasts. She's never worn a bra with underwiring before. The effect is magnificent, almost worth the discomfort.

She's glad he'd left so abruptly. She wouldn't have known what to say to him, *Thank you, it's very nice,* doesn't quite do it. Would he expect her to be wearing it at the next sitting? She's going to feel really awkward if she doesn't. Why couldn't he have just bought her a box of chocolates, for God's sake! And yet she is touched. No man has ever bought her anything so special. And it must have cost loads.

The way he had held her breasts had been so tender, as if he'd thought he might break them. She remembers the smell of Imperial Leather. It reminded her of her granddad. She'd done it out of a sense of kindness, of gratitude. She'd seen the expression on his face turn to confusion, then horror, when he realised what he'd said. And then how forlorn he'd looked when she'd asked him if he'd ever held a woman's breasts. He wasn't like an ordinary man. She didn't feel threatened by him.

Dan digs her in the ribs. She opens her eyes. She wants to wait until the credits have finished rolling but he's already making his way towards the aisle.

She takes a sip of her beer; wishes she had enough money to get drunk.

'I think it's better we buy our own,' he always says. 'Keeps it tidy, then.'

She hates meanness, especially as she knows he has money.

'So you enjoyed the film?' He grins. He has the most perfect set of teeth she's ever seen. Strange, she thinks, how you can fancy someone and then it not work in bed.

'Thought it was a bit pretentious actually.'

'How would you know? You slept through most of it.'

'The bit I saw was. So it stands to reason.'

He languishes back in his chair, legs apart. 'I hadn't been to the cinema for ages.'

'I went to see the Toulouse Lautrec film last week with...' No, she won't tell him that.

'I wanted to see that. Why didn't you give me a bell?'

She shrugs it away, 'How's your dissertation going?'

'Not good. I had what I thought was a really good idea and that bastard Alex says, it's shit, go away and think of something else.'

'Why do you take any notice of him?'

'What do you mean?'

'Well, if you think it works...'

'The bastard would fail me, I know he would.'

She stands up. 'Right, I'm off.'

'Aren't you having another half.'

'Haven't got anymore money.'

'There's a cash machine round the corner.'

She can't believe the meanness of this man. 'When I say I haven't got any more money, I mean I haven't got any money.'

He sighs a long suffering sigh, 'Sit down, I'll get you one.'

She sits back down, 'Why, thank you. Can I have a pint this time? I could do with getting drunk.' She watches him standing at the bar; faded jeans, clumpy boots, nice arse.

Back in his room, the sheets are even greyer than before. She sits down on the edge of the bed and watches him strip off. She loves his body, perfect even down to the slight tan. He jumps into bed, pulls her towards him. His kiss is sloppy, intrusive. She pulls away.

'Come on, aren't you getting undressed?'

'Not sure I can be bothered,' she yawns, stretching her arms above her head. This action causes the underwiring in her bra to dig sharply into her breasts. She lets out a little gasp and stands up. Dan hasn't noticed her discomfort. He is leaning out of bed scrabbling for something underneath.

She feels quite drunk and sits back down on the bed, 'What are you doing?'

He sits back up a grin on his face. In his hand he has a small clear plastic bag. He waves it at her, 'Thought this would liven you up.'

'What is it?' She knows what it is. Suddenly she feels afraid.

'Nice bit of spliff, best Moroccan.'

'I don't want it.'

'You've tried it before haven't you, you're not that square.'

'Course I have,' she lies. She has to get out of here.

'I think artists should to be made to take it.'

'I don't need it. I can be creative without all that shit.'

'Cocky, aren't we? Well, answer me this, Miss Think-we're-so-bloody-fantastic, how do you know if you've never tried. I think I've got an LSD pill under here somewhere,' he leans back under the bed. 'I'll split it with you.'

She walks back home through the terraced streets. No TV screens to watch tonight. Everyone's gone to bed. She could so easily have stayed, been persuaded. Spliff? LSD? And then what else? It would be so easy to be curious. She wasn't like that though. Not like him. She wonders if he's even noticed she's gone yet.

She studies her reflection as she passes a darkened window. She has the same loping gait as her mother.

CHAPTER THIRTY-SIX

The cold hardness of the concrete beneath the thin carpet seeps through and into his bones. He is lying on her grandfather's blanket again. The roughness of it irritates his skin.

When he had first entered the room he noticed that Angela had cut her hair and returned it to its natural colour. He thought how it softened her skin, making it even more translucent, the blue vein tracing down her left cheek like a blurred line in fine porcelain. She was already undressed. He searched for signs of the crimson bra in her pile of clothes, looked for marks on her body to see if she had been wearing it, but he could determine nothing. At first he thought she seemed a bit offhand but that had passed and they returned to their normal banter.

He shuts his eyes and imagines her sitting there, drawing him, her breasts encased in the crimson bra. He feels annoyed at her for placing him again on the grey blanket on the hard floor and for not showing gratitude for his present. But underneath the annoyance is a terrible longing. He grits his teeth and wills it to subside, to wait for darkness, for the privacy of his own room. This is private, between you and me he tells it; it has nothing to do with the girl. He concentrates his whole mind on trying to quiet the stirrings in his groin.

Tears of fury spill from his eyes and trickle down the upper side of his nose.

His penis continues to grow, protruding like a defiant limb. He listens for the faint scratch of charcoal. Yes, there it is. She said she was going to draw his back today. Please God, he prays, don't let her see my distress. If only he could shift his pose he could cover it with his hand, or pull it down between his legs. If he keeps perfectly still maybe, just maybe, she will not notice and it will subside and, he grits his teeth, it will become the baby mouse that they had laughed about the other week.

He hears her put down her board and cross the room to stand above him. She says nothing but crouches down and begins to gently stroke his hair. He sobs and moves his hands down to cover his groin. The sobs judder through his whole body. She removes her hand. He holds his breath, waiting for her to move away. But she doesn't and he is even more bewildered when she lies down beside him on the blanket. What is she doing? She shuffles her way inside the curl of his body. For a few moments they lie there like two spoons, his tears wetting her newly shorn hair at the nape of her neck, and then he puts his arm around her, seeks out the sweet softness of her breasts. She nuzzles her bottom against him and then, reaching behind her, she takes his penis in her hand and puts it between her legs. He pushes gently against her and, as if in a dream, enters her body.

Afterwards, he falls asleep, holding her in his arms. When he awakes he notices the light through the skylight has turned to charcoal grey. She stirs and gets up. He stays very still while she dresses, hoping she will leave in silence, but she kneels over him again and shakes him gently.

'Edward? Come on, wake up. The caretaker will be here soon.'

They leave together in silence. Parting with a nod on the Pelican crossing.

CHAPTER THIRTY-SEVEN

Saturday morning and Angela is lying in bed, half way between sleep and waking. She tries to drift back into slumber but her mind has already switched on and her thoughts are forcing her awake. She hears the phone ring downstairs.

'Ange?' someone shouts up the stairs, 'Phone.'

She sits on the bottom stair watching the dangling phone twist round and round. Is it Edward saying he can't make this week? She doesn't want to speak to him, but she picks up the phone. Her gran could have been taken ill.

'Hello?' she says, tentatively, into the mouthpiece.

'Hi, Ange. It's Alex. Sorry, did I get you out of bed?'

Thank God. 'Yeah,' she yawns. 'But it's okay, I needed to get up anyway.'

'Sorry to disturb your sweet slumbers, but I had to let you know I can't make it on Monday. I've got to go to Cornwall for a few days.'

'Cornwall. Christ, it's a long time since I've been there. I went on a field trip from school once. I loved it.'

'My mother isn't very well.'

'Oh yeah. Sorry, I forgot.'

'Come with me then.'

Silence. She couldn't.... 'I can't.'

'Why not?'

'I just can't.'

'I can draw you while my mother is sleeping. That way I won't get behind with my commission.'

'I don't know, Alex. I'll have to think about it. I'm supposed to be working on my dissertation, aren't I?'

'The house is right next to the sea. I'm only going to be a few days.'

'When are you going?'

'As soon as I'm packed. A couple of hours?'

'I can't.'

'You kids nowadays are so unadventurous. Fancy turning down a free holiday.'

'Yeah, but it wouldn't be a holiday would it.'

'You'd have plenty of free time to wander the cliffs at will. I'll have to spend quite a bit of time with my mother.'

'But that won't get my work done will it?'

'You never know. It might get your imagination working. You might even come up with something original.'

'Very funny.'

'I'll contact you when I get back then?'

'No hold on, I've changed my mind, pick me up.'

She soaks her head under the shower and breathes deeply. She is just putting a splodge of orange shampoo into the centre of her palm when she remembers Edward.

It is Saturday.

'Shit!' How could she have been so stupid?

She sits on the stairs, a towel wrapped turban-style around her wet hair, looking for Alex's number. There isn't an Alex Culver in the book. She tries enquiries but the number is ex-directory. She chews her lip, unconsciously flipping the pages of the phone book, wondering what to do. She could phone Edward and tell him that she can't make it this afternoon. She picks up the phone, hesitates, and puts it back down.

How can she ever face him again?

As they leave the city behind, Angela relaxes back into the heated leather of her seat. Alex keeps looking at her with a puzzled expression on his face, 'You've cut your bloody hair.'

'Do you like it?' She puts a hand to the back of her neck.

'You've changed your appearance.'

'So?'

'And I'm in the middle of drawing you.'

'Oh shit.' She puts her hand to her mouth. 'I never gave it a thought.' She pauses, gives him a sideways smile. 'Do you want to take me back?'

'Never mind.' He shakes his head. 'I'll manage, somehow.'

'I could do with being back by Wednesday,' she says.

'So could I,' he says. 'So we'll aim for that, shall we?'

'I must be crazy.'

'Good, isn't it?' He grins. She notices the gap between his front teeth.

'Has your mother taken a turn for the worse?'

'She's bloody unlucky. Breast cancer, recurring again after thirty five years. Not sure how she is. My aunt rang, said could I come down, my mother wants to see me. So I can only assume…'

She watches his hands grip the steering wheel, the nicotine stain on his index finger.

'I wonder what makes it recur?'

'Grief. She's never got over my dad dying. The grief seemed to eat away at her. It's almost as if she wished the cancer back. And now she's taken herself off to bloody Cornwall.'

'To die?'

'I'm not sure. Like I said the other week, I think she's into some form of alternative mumbo jumbo. I know her and my aunt are up to something. Her doctor in Nottingham wanted her to go for chemo but she wasn't having any of it. I tried to tell her it isn't like thirty years ago, but she still refused. Said she wanted power over her own body this time, and that she would decide how to fight the cancer.'

'Did she have her breasts removed the first time she got the cancer?'

'Only one, if she had done as the surgeon advised and had them both off… maybe it wouldn't have recurred.'

'Did she have reconstruction surgery?'

'No, I don't think so.'

'Have you ever seen it?'

'What?'

'The scar where she had the breast removed.'

Alex shudders, 'No.'

'I'd love to draw someone who's had a breast removed.'

'You're sick.'

'No, I'm not. If it wasn't your mother you might think differently.'

'What is it with you?'

'Why should you hide your body away just because it's not a replica of everyone else's?'

'Maybe you'd feel differently if it was you.'

'I don't think I would. I would say – look, this is me – this is what I am. Other people's tragedies are usually the most interesting thing about them.'

'Jesus, Ange, you do twist things around.'

'What tragedies have you had in your life then?' She asks.

'None really, except my dad dying.' He turns towards her, gives her a tight little smile.

'See. I make my point.'

'What?'

'No tragedies. Boring person.'

'And what tragedies have you had in your life to make you so bloody vitriolic.'

She is taken aback by the anger in his voice. She turns and sees the hurt in his face. 'Sorry.'

'You haven't answered my question,' he persists.

She stares out of the side window, 'My whole life's a bloody tragedy.'

'Poor little thing.'

'It's true.' She continues to stare out of the side window.

'Orphan, brought up in the workhouse were you?' He digs her in the ribs.

She turns, 'I might as well have been.'

'Why, what happened to your parents?'

'I was brought up by my grandparents.'

'So what happened to your parents?'

'They're both smackheads, total wasters. All right?'

'Jesus, Ange. That's awful.'

She looks at him. He's being sincere. She frowns, 'I bet you were brought up in a cosy little semi in the suburbs of Nottingham weren't you?'

'Yeah, I was, and I've been fighting it ever since.'

'Still trying, eh?'

'Not half as trying as you, my dear.'

She laughs and notices how he bites his lower lip with his front teeth, trying not to laugh.

He flicks his fringe out of his eyes. 'And did your grandparents treat you badly?' He asks.

The clouds are scudding across the grey winter sky. They are in the fast lane, skimming grey tarmac. Everything is grey, Angela thinks; the grass, the road, the fields, the trees, all grey, as if they were passing through a grey dream to somewhere else.

'They were lovely, but,' she pauses, 'How can I put this? I didn't belong. I felt like a cuckoo in the nest. I suppose my mother must have felt a bit like that too. Never thought of it like that before.'

'What do you mean?'

She shrugs, 'We never had any books or pictures in the house. It wasn't until I was about six and my Gran took me to the house of an old French lady she used to clean for, that I discovered there was a whole different world out there.'

Alex pulls over into the inside lane. 'I'm going to have to stop at the next service station. He taps the dashboard, 'She's overheating again, and more importantly, I've run out of fags.'

Later, back on the road, the sky darkens until she can no longer see the horizon. Alex talks to her of his work and his passion for colour. She drifts in and out of sleep. He puts on a cassette. She likes his choice of music and wishes she didn't.

They arrive late at night.

The sea crashes the rocks below like the roar of an animal out in the night. Angela kneels up in bed and pulls back the curtains, pressing her face against the cold glass. She can see nothing beyond the blackness of the night. She fumbles with the latch and pushes up the window. Sticking her shoulders under the sash to prop it open, she puts her head out and gasps as the salt air chills her lungs. Her first reaction is to draw her head back in, but she sees a faint glimmer in the sky, a sliver of light, the moon silvering the edges of the moving clouds. Just for a moment it pierces through, striking a path across the water in the cove, and she is glad she came. She waits for the moon to appear again, but the clouds thicken and soon the wind forces her back into the room. Through the wall, she can hear the faint murmur of voices in the sick room, Alex and his aunt. Angela has not yet met his mother.

CHAPTER THIRTY-EIGHT

At 4.45 the estate agent is already waiting for him, leaning smugly against his dark blue BMW,

'Mr. Anderson?'

'Yes.'

The estate agent extends a hand, 'Clive Bates, of Mutton and Hennion, pleased to meet you.'

Edward swaps his stick to his left hand and extends his right. 'How do you do.'

The block of flats is perched on the side of a hill. The flat he is being shown is on the first floor. Access to it is via a metal walkway. To reach the lower flats there are steps from the road above. The windows are large, both at the front and back and, once inside the flat, the estate agent points out the extensive views over the city. 'You can see right across to the other side of the valley.'

Edward runs his eye up and down the streets that diagonally cross the opposite hill and sees how the trees trace black against the skyline. The bedroom is at the back of the flat and looks out onto a bank covered in moss and grass. He hopes it will be dotted with crocuses and daffodils in the spring.

He takes the flat. He loves it and he wonders, going home on the bus, whether he should have looked at more before making a decision, but his need to get away from Mrs Ingram is so great he probably would have taken the flat even if he hadn't liked it. Up until a few months ago she hadn't irked him that much. In fact, he had taken a certain pleasure from the perversity of the situation, thwarting her at every turn, playing a game of rituals. But recently he had begun to long for his own private space away from her intrusion. Suddenly he needed to take control, to cook his own food, put his own soiled clothes in the washing machine, empty his own waste paper basket. To live his own life.

'Mrs Ingram? I'm moving out.'

There, he has finally said it, after all these years. She is so shocked that her jaw drops open and her bottom set of teeth slide forward. Edward watches, mesmerised, as she plonks herself down on a kitchen chair and pushes them back into place.

'Well now, Mr. Anderson. I'm sure I don't know what to say. What on earth! Why! Well, I don't know. I'm speechless.' Suddenly, and to Edward's horror, she begins to cry,

'What ever am I going to do without you? Since Mr. Ingram died you have been such company for me. You'll still come for your Sunday lunch, won't you?'

For a split second Edward thinks to put a comforting arm around her shoulder.

'No, Mrs Ingram. I'm sorry. I'm going to join an archaeology club. So I'll be out most Sundays.'

'Have you met a young lady? Is that what all this is about?'

He turns angrily away, 'No, Mrs Ingram, I haven't. I'll be leaving on Sunday.'

He takes the number off a card in the newsagent's window: *Home removals - cheap rates.* When the man answers the phone, Edward asks if he can move him on Sunday. But that is his one day off. He could fit him in on Saturday morning before the match. He accepts his offer. He had wanted to arrive just as the evening was drawing in or, at the very earliest, late afternoon, so that he could wake to a new day in his new flat.

On the Saturday morning as he is moving out, Edward surprises himself by feeling rather sorry for Mrs Ingram. 'At least you get your house to yourself again, Mrs. Ingram,' he says.

'And what if I don't want it?' she replies, her bottom lip wobbling.

'Goodbye, Mrs Ingram.' He closes the front door firmly behind him. As they drive away he sees her, a lonely figure in a floral pinny standing on her front doorstep.

While they are sitting in traffic on the dual carriageway, the removal man tells Edward that he has five children ranging from six months to twenty years. Edward, curious, asks why.

The man laughs, 'No idea, mate. Life, ain't it? As long as I get me fags and a pint on a Saturday night and get to go to home matches, I ain't really complaining.'

So, Edward thinks, I'm not the only one to be washed along by the tide of life. 'I've never been to a football match,' he says.

'Never? You're kidding me. You don't know what you're missing, mate.'

'Why?' Edward holds on tight as the van swings onto the roundabout.

'It's like being part of a big wave, roaring your team on. Bloody hell, mate, you don't know what you're missing. It's better than sex.'

Could it possibly be, Edward wonders? No. He doesn't think so. The sun is shining through the windscreen, warming him through.

'Explain more, I'm curious,' he prompts.

The removal man thinks for a moment, 'Belonging,' he says, 'It feels like belonging.'

They pull up outside the flat and the man turns to Edward, 'It's just as well you haven't got anything heavy. I usually bring my lad to help but he's cleaning cars this morning. I don't suppose you can lift much with that there disability.'

Edward is amused. He'd never heard himself referred to as if he had something extra but he supposed he did, if he thought about it.

When the removal man has left, Edward feels suddenly stranded. Should he go out, get a spot of lunch, see if he can find the courage to go back to the studio? Would she even be there? He shudders. He doesn't know if he can go back. The late morning light filters through the empty flat and for an instant he is afraid and wonders if he has done the right thing, until he sees a shaft of sunlight catch the stained-glass windows of the church across the valley.

Everything is a new adventure. Even catching a bus with a different number and unfamiliar faces on it. Going to the supermarket and picking carefully through the gleaming rows of strange fruit and veg. Buying soap powder. Choosing through all the peculiar names and then reading the instructions. Putting his books out on the shelves and walking naked around the flat.

He sees a notice in his local newsagents. *Good home wanted for cat.* She turns out to be an old thing, a tortoiseshell with white paws, and when he comes home from work she greets him on the metal walkway, meowing up at him. She curls her tail around his legs. He lets them both in and when he is seated, she jumps onto his lap.

He smiles to himself, smoothes his hand along the length of her back and thinks, how ironic, if only his mother, like Mrs Ingram, had been sad at his leaving all those years ago, maybe he would have had gone out into the world and made a life for himself.

CHAPTER THIRTY-NINE

Angela wakes early and lies snuggled up in her bed, listening to the scuttle of pebbles on the beach. The tide must be on its way out. The wind is dancing through the house, rattling the latch on her bedroom door.

She slips on her jogging bottoms and jumper. Downstairs, the house is waiting for its occupants to rise and draw back the curtains to let in the world. Angela shivers and looks for the radiators. There are none. Just the warmth of the Rayburn, its damper clank-clanking to the singing of the wind in the chimney. She leans her bottom against the stove's rail and surveys the kitchen. There is a small window cut out of the wall. Outside, the grass bank rises steeply.

Angela walks up the hill through the narrow street of fishermen's cottages, long since turned into holiday lets; some still shuttered and closed against the gales of winter. She comes to the end of the houses and sees the road continue on up the hill through high, narrow hedges. Looking back down the valley, Angela can see the cut-out of the black cove; the sea flat and glistening in the distance, and nearer, a collection of crooked chimneys, all sleeping, except for one.

She follows the smoke, taking a small path that leads her down towards a stream, then along beside the clear water, slipping over wet stones and through green cress. Boat sheds with slate roofs and walls of slatted grey wood lie empty, except for one rotting dinghy.

An old woman holding a cat stands outside the cottage with the smoking chimney and watches her approach, 'Mornin'.'

'Good morning,' Angela shades her eyes from the sun. 'Could you tell me where the nearest shop is please? I want to get a paper and some milk.'

'You're not from round these parts, are you? Near on three

miles. You'll need to go into Port Isaac, my dear. It's a fair old walk.'
The old woman looks at Angela over her glasses. 'Staying down on
the front with Hilda, aren't you?'

'How did you know that?'

The old woman laughs, 'I could tell you it's because I'm the
local healer, but since Hilda's is the only other occupied cottage,
don't you think it's a pretty fair bet? And speak of the devil.'

They watch as Alex's Aunt Hilda strides up the hill towards
them.

Hilda stares straight at Angela, ignoring the faith healer,
'What are you doing up here?'

The healer nods at Angela. 'We was just talking, Hilda. She
was asking me where she could get a newspaper. This young maid
staying with you, then?'

'Yes.' Hilda puts her hands on her hips. 'She's a friend of
Alex's.'

'I was just coming down to see you. Not so good this
morning, is she?'

'No.' Hilda shakes her head. 'Alex is with her at the
moment.'

'Well, 'Maid here,' the old woman nods at Angela, 'wants a
paper and some milk. So happen he can take her into Port Isaac then
I'll come down.'

'It's true then, Alex's mother has come down here for a
cure?' Angela asks, looking from one old woman to the other. Hilda
gives her a cold stare. The woman's whole demeanour reminds her
of stone; the grey sculpted hair, the angular features, and now this
look that says in no uncertain terms, mind your own business. The
faith healer cocks her head at Angela and winks.

Angela and Hilda walk back down the hill in silence. The
sun, still low in the sky, slants up the valley making them shield
their eyes. As they near the house, scrunching along the pebble
path, Hilda says, 'I'd be very much obliged if you'd not mention
any of this to Alex.'

Angela stops. 'Can I ask why?'

'He would start going on at his mother if he knew, and at the
moment that's the last thing she needs. So please, I'd be grateful if
you kept it to yourself.'

'Do you believe in healing?'

Hilda shrugs, 'I have an open mind. My sister believes in it and that's what's important.'

Alex is stirring tea in a large brown teapot. 'Want some black tea?'

'No, thanks.' Angela shakes her head. 'How's your mother?'

He wrinkles his nose. His aunt speaks from the doorway, 'Will you take Angela into Port Isaac for some milk and a paper? I found her out searching for a shop.'

Alex puts the teapot on top of the Rayburn to keep warm. 'I'm a bit tired this morning. This afternoon maybe.'

'Oh, come on, Alex. Don't be so miserable. It's a lovely morning. The least you can do is show me the sights.' Angela winks at Hilda. The woman turns and leaves the room.

The car groans its way up the winding hill. The lane is so narrow that the grass from the uncut hedgerow sweeps against the side of the car.

'It almost feels as if you're on rails, doesn't it?' Angela says, perching forward in her seat.

The car swerves slightly as Alex fumbles in his pocket for a cigarette. 'That's how the locals get home after a night in the pub you know. The car just bounces between the hedges.'

The early morning sun drains the natural colour from the landscape, making the fields look sad and neglected until, cresting the brow of a hill they see, far below them, dancing with colour and sunlight, the fishing village of Port Isaac.

Alex brings the car to a halt and they stare in silence at the random clusters of grey roofs, the smoke rising in twists from tall, crooked chimneys, the stranded fishing boats lying skewed on the pebbled beach and further out, the glimmering blue of the sea turning to white where it crashes against the high black cliffs.

'Wow.'

'Glad you came now?' Alex asks as he starts to let the car roll slowly forwards down the hill.

The gulls are circling above the quay. The cottages, many with sides hung in grey slate, huddle together in the bottom of the valley. Double yellow lines on both sides of the tarmac define the downward weave of the road.

'We'll have to park up on the top and walk down,' Alex says. 'Unless you want to just jump out when we get to the shop, and I'll keep the engine running.'

She thinks of the women back at the cottage and relishes her secret. 'Let's have a walk down shall we?'

He groans, 'I knew you'd say that. I had a long drive yesterday you know? I was hoping to get a bit of a rest today.'

'Don't be so feeble,' she laughs, 'Old man.'

They park the car on the other side of the valley, where the port has spread into a holiday resort of crouched bungalows for retired people and tall rendered houses with peaked gables and bed and breakfast signs swinging in the breeze.

'Look,' says Alex. "You can follow the line of the cliffs right up to Tintagel. What a clear day, shall we stay in the car and enjoy the view in comfort?'

She opens the car door. 'You can if you like. I'm going for a walk.'

They make their way along the cliff path. Alex links his arm through hers. She looks at him sideways.

'Just making sure you don't fall over the edge,' he laughs.

She pulls away and looks down at the gulls screaming around the deserted fishing boats, searching for scraps. 'I'm going for a walk along the quay.'

He stops to light a cigarette, cupping his hand around his lighter. 'I'll come with you.'

'No, it's okay, you get the paper,' she calls out, skipping off down the narrow street. She makes her way carefully along a concrete ridge to the quay, breathing in the smell of salt, fish, and something else that is either putrid seaweed or sewage.

The slate steps up the side are still wet from the outgoing tide. She holds on to the rusty handrail and splashes her way to the top. The walls of the quay are hung with strands of bright green seaweed and studded with horn-coloured winkles. Leaning over the wall, she can see the mouth of the cove and the sea-spray as it crashes against the rocks at the entrance.

'Mornin'.'

She jumps. Sitting amongst the lobster pots further up the quay is a man, a youth, of about her own age.

'Morning.'

"Tis a bit brisk for it, in'it?'

'For what?' Angela wishes she didn't sound quite so posh.

'Anything you like!' He smirks.

His tone annoys her.

'What, like a good fuck, or something?'

He laughs, surprised, and slaps his thigh in delight. Angela likes the weathered blue of his jeans. He wipes his eyes, 'Where in the bloody hell did you come from?'

'Mind your own business.' Again she sounds too posh.

He smiles at her. 'I like you. You can stay.'

She laughs in spite of herself, 'Thought I was an Emmet, didn't you?'

'You are.'

'Maybe.'

'Maybe! There's no maybe about it, you are.'

'So, is being a tourist a problem?'

'Most Emmets are, but I like you.'

'Well thank you, how gracious.'

'I could show you the night life, if you like.'

'Night life!' she laughs.

'You'd be surprised, we can have a bloody good time.'

'Doing what?'

'Like I said, I'll show you.'

'You don't waste any time do you?'

He pulls off his woolly hat. His hair gleams crow black, 'Can't afford to. You're only here for a couple of days, I suppose.'

Angela perches cautiously on the rim of a lobster pot. 'What about your girlfriend?'

'Oh, don't worry about her. She's up at Cardiff University.'

'A clever woman. What's she doing with you?'

'Well, that's the point, in'it? She's not with me.'

'Like I said, a clever woman.'

He snaps shut his penknife. 'Cornwall is somewhere you either never want to leave or somewhere you can't get away from fast enough. I could have gone to Uni, but I like it here too much. Where else could I sit, in winter, in my shirt sleeves, admiring your lovely arse bent over the quay wall?'

She tries to stop her face turning to red, but she can already feel the heat creeping up her neck, 'Oh, and I thought it was my intellect that attracted you.'

'It wasn't your intellect I first saw bent over the wall.'

'ANGELA!'

She looks back up the Harbour; Alex is waving at her.

'That your boyfriend?'

She twists her mouth. 'No.'

'Looks a bit old for you.'

'Do I get a lobster for entertaining you with my arse?' She says, inspecting the lobster pots.

'I haven't got any. Little buggers was hidin' last night.'

Angela grasps the handrail at the top of the steps, 'See you, then.'

'I'll pick you up tonight. It'll have to be about half eleven, 'cos I'll be going out tonight.' He nods in the direction of the sea.

'There won't be anywhere open.' She puts a foot on the first step.

'Where you staying?' he asks, standing up.

'Port Gent.'

'That cottage on the front?'

She half nods.

'I'll park outside. Listen for me.'

'ANGELA!'

'I'll have to go.'

'See you tonight, then.'

She pauses, 'Maybe,' she shouts, splashing down the steps.

'Until tonight then, Angela?'

She halts, 'How in the...' then she laughs, and makes her way carefully back along the concrete ridge. Alex is propped against a wall reading the paper.

'About bloody time,' he says, folding up the paper. 'Who've you been talking to?'

'A local lad. A fisherman, I was trying to get us some fresh lobster.'

'Where is it then?'

'Little buggers was hidin' last night,' she mimics, 'He hadn't got any.'

'Is that all you were talking about?'

'No, he said he'd been sat there admiring my arse.'

'Bloody cheek, didn't you slap him?'

'He was rather nice actually.'

'Come on, we'd better get back.'

'I thought we could go in the pub.' Angela says nodding up the alley. Suddenly she feels in a holiday mood.

'If you remember, I came down to Cornwall because my mother was ill, not to entertain you.' His words crush her. She feels a lump rising in her throat. Bastard.

'I'll stay here then shall I?' She retaliates, 'Make my own entertainment. I'm sure he'll,' she nods towards the quay, 'take me for a drink.'

She watches as Alex attempts to light a cigarette. He turns his back against the wind to shield the flame. 'I was hoping you'd sit for me when we got back?'

'Alex? Fuck off.' She strides out ahead, choked by her anger and the wind whipping in from the sea. She looks down into the harbour. He is still there among the lobster pots.

'Oh please, don't sound so bloody enthusiastic.' She hears Alex's voice on the wind.

She sits on the wall of the car park, waiting, tracing the coastline with her eye. She shouldn't have come. She should have gone to the studio, confronted Edward. But what would she have said? She shivers, clasping her arms around her body. Trust her to fuck it up. How in the bloody hell was she going to complete now? She'd had something so unique, and now she's been and spoilt it. All her dreams wiped out with one action. What had possessed her to make love to an old man? Edward, of all people. She shudders, thinking back to the sittings, building week by week, them growing inexplicably closer. She can't face him, not ever. She'll just have to see if she's got enough work to pull it off.

Alex stands next to her. 'Penny for them.'

'Worrying about my work, I shouldn't have come.'

'Would you like to go for a walk along the coastal path later?'

'How could we possibly? We are here because your mother is ill, remember?' She jumps off the wall. 'Mind, I could always go for a walk on my own,' she mutters, striding over to the car. Inside the car they wait for the windows to demist. He leans over and ruffles her hair; tries to look into her eyes.

'Hello, Grumpy. Wishing you hadn't come?'

She grunts and wipes the mist off her window with her sleeved hand. 'You should have brought your pale wife instead.'

'Who? Oh, Barbara. She's not my wife.'

'Who is she, then?'

He ponders, 'My woman, I suppose.'

'Thought with your passion for colour you would have gone for something slightly less insipid.'

CHAPTER FORTY

Rachel waits for Edward. It's now half past twelve and he is never late, so what can have happened? She orders a glass of white wine and tells the waitress she is waiting for her son; he will be along soon.

At one o'clock, sheltering under her umbrella, she crosses Fargate and hurries up Surrey Street. The Yorkshire flagstones outside the library shimmer in the rain. She is not quite sure who to ask. She stands hesitantly in front of a man seated at the Enquiries desk, 'Excuse me.'

He looks up and smiles, 'Yes?'

'I wish to speak to Edward Anderson on an urgent matter. Can you help me?'

'I'm sorry. Edward's off sick.'

'For how long?'

'I'm not sure.'

She drops her voice and leans forward, 'Do you know what's wrong with him? It's not serious is it? You see, I'm his mother.'

The man breaks into a smile, 'Well I never! So you're Edward's mother. How do you do?'

'Very well, but you didn't answer my question.'

'I'm sorry. I can't give out details of such a personal nature.'

'But I'm his mother.'

'Why don't you phone him?' The man asks patiently.

She begins to back away, 'Yes, I suppose I could,' then, changing her mind, she moves forward again, 'Can you tell me how long has he been off?'

The man frowns, trying to remember. 'At least a week, I think. Most unlike Edward to have time off.'

Rachel stands on the library steps and waits for the rain to stop. She has butterflies in her stomach. She is not sure whether it is because she is hungry or because she feels unnerved by Edward's disappearance. Is he really ill? Unfurling her umbrella she steps out into the rain. He could be in Henry's waiting for her this very minute. She will go back and see; have something to eat and try to clear her head.

Seated in Henry's, Rachel sips at her white wine and scans the restaurant for any sign of Edward. When the waitress comes she orders the salmon, as she had the time before.

'Excuse me?' The girl is just turning away. 'Has by any chance my son been in?'

The girl comes back to the table and smiles, 'But I don't know what he looks like, do I?'

Rachel finds her tone rather patronising. She gives her a tight little smile. 'It doesn't matter.'

'What does he look like?' The girl persists.

'It really doesn't matter.'

'It would be a shame though if you'd missed him.'

'He walks with a stick.' Rachel crosses her arms defensively. 'He has a hunched back.'

'Oh. I know who you mean.'

'So he has been in?' A sense of relief washes over her. 'Thank goodness.'

'He knows Angela, one of the other waitresses,' the girl adds. 'He's been in recently but not today.'

'And is Angela working?' Her name sticks in Rachel's throat.

The waitress pulls a face, 'Not turned in. I'm run off my feet.'

Rachel waits for her food. She wishes she was sitting where she could see the door instead of having to turn every time she hears it open. She puts her head in her hands and closes her eyes. She is overcome by a sudden sense of overwhelming loss. What does she know of his life? Their lunchtime meetings had kept things exactly how she had wanted them and now, looking back, she realises how much she had enjoyed them, maybe more than she had ever admitted to herself.

She opens her handbag to look for a handkerchief. Tucked in the side pocket she sees the envelope of Edward's last letter.

80 Hancock Rise
Sheffield
Dear Mother,
Thank you for your letter, I am glad you remembered to buy the

crocus bulbs last year. The flowers will give you a lot of pleasure in spring. (If you also remembered to plant them.) When I was little, father never missed taking me to see the crocuses in the park. I always used to find it magical that the sad green winter grass had suddenly been littered with yellow and purple flowers and that the next time we went they would be gone and all there would be was green grass again.

I will see you next Tuesday at Henry's, for lunch.

Love

Edward

PS I have a really good book for you this time, which I am sure you will enjoy.

No, she hadn't got the arrangements wrong. As she sees the waitress returning with her food, she refolds the letter and puts it in her bag.

The salmon, although cooked to perfection, is hard to swallow. What can be the matter with him? It must be something very serious for him not to ring. She thinks back to the time when, as a child, he had contracted polio. He had spent weeks in a hospital bed and the only contact she and George had with him was to wave to him through a small window opposite his bed. The memory of Institution Green walls hits her like a bad smell. She can still see him now, clattering down the corridor towards her. The calliper on his leg resonating around them as his foot hit the floor. Strange how his leg had healed and he had been perfectly all right then, until that day when Ruben had brought him back on the train. She had been so glad to see her brother. He visited them so rarely.

'Haven't you noticed?' he had raged at them. 'Are you blind? Your son is turning into a hunchback and what have you done about it? Nothing!'

And what could they say? Neither of them had noticed anything unusual. Maybe Ruben had been right. Maybe they hadn't wanted to.

Rachel knocks on the bottle-green door with the round, stained glass window and waits. She hears someone shuffling from the back of the house, then the bolts top and bottom being slid back and the safety chain clanking against the door. The door creaks open. A woman with a floral pinny and a ginger cat in her arms regards her curiously.

'Hello. I'm looking for Edward Anderson?'

'He doesn't live here anymore, he moved out a few days ago.'

Rachel is stunned. 'But, but this is the address on his last letter.'

'Must have been before he moved.'

'Yes, but... '

'Shall I say who called, if I should see him?'

'Oh, do you see him?'

'Ah, no, but you never know, he might call round.'

'What for, his post?'

'No, he's had that forwarded to his new address.'

'And do you have that?'

The woman shakes her head, 'Never even left me his address. He's lived here all these years and then he ups and leaves just like that.'

'And was he well when he left?'

'Fine, except for his disability like.' She nods knowingly.

'Well, I'm sorry to have disturbed you.'

'You know, I said to him, why don't you still come for your Sunday lunch Mr. Anderson, but no, he would have none of it.'

Rachel backs away and puts up her umbrella.

'Who shall I say called?' the woman calls after her.

Without answering, Rachel turns away. She waits for the bus, sheltering from the rain under the canopy. So that is where Edward has lived all these years. She can see the house from the bus stop, and that must be the awful Mrs Ingram.

How is she going to find him now? A bus comes but it is not the one she wants. She shivers and pulls her coat tighter around her. She searches her mind for a solution, wipes her gloved hand across the glass of the shelter so that she can look out for the bus. Why would he suddenly cut off all contact? At least it didn't appear as though he was ill, well not seriously anyway. But why would he want to cut her off just like that. She feels a desolation begin to creep in around her. Desolation she has not felt since her uncle's death.

She'd felt all right while she was at the farmhouse, helping her aunt sort out his belongings, but when she had returned home this terrible sense of loss had swept over her. It came from nowhere like the mists up on the moors, shrouding her in a misery from which she could not escape. What they'd had was solely between them, and she could share it with no-one else. George irritated her even more than usual and Edward, well, he was his usual sullen self. A boy turning slowly into a man. Once, and only once, she'd attempted to confide in her brother Ruben. She'd cried and told him how much she missed their uncle.

'I don't know why. I never liked him anyway. They always said he was a bad egg.'

She looked for solace in many places, but the only comfort she'd found was to sit in the attic and hold her necklaces up to the light. It was not until ten years later, after George died, when she started modelling for the college, that she felt her life begin to come right again. And when the shy boy came to her house, finally things fell back into place.

But where could Edward be? She thinks back to their last meeting. They had not really argued, not badly anyway. Just about him modelling.

The rain sweeps in under the canopy and wets her stockinged legs. Mrs. Ingram is watching from her front room bay.

She wishes a bus would come, and that she could go home.

CHAPTER FORTY-ONE

Back at the cottage, Angela puts the kettle on while Alex goes upstairs to see his mother. Angela holds the teacup to her face, warming her cheek. Hilda comes in through the back door.

'I've just made a pot of tea. Would you like one?' Angela says.

'No, thank you.'

Her manner is still cold, and Angela wonders if she resents having to share a confidence, 'I would like to meet Alex's mother,' Angela says.

'Why?'

Angela is taken aback by the sharp response of the woman.

Hilda looks at her coldly and says, 'Alex has had such a string of women over the years.' She shrugs, 'I don't think his mother would see any point in bothering to establish any further relationships.'

Angela laughs, incredulous. 'Excuse me, but can I put the record straight? I'm not one of Alex's women. I'm one of his pupils.'

'It wouldn't be the first time he's had a relationship with a student.'

'Well, not in this case.' Angela plonks her cup down on the table.

Hilda fingers the edge of the tablecloth, 'I'm sorry. We just assumed.'

'Sorry to disappoint you.'

'What are you doing with him, then?'

'I'm doing some modelling for him. For which I am getting paid. He has to get this work finished so I said that I'd come down with him so he wouldn't fall behind. Does that answer your question?'

The woman shifts on her seat and looks across at Angela, 'I'd never trust Alex where women are concerned.'

'You sound as if you don't like him very much.'

'You're rather a rude young woman, aren't you? What gives you the right to accept my hospitality and then think you can ask me personal questions?'

Angela feels stung. Without another word she leaves the room.

She pokes a stick into the centre of a sea anemone, swaying pink fronds and no brain. The fronds suck into the stick like an infant on a mother's nipple. Her heart is still pounding like the sea tunnelling up the cave. She is angry with herself; angry at the tears that are stopping her from swallowing; angry that she can never cope with confrontation; angry because she always feels so alone.

She picks a pebble out of the pool and rolls it in her hand. She feels its cold wetness, and the way it warms to her touch. She sees, as the stone begins to dry, that the vivid blackness, ingrained with gold and brown begins to fade. She throws the stone back into the pool and watches as it settles back down into the sand, taking on its former glow. It's like a tiger-eye she thinks; like Rachel's beads.

'Ange?'

She crouches into her haunches. 'For God's sake,' she mutters, 'go away.'

'Are you all right?'

'Why shouldn't I be?'

'Just your body language.'

'Do you want me to come and sit for you now?' She looks up at him.

Alex brushes his fringe backwards and holds it tight against the top of his head. 'I thought we might go for a walk first.' He shades his eyes and looks up at the square house perched on the end of the headland.

'Nah.' Angela balances on the edge of the pool, rocking back and forth. 'I feel too lazy to go for a walk. Which room are we going to work in?'

'I thought your bedroom.'

Angela lies on the bed, propped on one elbow. The pink satin of the eiderdown gives her skin a soft glow. Like her new bra, she thinks.

'Keep still.'

'I'm trying to but the feathers from the eiderdown are

tickling my nose. How much longer are you going to be?'

'You know what you were saying about your parents on the way down? Well aren't you curious about them?' He looks over at her, studying her.

'No,' she replies, in a sullen tone.

He continues, 'I thought you said they were artists too.'

'So?'

'Well, aren't you interested in their work?'

'Alex, will you stop going on about them?'

'You know,' he seems to be miles away. 'I'm sure your breasts are getting fuller. They're magnificent. So nubile and,' he cups his hands, 'so ripe. I want to eat you. Devour you. Imagine you as a finished model of creamy marble, a Greek goddess.'

Angela sits up and pulls the eiderdown around her. 'I hope you break your bloody teeth.'

'Why did you have to move? I'd nearly finished. I was speaking to you as a fellow artist. Christ, you're touchy.'

'You know your aunt Hilda? Well, she thought we were an item.'

'How disgusting.' There is a note of mockery in his tone. 'To think I'd want to bed you. How can the thought have ever entered her head?'

'I told her I'm your pupil. Alex wouldn't take advantage of me like that. He has principles.'

'Ah, how black and white the young see the world.'

'What do you mean?'

'Do you know the colour of that eiderdown complements your complexion perfectly? I wish I'd brought some paints.'

She gets up and goes over to the window, her eiderdown wrap trailing behind her. The light outside is beginning to fade. He comes and stands behind her. She can hear his breathing, feel its warmth on her shoulder. His words are spoken so quietly they are hardly audible, 'You're very lovely you know.'

She turns and walks across the room, putting the bed between them, 'I'm going out for a breath of fresh air.'

'I'll come with you.'

She collects her clothes off the floor, 'Alex, don't you ever want to be on your own?'

She walks up the village street. Dusk is falling and the air is purple, misting to mauve. She can smell wood smoke. She pulls her coat tighter around her, fishes in her pocket and pulls out a razor shell that she had picked up off the beach earlier that day. She smoothes it between her palms and sits down in the darkness listening to the trickle of the stream, breathing-in the salt air. She feels so confused. Nothing is as it should be. She lets out a soft moan and wraps her arms around her body, shivering as she remembers. Oh God, it had felt so good, so natural with Edward. And yet how could it be? She shudders. It was disgusting. She had made love to an old man with toe nails like claws. She closes her eyes and lets the roar from the sea filter through her body.

Hilda is sitting alone in the kitchen reading Alex's paper. She looks up as Angela enters. Angela places the razor shell on the table. Hilda takes off her glasses and examines it. She picks it up and holds it between her fingers, stroking the smooth surface, 'Thank you.'

Angela nods. 'That's okay,' she says quietly.

Hilda turns the shell over, 'I don't know what to make of you.'

'Then just accept me as I am.'

'Do I have to?'

Angela laughs, 'No, I don't suppose so, but at least let's not quarrel about a man.'

Hilda holds the shell up to the light. 'This is a village of women, you know?'

'How'd you mean?'

'All the men went out to sea one day and never came back. Left a village of widows and young children.'

'Is that why it seems so sad?'

Hilda frowns, 'Do you feel that?'

Angela nods, 'I noticed it this morning. What happened to the widows?'

'They tried to hold things together here, but gradually they all drifted off until the village was deserted. It's only in recent times that the cottages have been restored.'

Alex comes down the stairs. He looks sad and tired, 'What are you two talking about?'

Angela wants to hear the rest of the story, but Alex has broken the spell.

CHAPTER FORTY-TWO

Edward has been to the supermarket for his weekly shop. He has been very judicious, knowing that he will have to carry it home and that he will only have one hand free. The other he will need for propelling himself with his stick. Among his purchases is an aubergine that he had been unable to resist. He'd picked it up and felt the cool, polished flesh against his skin, the prickle of the pale green cap on the underside of his wrist and - this week's special offer - Aubergine Recipe Cards.

Next day, he slices the aubergine into black-rimmed discs and places them one layer thick on a dinner plate. He picks up the salt and studies the picture of the boy throwing salt over his shoulder before, liberally, as the recipe instructs, sprinkling the grey-green flesh of the aubergine. He places another dinner plate on top of the aubergines and then, on top of the plate, a brass weight from his new scales.

He walks down to the delicatessen for some Parmesan cheese.

'Would you like it grated? Or a slice off the wedge?'

'I didn't know I had a choice,' Edward says.

'What are you making?'

Edward fishes in his pocket and pulls out the recipe card, 'Mou-Moussakka.'

'Mm, lovely. To be honest I'd go for the ready-grated. It's a bugger to grate if you're not used to doing it. I hate it. Always get the wife to do it.'

In the late afternoon sun, Edward hobbles back up the hill. He sees his reflection in a shop window and tries to straighten up. He stops outside a shoe shop and studies the merchandise in the window. He likes what he sees and on impulse, enters the shop. He asks for his size in a light tan slip-on that he has seen in the window.

'Would you like to try them on?'

Edward shakes his head, 'No, but may I bring them back if they don't fit?'

'It would be much easier if you tried them on here, Sir.'

'For you, maybe. Never mind, I'll leave it,' he picks up his stick.

'I'm sorry, Sir. I didn't realise. Of course you can bring them back.'

As Edward is paying for the shoes with four crisp twenty-pound notes from his wallet, he notices at the side of the till a long shoehorn, the colour of the buttons on his tweed jacket. He reaches out and runs his thumb and finger down its length.

'What a lovely thing. It's just what I need. It would make life so much easier having one this length. How much is it?'

'I'm sorry, but it's not for sale. It's real horn. I've had it years.'

'My father had one just like this. I think my mother threw it out. Oh well, never mind.'

As he pulls the shop door open the bell tinkles. The tone is the same as at the delicatessen.

'Excuse me, sir.' The assistant is extending the shoehorn towards him. 'Pop it in your bag'

'Are you sure? Won't you get into trouble?' he asks.

She shakes her head. 'It's my shop, but not for much longer. I've sold up. I'd like you to have it.'

The shoebox bangs against his leg as he walks. He should have asked her to take them out of the box but he can never resist a shoebox. They are useful for so many things. As he walks along, he hums to himself and thinks, is this what happens when you feel happy? Other people want to buy into it? How kind of her to give him the shoehorn. As he passes the bus stop he taps his stick against the metal of the shelter to listen for the echo. He walks along the ridge of the hill and down past the park. He watches the park keeper coming through the big wrought-iron gates and remembers long ago, when he was a boy, being chased out of the park at dusk so that the park keeper could lock the gates. He is suddenly overcome by a strange sadness. He does not want to go home yet. He wants to be among people. He stops for a coffee - two coffees – and a light salad. It was yesterday that he had arranged to meet his mother for lunch. He wonders how long she would have waited for him; imagines her growing state of confusion, her flux about whether to order or not. He watches the light outside begin to fade, listens to the chatter of the other people in the café. He will cook the Moussakka tomorrow.

Edward opens the door and feels inside for the light switch. He hears a ping as the light bulb in the hall blows, fusing all the lights.

'Damn.' He comes into the darkness and closes the door. He can see the shape of the keyhole lit up by the streetlights outside. He puts his key in the hole and turns it. He feels his way along the wall and notes the roughness of the woodchip wallpaper under his hand. He grasps the handle of the lounge door and pushes it open. There is a faint orange glow on the ceiling from the streetlights across the valley. His high-backed chair is silhouetted against the window. It resembles the head of a black horse. He walks over to the window and stares out across the valley. A double-decker bus is making its way up the hill on the opposite side.

He undresses in the dark. It is much darker in the bedroom than in the lounge. He stands by the chair and as he takes off each item of clothing he drops it onto the chair. In the morning he will have to search out the fuse box. Coming into the flat in darkness has made him think about things he'd rather not. He fumbles his way along the bed, searching for the top of the sheet. The cotton is cold against his skin.

CHAPTER FORTY-THREE

Angela is in bed and fully clothed. She has had a flannel wash and combed her hair, just in case, and tries, without success, to concentrate on her book. Surely he was joking, a throw away line, a final tease so that he could say that he'd stood up an Emmett.

She listens closely to the sounds outside; the sea is quieter now. She turns out the light and sits by the window. A headlight beam is tracing its way down the opposite hill. She gulps, hoping it will make its way back up the other side of the cove. A white van turns into the pebbled lane and comes to a halt under her window, its engine thrumming quietly.

'Shit!' She pulls open the sash and carefully eases herself onto the wall below. She taps on his window. He motions her to get in. Again, she taps on the window.

He lowers it. 'Get in.'

'I'm not coming.'

He arches an eyebrow and smiles. 'Bottled out, have you?'

She laughs and shakes her head, feeling the sea breeze lift the hair on the back of her head. 'This is crazy.'

'Come on, get in. They won't let us in the pub if we're much later.'

The wheels spin on the pebbles as he reverses out.

'That was clever,' she hisses. 'Wake them all up, why don't you?'

'Sorry,' he grins.

'Where are we going?'

'Padstow.'

'Isn't that miles away?'

'It's not that far. It'll only take us twenty minutes.' The engine screams its way up the steep winding hill.

Angela grasps the door handle. 'Yes, at this speed it probably will.'

'You think this is fast?'

They come to a junction where the road is wider and the hedges seem lower. A rabbit runs across in front of the van. 'Bugger! I could have had him.'

She ignores him, closes her eyes and for a while they drive in silence.

'Have you been out fishing then?' She finally asks.

'Yeah, we had quite a good catch. You must have brought me luck,' he says turning down towards the harbour.

'Your lucky night, is it?'

He pulls up on the harbour front with a screech. 'Let's hope so, shall we?'

He winks, and comes around the car to open her door. He extends his hand, bows low and pulls her out of her seat.

She laughs, 'Mister Gallant.'

He leans forward, pushes her up against the side of the van and kisses her, seeking out the inside of her lips with his own. 'You taste wonderful, Maid.'

'Christ, you don't waste any time, do you?' She says pushing him away. She runs her tongue over her lips. She can still taste him. Peppermint.

He takes her hand and they walk along the harbour where the streetlights are reflected in the water. The moored boats chatter gently amongst themselves. I'll have to get Alex to bring me here during the day, she thinks.

'I like to get all the crap out the way. Get everything up front and out in the open.'

'Sorry,' she turns away. 'What were you saying?'

He stops and kisses her again, longer, slower this time. She presses herself up against him.

'And it's obvious you agree,' he says.

'I wasn't listening,' she says, laughing.

'So, you agree then?' He turns up a side alley pulling her with him.

'About what? Where are you taking me?'

He steps down off the street and opens a door. Inside she can see a bar.

'Ev'nen, Paul.'

Paul, she muses, yes I suppose it suits him. Three men playing darts turn to look as the barman speaks. They nod over at

Paul, giving her the once over.

'Two rum and shrubs please, Albert.'

Angela wriggles herself onto a barstool. 'Don't I get asked what I want to drink?'

'Listen, I'm take'n you out for a secret evening, so we're having non-Emmett drinks.'

Angela takes a swig and gasps. 'Christ, what's that? It's like bloody rocket fuel.'

Paul and the barman laugh. 'Do you like it?' Paul asks.

'Yeah, it's wonderful.' Angela takes a cautious sip. 'Are you trying to get me drunk?'

'I wouldn't think I needed to. Fresh, young, maid like you.'

'Depends if I think you're any good.'

'And?'

'Not sure.'

'How are you going to find out?'

'Mmm.' She leans forward and sniffs his neck, and then nuzzles it with the end of her nose.

'What you sniffing for? Aftershave?'

'No.'

'Good, 'cos I hate the stuff.'

'You smell nice, sort of outsidey, like washing that's being on the line all day.'

'Going to hang me out to dry are you?' They laugh. He leans forward and sniffs behind her ear. His lips graze her neck down to her shirt collar. She shivers and pushes him away. He laughs, 'Mmm, lovely. You smell like a foxglove.'

'What does a foxglove smell like?'

'I've no idea, but you make me feel like one of those days in June, when I'm driving along with the windows down and all the foxgloves are bending towards me from the hedgerows.' He places his hands on the top of her thighs and rubs up and down her jeans, opening his eyes wide. She puts her hands on top of his and stills them.

'Would you like another drink, Angela?'

'You think you're so clever 'cos you found out my name don't you, Sherlock?'

'That's not my name.'

'No, I know it isn't your name, Paul.'

'What makes you think that's my name?'

'The bloke behind the bar thinks it is.'

'Yeah, but that don't mean it's my name, does it? I call you Maid, but that's not your name is it?'

She holds up her hands. 'Okay, you win. I suppose I shouldn't have expected to follow the logic of a man who calls me maid. I've never been called maid before, it's quite quaint.'

He puts his hands on her shoulders. 'Quaint, am I?'

She raises her eyebrows, 'We'll see, shan't we?'

He laughs and shakes his head, changing the subject. 'They made a Sherlock Holmes film near where you're staying, you know? Have you seen that castle-looking place out on the headland?'

'Yeah, I keep wanting to walk out to it. What was the film? *The Hound of the Baskervilles*?'

'Oh yeah. The hounds rose out of the sea. Hey, I've got the key for that place. We could go there tonight.'

'I hadn't got you down as a between-the-sheets man.'

He laughs, 'What do you reckon then, in the back of my van? You might get a fish hook in that lovely rump of yours.'

'What makes you think it will be my rump?'

He rubs his hands together. 'This gets better by the minute.'

She takes a sip of her drink and leans her elbows on the bar, pressing her hand into her forehead. He takes her other hand between his burred palms and rubs it gently. He plays with the underside of her Gran's eternity ring, turning it so that the green stones are on the underside of her finger. He bends forward and kisses her on the cheek, as if he senses her doubt.

'I'm just going to the bog,' he says, letting go of her hand.

She watches him walk the length of the room. He has the self-assured swagger of a man that she would normally detest but there is something animal about him; an honesty that appeals to her, a raw sexuality. Even their conversation she finds sexual. She can't remember the last time she fancied anybody so much. Yeah, she'd fancied Dan, he'd had all the right ingredients, but that magic spark just wasn't there.

She thinks back to earlier that evening, sitting in the dark, listening to the stream, remembering what had happened between herself and Edward, and trying to make sense of it all. If only life were a dream from which she could awake.

She leans on the bar and gazes into the gaps of mirror

between the bottles. The subdued lighting twinkles and sparkles amongst all the polish, glancing off from the oddest of places. She smoothes her hand along the bar rail and watches the glow blur and then clear. She feels warm inside, and wonders if it is the rum, or the dream.

CHAPTER FORTY-FOUR

Rachel had always wanted to draw, to become an accomplished painter. It was a dream she'd held from being a very young child and, after all, George was dead and Edward had left home, so she was free to do whatever she liked, but she hated the fact that most people in the class were not there to paint, or recreate the world in the way they saw it, but to pass a bit of time, have some company. She stuck it out for three Wednesday afternoons and then never went back. She saw her teacher one day while she was sitting in the gallery.

'We missed you. You were my best pupil.'

Rachel had grimaced and told her, 'That wasn't saying a lot, was it?'

The woman had laughed and asked her to explain.

'I came to paint,' Rachel explained. 'To be part of the excitement, and what I got was the reek of boredom. People just dabbling into something as a way of passing time, not because they had a passion for it.'

'And is that so wrong?' The woman had asked.

Rachel shrugged, 'Maybe not, unless you're looking for lost dreams.'

'How about coming to my life class, then? That's a totally different experience.'

'I think not. I really wanted to do landscapes, but you know, maybe I should have just left it as a dream. It felt like visiting a place you'd held dear in your memory for so long, to find that going back destroyed the image. Yes, I should have left it as a dream.'

'I don't suppose you'd consider modelling for us, would you?'

Rachel could absorb the atmosphere around her without having to become a part of it. All eyes were on her. At first it seemed strange, but then she began to take a pride in it and over the years she became a regular fixture, someone the tutors talked to with respect, and yes, there were those who desired her too. Those who, from the look in their eyes, wanted to do more than just draw her body.

Rachel had always been attracted to men who desired her. One boy had followed her home and stood at her gate in the falling dusk. She'd gone upstairs, turned on her bedroom light and undressed for him, turning around in the window so that he could see her silhouetted shape. When she looked out again he was gone. He didn't come to class for two weeks. When he returned she slipped him a note, invited him to tea without giving her address.

He came one Sunday afternoon, tongue-tied, with no flowers. She asked him if he had ever had sex. He shook his head and reddened. He stood up to go. She asked him if he would like to have sex with an older woman. Then he'd looked at her, and said she was the most beautiful woman he had ever seen, and that he'd dreamed all day of stroking the soft, white, dimpled flesh of her inner thigh. She took him; not upstairs in her bed, but out of the house and round the back, down the steps and into the gentle, must smell of the cellar, where George's workbench with all his tools were still arranged as neatly as he had left them the weekend before he died.

There were others after him; a lecturer, shabby, bored and waiting for his retirement. She didn't take him home. The boy was her only special one. He would seek her out at the oddest of times. She would hear a soft tap on her door and know by the timidity of the knock that it was him. She would shut the front door behind them and take him around the back of the house and down the cellar steps. As his confidence grew, he visited less often; spending more time with people of his own age. She had loved the passing secrecy of it, even though she no longer had to keep these things from George.

CHAPTER FORTY-FIVE

Edward sits in the darkened room. All day he has sat in his chair, watching the changing light through the curtains. He had got up as normal and organised himself for work but, again, he had not gone, not even rung to say he would not be in. He sits silently until darkness has swept in across the valley. Tabitha mews and rubs against his legs. She is hungry. He gets up and presses the light switch, darkness. He's forgotten to look for the fuse box. Edward Anderson, what is wrong with you? He sits back down again.

He lays his head against the wing of the chair and feels the wet of his tears drop to his bare shoulder. The pain in his belly is hard, jagged like a rock, as befits a man who has waited until he is forty-nine to fall in love. The rawness of it all eats away at him, how is he to go on? He closes his eyes and again, behind his lids, sees the same scene – he and Angela lying naked. It is as if he had not been part of it, but looking down from above where he can see the mushroom texture of her skin, the glistening where the flesh is full and plumped and the slightly tawnier colouring where the bones touch the surface. He can see her hair cut into the nape of her neck and, if he takes a deep breath, he can smell her; that slightly cloying, musky smell. He groans out loud, 'Oh God!' If only things could go back to how they were. If only this awful ache would go away. Is he going mad? His head feels as if it wants to explode, to spill out pink flesh like an overripe pomegranate.

He had meant to go back on Saturday but the mounting anticipation had been too much. If only he could have reached inside his chest and clawed out the angst that he'd felt. His whole life now feels like a dream. Every night he wakes, his body throbbing with confusion and excitement. 'Oh God, Oh God,' he sobs, rocking back and forth in his chair. Tabitha jumps onto his knee and nuzzles him like a child.

Tomorrow he must go back to work, or to the doctor.

The doctor says he is suffering from depression. Edward wonders how he knows. He hadn't said anything except, 'Well, I'm not sure what I've come about really.'

'Quite normal these days, stress of work and all that.' From his printer the doctor takes a pale green prescription and then, as if noticing Edward for the first time, waves it at him, 'This should do the trick, and I'll do you a sick note for two weeks.'

Edward drags the rubber-clad end of his stick along the polished floor as he makes his way back to the pale-green waiting room. He feels suddenly angry, disempowered, as if the doctor has stripped him of his shell.

The pharmacist shakes her head as she reads his prescription. 'I'm sorry Mr Anderson, I'm waiting for some more Prozac to come in. Can you call back later?'

'No. I can't.'

She shrugs her shoulders and hands him back the prescription, 'Sorry, seems to be a run on them today, already done 19 prescriptions this morning.'

When he gets outside, Edward puts the prescription in his pocket and, closing his hand around it, crumples it into a ball. He takes it out of his pocket and crumples it some more and, as he passes the doctors' car park, he throws it under a car and watches it go scurrying away into a puddle.

Walking home, he shuffles his stick through some scattered leaves on the pavement. He feels better now, as if he has taken charge of his own life. However painful his new feelings are, for the first time in many years he is experiencing emotion. Emotions that he'd forgotten, and some that he'd never believed existed. He is not depressed. He is the opposite of depressed. But no, not elated. He wonders what the word is for his condition? Happy? No, alive, maybe.

He must use his sick leave to get away. Clear his head. When he gets home he phones the archaeology study centre. There is a dig starting the day after tomorrow just outside the city walls at York and yes, they still need volunteers.

Edward feels pleased with himself and decides he deserves a proper cup of coffee. He pours the beans into the grinder and places his hand on top of the clear plastic cover. He feels the throb of the beans grinding through the palm of his hand. He lifts off the top and smells the oil of the beans. Coarse ground, just right.

He carries the mug and then the jug and cafetière through to the sitting room and seats himself in his rocker. He waits four minutes then places the centre of his palm on the gold plunger. It is warm to the touch. He gently pushes down until all the coarse grains are crushed to the bottom. The coffee is exactly as he likes it. He can tell by looking at it. It has that slight grainy froth settling on the top.

He watches the sunlight dancing on the pale apricot walls. He will go to York today. By the time he gets there the sun will be so high in the sky that the sandstone of the walls will be turned to the colour of honeycomb. He will see if they have rooms at that B&B just outside the city walls. He will pack now before he changes his mind.

He turns the key in the lock and puts it carefully in the zip pocket on the flap of his bag. Tabitha brushes round his legs and Edward coaxes her to jump up onto the side wall where he rubs his knuckle under her chin. He picks up his bag and taps his stick on the metal floor of the walk way. I'm feeling better already, Edward thinks to himself.

But he stops and turns back towards his flat. He can't go away, what about the cat? He can't leave her for a whole week.

CHAPTER FORTY-SIX

Angela pokes her head round the door at the bottom of the stairs.
Alex is sitting alone at the kitchen table with yesterday's paper
spread out before him.

He grins, 'I thought it was Aunt Hilda. You look wonderful.'

'Can I have a bath?'

'Okay, as long as you leave the water in for me.'

'Yuk.' Angela turns up her nose.

'There's only enough water to run one bath. I don't mind
bathing in your soup, so knock on the floor when you've done.'

Angela lies back in the bath and closes her eyes. She thinks
of the night before, feels half-ashamed. A shame that brings warm
blood to her belly. She laughs to herself and, spluttering, submerges
her head under the water.

She gets out of the bath and sits on the mat with a towel
draped around her, like a white island in a sea of turquoise lino. The
door opens and Alex enters.

'I didn't say to come up yet.'

'I'm sorry, I thought I heard you knock on the floor.' He
comes in and closes the door. 'Do you mind?' he says, nodding
towards the bath.

'No, I'll watch you undress.' She looks at him, daring him to
back away and out the door but he unbuttons the top two buttons
of his check shirt and pulls it off over his head. His flesh has an
uncooked texture about it, like a pie waiting to go in the oven. His
stomach muscles are flabby, his belly slightly protruding. He grasps
his forearms, flexes his muscles and laughs. His arms are thin and
have a fine covering of black hair.

'Carry on,' she says.

He undoes the buckle on his brown leather belt, breathes in
to undo the metal stud of his jeans and lets them slip to his ankles.
He is wearing tight fitting grey boxer shorts.

Not bad, she thinks, then 'Go on,' she urges.

He turns his back and pulls down his shorts, wriggling his non-existent bum. Sheepishly he turns round, covering his genitals with his hands. She feels an overwhelming urge to laugh.

She pulls her towel tighter. 'Get in the bath, will you.'

She smears her hand over the mirror, sees a blurred vision of herself, and hears Alex lowering himself into the water.

'You know?' Alex turns on the tap.

'What?'

'Most artists end up making love to their models. It's a natural part of the creative progress.'

She laughs into the mirror. 'Nice try.'

'I didn't particularly mean us.'

'Good.'

'I was just thinking about it, that's all.'

'We talked about it before, don't you remember, you were going on about the pre-Raphaelites, said it was a different era, that they weren't their pupils. Remember?' She squeezes someone else's toothpaste onto her brush. 'What do you mean though, it's part of the creative process'?'

He sits up in the bath. 'Not sure really, I suppose it's like when you get two actors working together they have to form a bond to make it work.'

'And what if a bond doesn't form? I suppose that explains why artists always choose beautiful models.'

'Interesting question, I think you'd find that the work lacked a certain something.'

'Expand.' She puts her toothbrush to her mouth.

'Intensity, I suppose. I dunno, that unexplainable ingredient.'

She uses downward strokes to clean the inner sides of her teeth. So if Alex is right, what happened between Edward and her had been inevitable, and was her work improved by it?

'Ange?'

She turns, toothbrush in mouth.

'I don't think I can go back tomorrow. Mum had a bad night and I want to wait and see if I can find a doctor in this Godforsaken place.'

She turns, frowning, 'I think I'll go back today then.'

'There's no way I can make it today.'

Trapped here with Alex for days, even weeks? God, she's got

to get away.

'I'll get the train then.'

'Do you have to go today?' He asks, a plaintive note in his voice.

'Yes.'

'But surely you can wait until I go back.'

'No, I can't. You forget. I've got my work to complete.'

'Oh well,' he sighs. 'I'll find out the train times then.'

Hilda is standing in front of the Rayburn stirring a saucepan with a wooden spoon. Angela observes how closely her steely grey hair is shorn into the nape of her neck. She turns, and as she does so her fringe falls across her face. Like Alex, Angela thinks. Even the teeth are the same. Hilda continues to stir the pot using graceful, swivelling motions from her wrist,

'Would you like some porridge?'

'Porridge? I haven't had porridge for years. I'd love some.'

'You must be hungry after your little session in the bathroom.'

'I'm sorry, I don't get your meaning.' Angela says pulling a chair out from the table.

Hilda pours porridge into two bowls and places one in front of Angela. 'Does this mean he's won you over? That you're now one of his women?'

'Have you got any brown sugar?'

Hilda nods to the cupboard behind Angela.

Angela swirls the brown sugar into her porridge until it all becomes a dull brown. 'You probably won't believe this, but there is nothing between me and Alex and nothing,' she looks upwards, 'happened upstairs.'

They hear Alex coming down the stairs. He pokes his head around the door.

'Would you like some porridge, dear?' Hilda asks, rising from her seat and turning towards the Rayburn.

'Yes, please.' He rumples Angela's wet hair. 'What have you two been talking about?'

'We were just discussing how you've got the hots for me.' Angela watches him turn bright red. She tries not to laugh.

He pulls a face at her and looks over at his aunt to gauge her reaction. Hilda is standing with her back to them, reheating the porridge, her shoulders shaking with silent laughter.

Alex pushes back his chair, 'I'm going for a walk.'

The sun has already warmed the top of the garden wall. Angela has said goodbye to Hilda and now she is waiting for Alex. Pressing her palms into the slate she lifts her bottom and swivels round, stretching full length along it; absorbing the warmth into her back. Shading her eyes, she looks up at the cottage. The green curtains in the sick room are closed, but the window is slightly open. Angela can hear the low murmur of Hilda's voice; on and on it carries in the same tone. She must be reading to Alex's mother. Angela strains to catch a word, but the breeze coming in off the cove is against her. She is almost tempted to stand on the wall and peek in. To see if, propped up against the pillows, there is a female version of Alex listening to Hilda read. She sits back up, and starts to bang her heels impatiently against the wall.

Below her, the beach is a spread of wet pebbles, the tide lapsing slowly outwards and then, as if changing its mind, rushing back again. No sign of Alex yet. Where can he have got to? She spots him up on the headland; a small figure silhouetted black against the sun. He is standing by the house on the cliff-top, the Sherlock Holmes house. She waves. He sees her and turns away. 'Shit.' She slips off the wall, throws her red holdall into the garden and starts to make her way up the cliff path towards him. She stops half way up and looks back. The sick-room window is now fully open, the green curtains flapping in the breeze. Smoke is drifting lazily from the chimney. It all feels so serene. Angela thinks back to Hilda telling her about the fishermen being drowned at sea. The place did have an other-worldly quality about it. A feeling of both sadness and tranquillity, and she knows now why Alex's mother wanted to return. It would be a good last resting place.

'Alex!' she shouts. He hears her and turns away, peering in through the diamond-paned windows of the house.

'The rooms are quite small, aren't they?' She says, coming up behind him.

'How do you know?' He turns away from the window.

'Oh, um, Hilda told me.'

He puzzles for a minute. 'That dried up old prune.'

'Actually, I rather like her.'

'You would. Two bitches together.' He turns back to peer in

the window.

'Witches?' she says, her voice rising.

'I said bitches, bitches,' he repeats. 'You're a bitch.'

'If you find my company so distasteful, you won't mind running me to the station then, will you?'

Shading his eyes, Alex sits down and gazes out to sea. 'Why were you discussing me with her?

'Listen idiot, I wasn't. She thought we were having sex in the bathroom. I had to dispel that notion,' she pauses. 'I mean, it would have seemed really callous, us fucking, with your mother ill across the landing.'

He peers up at her, shading his eyes from the sun. She offers him her hand and pulls him up.

'You ought to see it up here when the sea-thrift is out. Everywhere there are huge clumps of pink, and back there against the wall, Foxgloves and Campion.'

'Do you like the smell of Foxgloves?'

'They don't smell, do they?'

She smiles, 'Not sure.'

'How do you know there's a train?' he asks.

'Hilda has a timetable. There's one at twenty past twelve.'

He looks at his watch, 'We'll have to hurry.'

They slip and slide their way back down the steep path. Angela leans over the garden wall and pulls her holdall out from among the catmint.

'Aren't you going to say goodbye?' he asks.

'I already have.'

'I'll just see if they want anything.'

'Hurry up, I'll miss the train.'

The station is inland, hidden from the main road by a mass of rhododendron bushes. Everything is quiet, polished, and painted in brown and cream.

They sit on the platform bench in silence, waiting. Alex takes her hand. She lets him.

'I wish you could have stayed,' he says, studying her palm.

The track begins to vibrate. Angela stands up. 'Alex, don't go there, okay? Thanks for the break. It's been good.'

'Good? It's been wonderful.' He leans towards her and kisses her lightly on the cheek. He smells of stale cigarettes. She remembers the smell of Edward, Imperial Leather, a warm, clean smell, comforting. She jumps into a carriage and clatters the door shut.

Alex holds an imaginary phone to his ear. 'I'll ring you,' he mouths. She looks at his teeth. When he smiles, both his bottom and top set are revealed. Like little tombstones; slightly protruding, weather stained tombstones.

CHAPTER FORTY-SEVEN

The auction boards were already up when Rachel arrived. Her aunt asked her to stay on to help her sort out the house and reluctantly she'd agreed. She had wanted to get back for Edward. He was in his last year at school and she had hoped that he would come with her to his Great Uncle's funeral. He'd been twelve years old the last time he visited the farm. When she'd pointed out to Edward that Uncle Jack was of his own flesh and blood, he seemed to get angry. He'd refused point blank to speak to her, even when she was leaving to catch the train.

She had wanted to go to the Chapel of Rest to see her uncle, but her aunt had already instructed that the coffin be sealed. To Rachel it all seemed too sudden: The nailing down of the coffin, the house up for auction. It all felt like a chapter in her life snapping shut before she'd had time to finish reading it. Her aunt's sister lived in a bungalow in Bournemouth and she was going to live with her.

'I thought you'd want to stay on a while,' Rachel said, as they stacked the crockery on the dining room table.

'Stay on? Why ever should I want to stay on here? What has this farm ever given me? My little boy drowned. What was left for me after that? We could have sold up and gone. He could have got another job. But oh no, he wouldn't hear of it. So we stayed and soured each other with our memories.'

'Did you never want any more children?'

Her aunt snorted, 'Your uncle wasn't capable, not after Robert died. It seemed to, I don't know, take away his manhood. He never said but I think he felt that Robert dying was a punishment for him marrying a gentile like me. And anyway, I felt so bitter towards him.'

'Why?' Rachel asked quietly.

'For making me stay. And now here I am at seventy and too

old to do all the things that I thought one day I would. So, no, I don't want to stay, and the sooner I am out of here the better.'

Around her waist her aunt wore the bunch of keys that Uncle Jack had always carried. It was strange to see them jangling on her hip instead of his. They tried nearly every key before they found the one for the padlock on the cabin trunk in the attic.

'I've always wondered what he had in here,' her aunt said as she twisted the rust from the lock.

'Did you never think of looking?'

'Did you ever know him not to have his bunch of keys with him?'

Rachel shook her head and waited as her aunt lifted the lid. Inside was a shallow tray that sat around the rim. It was divided into little square compartments, most of which were empty but in some were neatly folded packages of yellowed tissue paper. Her aunt carefully unwrapped one: nothing. It was the same with all the rest until she got to the last one and as she opened it, out fell a shower of small twigs of orange.

'What on earth?' her aunt said.

'I think it's coral.'

Her aunt laughed, 'Plastic, more like.'

'Can I have them?'

Her aunt looked at her. 'Whatever would you want rubbish like that for?'

Rachel picked a piece up off the floor. 'Look, each one has a tiny pinhole. I could make a necklace.'

'Umph! You're welcome to it.'

Rachel picked up all the bits that lay scattered on the floor. One long bit, maybe even the centrepiece, was wedged between the floorboards. She carefully prised it out with one of the keys on her uncle's chain. Her aunt lifted up the tray. The trunk was empty, except for a sheet of old newspaper in a strange script lining the bottom.

Rachel stared down at the newspaper. 'This must have been my Grandmother's trunk. I think this newspaper is Russian.'

Her aunt struggled to her feet, 'That can go in the auction, along with its contents.'

'Aunt? Would you mind if I had it?'

'I suppose not. Is there anything else you want?'

'No, nothing.'

The next day strangers came and took away the contents of the house; trampling with their muddy feet, not having a care for what had been before. All those years they had kept their secret, and now it was gone. She could still hear her mother, every year it would be the same, even after she was married. 'Why do you always want to go trailing off to your uncle's farm for your holidays? Why don't you go on a proper family holiday?'

Why, indeed.

Her aunt wanted her to take some Siberian Saxifrage. She had been digging up a clump for herself when Rachel came back from the barn and because she'd dug up too much she insisted that Rachel took some too. Her aunt had never been interested in gardening, so why was she taking this plant?

'It was the only thing that I brought with me, along with myself, that has survived. So it's coming with me.'

Rachel hated it. The big green tongues flat to the ground and the failed promise of the pink stalked flowers. She thought the saxifrage would probably be happier in suburban Bournemouth than in the flower border up against her house. Many times she had been tempted to dig it up, but it reminded her of her uncle, and so she kept it.

She never saw her aunt again. They exchanged Christmas cards for ten years. After that, she presumed her aunt had died.

CHAPTER FORTY-EIGHT

The air is yellow and heavy with floating dust particles. Angela sits in Edward's chair under the skylight and basks in the sun. She closes her eyes and falls gently into slumber; just for five minutes. When she wakes the sunlight is gone. She shivers, just like when she woke the last time they were here…

When she'd asked him to lie down on her granddad's blanket he'd grumbled as usual. He always seemed to enjoy a good grumble. *Hadn't she even thought to bring a duvet to put underneath to soften the impact of the floor on his poor bones?*

'Please Edward, it won't be for long, I promise. I just want to do a few quick sketches.'

'Help me get down then. Hold me from behind so I can give myself a bit of leverage.'

She'd sketched in silence. It was a good pose. Edward lay on his side with his legs slightly bent, his arms folded across his chest, his body slightly curved. The light from the window behind her caught the most prominent part of his back, accentuating the irregularities, casting the flatter side into dark shadow. She'd realised after a while that Edward was unusually quiet. It had made her feel suddenly ill at ease. She took her eye away from his back and glanced upwards to his face. The glint of something on the side of his nose caught her eye. Puzzled, she glanced again. Whatever it was, it was moving. She realised with horror that he was crying. Silent tears slid down the side of his nose and dripped onto the grey army blanket, forming a darkening circle.

She returned her eye to his spine, smudged a little with the ball of her thumb, looked again, still the tears were there, the damp patch on the blanket increasing in size. I must keep drawing, she thought to herself, he will know if he can't hear the scratch of charcoal. She traced the lower part of his back, the flat roundness of his buttock. A slight movement made her change her focus.

Protruding at an almost exact right angle from his body was his erect penis.

She had wanted to put down her board and run out of the room, out of the building, away from this man. What was Edward doing with an erection? Why was he crying? She could pretend not to notice. She grasped the back of her neck with her free hand. That week she had cut her hair and she missed the warmth of it on her neck.

She continued to scratch with the charcoal in the bottom corner of her paper. Her hands shook too much to continue drawing. But if she could keep drawing maybe his erection would subside and he could manage to regain a degree of dignity. They could pretend that this had never happened. She looked up. If anything, his erection seemed to have increased. He was still crying. She felt her own eyes fill with tears. She stood up, bent over him, stroked his hair, shuffled her way inside the curl of his body until they lay together like two spoons, his tears wetting her newly-shorn hair, her taking his penis, wanting it inside her...

She shivers to herself, if only she could have drawn them, lying there together. Angela O'Donnell, you're strange. She looks at her watch, 3.30 p.m. She hears the first spatter of rain on the skylight. How long should she wait? The man at the library said he would give him the message if he phoned or came in. She should have returned the following Saturday instead of going off to Cornwall. Had he been here waiting for her? Like the time they had that row and she had waited for him for two Saturdays in a row. Well, serve him right. She had almost convinced herself that she wouldn't need Edward to sit for her again. She could manage, she supposed, but it didn't feel quite complete, not yet. She needed to add something. What, she was not sure.

There is a knock at the door and like a scalded cat she jumps up from her chair. 'Come in,' She notices her voice is trembling.

The caretaker puts his grey head round the door, 'Be locking up in a bit, duck. Have you got a key?'

She shakes her head.

'Another five minutes then, eh?'

'Excuse me?' she calls after him. He puts his head back round the door. 'Have you been here all day?'

'Yeah, off and on. Why?'

'Have you seen a man with a stick?'

'That hunchback fellow that comes?'

'Yes, that's him.'

'No, can't say I have.'

'What about last week?'

He shakes his head. 'No, but he was here a few weeks back, the beginning of the month it was. I remember because it was my birthday. He was walking along the corridor singing to himself. I nearly shouted after him, *how about Happy Birthday?'*

Angela smiles, 'I know. I was here that week too.' She zips her portfolio together and both zip ends meet at the handle.

'Artist, are you?' I shall miss it when they finish the rebuilding up at the art college. I've enjoyed having you lot down here.

She nods and picks up her portfolio. Yes, she thinks to herself, I am an artist.

CHAPTER FORTY-NINE

Edward spends all week in the flat, going out only occasionally after dark to buy provisions, and even this he wouldn't do if he didn't need food for the cat. He lies in bed all day waiting for the darkness, only getting up to feed Tabitha or to go to the toilet. He wishes he had a curtain to cover the glass in his front door. He leaves the curtains in both his bedroom and the lounge drawn all day. As darkness falls he opens them and pulls his chair up to the window to watch the city at night. He notes the changing of the traffic lights from red, to amber, green. He watches the cars stop by rote as they advance up the hill, slowing as they meet the red lights.

He is fascinated by the blue light of an ambulance and, from where he sits, the silence of its night-time siren. Every night the ambulance takes the same route out of the hospital before branching off to its final destination along the ring road. He waits for the return journey, but knows he can only make that out if the blue lights are lit for the immediate and the dying.

On the way up the hill he passes the doctor's surgery. Maybe the doctor was right; perhaps he should have taken the Prozac. But he wasn't depressed. It was just that he needed time to adjust. Something wonderful had happened in his life. A beautiful young woman had wanted him to make love to her. He stops to rest, shivering himself deeper into his coat. All week he hasn't bothered to wash or shave, and on one of his night time forays he'd caught sight of himself in a mirror. He'd stared back at his reflection, and put his hand up to his face to feel the stubble that he saw. He'd looked like a tramp.

When he gets home he must have a bath.

After he has fed the cat he sits down at the kitchen table. He feels too weary to have a bath. He has been lost to the world for one whole week and who has noticed? He wonders if he would be in this state if he'd gone to York, if he'd never got the cat. She looks up at him as if reading his mind.

'Well at least you love me, don't you puss?' Is this what he is afraid of? That Angela does not love him? Pity, that can be the only reason why she had done it. The word is finally there, forming in his mouth: 'Pity.' He covers his face with his hands and groans. The groan softens to a hum, one long drone trying to drown out the emotions that swirl inside him. If only he could hold them, examine them, find somewhere to put them down when they became unbearable. He holds his hands a short distance apart, imagining a ball of glowing light between them, a sphere of twisting blues and purples. It warms to his touch, gives him pins and needles in his finger ends, making him weary.

He wakes up. The cold of the kitchen table has soaked into his cheek. He looks at his watch, two o'clock. He gets up and goes into the lounge to stare out into the darkness. Tonight there is a full moon, a poacher's moon, misty and ethereal. He will go to bed. Try to make a new start in the morning. He could even go to York for the day. Why had he not thought of that before? He goes to close the curtains and then thinks better of it. It will give him courage in the morning if he leaves them open.

He stands at his bedroom door. Tabitha is already curled up asleep at the bottom of his bed. He wishes he had slept all night at the kitchen table. The darkness, and the cold of the sheets on his skin, bring back the yearning two-fold.

CHAPTER FIFTY

As a child, there was a sadness in the house that Rachel could never quite fathom.

Sometimes a deep depression would descend upon her mother and she would stay in bed for days, only getting up in her nightdress in the early morning to do her piecework. She said the rhythm of the sewing helped to soothe her nerves. Rachel would lie in bed listening to the hum of the sewing machine. Her mother was a pocket hand. She sewed pockets into the suits that her father cut and brought home from the factory. If Rachel listened carefully she could tell the style of pocket her mother was making. Slow short bursts and then silence as she mitred the corners, and then two very quick bursts as she tacked the tongues of the welt to secure them, and then the long bursts as she attached the silesia bag meant she was putting in a welted pocket. Patch pockets were one continual steady burst, like sawing wood, as she attached it in one skilful, juddering flow.

When her father got up to go downstairs, Rachel would hear the whine of the sewing machine change as her mother pushed in the big black button to turn it off followed by her slow steps ascending the stairs. Rachel knew then that her father would soon call her to come and get breakfast.

At these times, if she was not at school, Rachel's father would take her to work with him and at lunch times, and on the way back home, he would take her to the corner café and order them bacon and eggs, or liver and onion casserole. Food she had never experienced before her mother's depressions; food that she, like her father, found delicious. When he finished his meal he would sit back in his chair, pat his stomach contentedly and sigh, 'Now that's what I call proper food.' Then he would lean forward across the table and whisper conspiratorially, 'Don't tell your mother, that's a good girl.' Rachel liked these secrets. It made the food taste even better.

'You women,' her father would tell her. 'Why can't you learn to cook food other than what you were brought up on? Is it so difficult? My mother was exactly the same. She was French, you know? There's a lesson for you, lass. Always marry your own kind. Causes much less trouble in the end.'

Rachel would often pester her father to tell the story of his childhood and of her grandparent's romance. My father, he would begin, your granddad, was a fabric buyer. He must have been good at his job. A gentile working for a Jewish haberdasher was very rare in those days. He was often sent to Europe to purchase silk and on one of these trips he met your grandmother, married her and bought her home. When I was fourteen, Father died. He wasn't even cold in his grave before my mother had packed our bags. You see, he said, she'd always hated Leeds. I suppose she was homesick for her own country.

As she grew older, Rachel learned that her father had refused to return to France with his mother. She had found him an apprenticeship with a Jewish tailor and, as soon as he was settled in lodgings, she left. He never forgave her. She often wrote to him and begged him to come to France to visit her, but he remained in Leeds where he married the boss's daughter. A boss who, until he announced that he'd fallen in love with his daughter, had treated him like a son. Strangers off the street were witnesses at their wedding, and on their first night he carried his new bride across the threshold of the house they were to occupy for the rest of their lives.

The letters from France went behind the clock on the mantelpiece. They were still there, most of them unopened, when Rachel cleared the house after her father's death. She put them in her handbag and on the train home she read them.

She discovered that her French grandmother remarried and had a daughter and that when the daughter was in her early twenties, just before the outbreak of the Second World War, a rift had occurred between them and the girl had run off with a Jewish artist twice her age. Rachel's father was urged to visit his mother now that she was all alone in the world.

Rachel wrote a letter to the address at the top of her grandmother's letters. For a year she heard nothing and then she received a letter from Manchester, in a hand she didn't recognise. It was from a Claudette Mason, informing her that her grandmother had died five years previously and that she was her father's half-sister who had come to live in England during the war. She now lived in Manchester. They corresponded regularly, gradually building up a picture of each other's lives until one day, several years later, Rachel went to Manchester to visit her.

Rachel would have given anything for Claudette's house. Not for the size or location, but for the life, the experience, the knowledge, the culture all held there between the walls. Claudette was quite elderly and walked with the aid of two wooden sticks, which, when seated, she placed together as a pair to one side of her chair. Rachel could still see the remnants of great beauty in the woman's face; the high cheekbones, hair pulled back into a soft bun and streaked like a horse's mane, eyes dancing with humour and intelligence.

The two women had tea, and Rachel asked about the rift between Claudette and her mother.

The muscles in Claudette's face stiffened. 'It was sad for her, maybe, but not for me. She was a very hard woman. I was better away from her.'

'And the artist?' Rachel asked.

At this, Claudette became wistful. 'Ah! Isaac. How I loved that man, and his work. I'm not sure now which I loved the most,' she laughed. 'It's strange how things turn out. I have a friend who comes to visit me, well, she is also my cleaner actually, and with her she brings her granddaughter, a girl of seven or eight and, you know what, that child, of all the books I have, that is the only one she wants to look at; the book of his work. It's almost as if he's come back from the dead to poke me alive. To say, *don't forget me.* When the Germans invaded we were living together. One day when he went to the shops they arrested him. I learned this from the baker. I never saw him again. I packed a few things and fled with my life. I came over here and I waited for Isaac to follow. After the war I went back and searched for him. I heard that he'd died in a concentration camp. When I finally believed he was dead I came back to Manchester and married Mr Mason. I'd met him soon after I arrived in England. He was a kind man, an English teacher who helped me with my language. At first I didn't love him. I thought I could never love anyone as I had loved Isaac, and that was true. But one day I woke to find that a relationship I had expected so little from had brought me great happiness and contentment. We found so much in common. Ours was a gentle love, a love of quiet happiness.'

'And what of my father? Did you never think to find him?' Rachel asked.

'I often thought of your father and one day, a year after my husband had died, I travelled by train across the Pennines to Leeds. I never knew before that England had such wild and dramatic countryside. The only clue I had to your father's whereabouts was an address that was pasted on the side of an old trunk of my mother's. That address was burnt on my brain, so I couldn't forget it. '33 Green Mouse Street'. What a strange address that is. I found the house but no one could remember my mother or her married name. So I had nothing left to go on. All I knew was that your father was called Richard. I don't think he ever wrote to my mother. All we got was a card at Christmas written in a woman's hand until one year, for some reason, maybe my mother had asked for it, a photo of him. Just him, none of the rest of the family. There was also another brother, you know? A child my mother had in her old age when I think she thought she was too old to have any more children.'

'Did he die?'

She'd shrugged, 'I never knew him. He was sent away, put in a home. There was something wrong with him you see. His body was bent and twisted. It was rumoured that the child couldn't have been my father's because he was already in a wheelchair by then, disabled by a stroke.'

'And your mother let the child go?'

'It was done in those days. I think she used to visit him because every year she would go away on her own to the coast for a week. Somewhere I have some photos of her with this boy grasping a bucket and spade to his twisted body. So she had the three children. Your father when she was twenty-one, me when she was forty-one and the other when she was fifty-four. Maybe I should have tried to find him after my mother died, but as you say in this country, I let sleeping dogs lie. You have a son, don't you?'

'Yes, I have a son.'

CHAPTER FIFTY-ONE

Alex stares at each drawing intently, holding each one out at arms length. Sometimes he goes back to look at one he has already studied. He says nothing. Angela wants to say something to lessen the tension, but she feels unsure of her ground. She has never seen him this serious. She stares out of the window, watches the crows circling the black branches of the trees on the brow of the hill, waiting for him to speak. A bus is making its way up between the houses. Still he says nothing. She watches him, studies how his brow corrugates into a frown; his legs crossed, one moccasin dangling loose at the heel.

He glances up at her, and then back down at the page where Edward lays curled into himself, his hump pulling off in a different direction,

'I don't know what to say. This work is outstanding, totally, absolutely!'

He looks up at her again. 'How old are you?'

'Twenty-two.'

He scratches his head. 'I didn't think anyone of twenty-two could draw like this. It's that old bloke isn't it?'

'Edward? Yes,' she says.

'Where did you get the idea from? How did you get him to pose? Bloody hell, I'm jealous. Do you think he'd model for the college?'

She shakes her head. She can't take in what he's saying. '*Outstanding,*' is that what he'd said?

'He'd be a great bloke to sculpt, don't you think?' He picks up another drawing. 'Fabulous.'

She feels a warm glow rising in her chest. She wants to cry. 'You're being serious, aren't you? You're not just kidding me?'

'I've never been more serious in my life. I knew you were good, but not this good. This work is truly inspirational.'

She doesn't know what to say.

'I'm proud you're a student of mine.' He looks up at her, searching her face as if seeing her for the first time, and then back down at the drawing he has in his hand,

'You've really captured something here. There is a great vulnerability and,' he pauses, 'a tenderness, an intimacy... all his life... this man... '

'Edward,' she interjects.

'...has probably been regarded as a freak, grotesque even, and yet you've totally transformed him, shown that beauty is not only in... in uniformity, in the expected. Such honesty is breathtaking, outstanding. I have only one criticism. I can't accept the work just in one medium. It's not enough. I need to see your use of other materials, other colours. Oils? You've done some fantastic work in oils.'

'I knew you were going to say that.'

'Then why...'

She interrupts, 'I have done a few in red pastel.'

He shuffles through the drawings, 'Two. It's not enough, Ange, I need more.'

'Well, you see,' she clasps the back of her neck. 'I might have a problem there. Edward seems to have done a disappearing act, doesn't he?'

'How do you mean?'

'We sort of had a bit of a fall out before I went to Cornwall, and when I came back he was nowhere to be found. He's not at work. He's not at his lodgings.' She shrugs, 'I don't know where he is.'

'I saw him, you know, the other day, he was sitting in that café down the road from here. You know, the one just down from the shoe shop.'

'Damn! I wish I'd seen him.' She nods towards her work. 'I could do some colour wash.'

He holds a picture, looks down at it. 'Do you think people might think you've exploited him?'

'No, I don't. I did occasionally think about that when I was drawing him and, oh, I don't know. What do you think?'

'If you had portrayed him like the Hunchback of Notre Dame, then maybe there would be an element of exploitation. But you haven't. You've shown him warts and all, so to speak. There is such an honesty comes through that you can't help but see the person – the man behind the deformity. In fact you've even captured, well, I hesitate to say this, a certain sexuality.' He holds up a drawing of Edward, legs spread out, his bottom on the edge of his chair.

'Sexuality?'

She looks down at Edward, a languid pose. He is looking straight at her and yet her eyes are inclined to his genitals which he is displaying with pride. She had drawn it, and yet not seen it. She is taken aback, how can this be?

'Can't you see it?'

'Yes,' her voice is almost a whisper. 'I suppose I can.'

He looks over at her and smiles, shaking his head. 'You're a funny girl, never have been able to work you out.'

'And now?'

'Now even less. I wonder what your parents would say.'

'Why do you bring them up, for God's Sake?'

'You said they were artists, didn't you?'

'Yes, but they're smackheads. What would they care?'

'Have you never thought they might still be artists? Where do you think you inherited your talent from?'

'What?' She wishes she'd never told him about her parents.

'For drawing. A double measure if both parents are artists. I think you ought to seek them out.' He looks down at one of her drawings. 'They would be really proud of you.'

'What the fuck do you know about it?' She bites her lip to stop it wobbling.

He shakes his head and smiles at her. 'How judgemental are the young.'

She screws up her face, tries to stop herself from crying. 'Why do you have to be so bloody patronising?'

'Look at this work,' he says. 'Can't I be excited for you?'

She stands up, crossing her arms over her chest, steadies her voice. 'So what shall I do?' She indicates her work laid out on the bench, 'About submitting.'

'Leave these with me.' He looks down at her portfolio. 'Not only is your work exceptional, you've presented it beautifully too. You're a real professional. I'm going to recommend you to be put forward for the post-grad scholarship. I'm being picky about the different mediums, you'll walk a first with these, but I just want that extra mile from you, so I'll hold off for a week, see if you can do some oil.'

'And if I can't?'

He picks up the drawing of Edward on the couch. 'I just want to move you up a notch from outstanding to phenomenal. It goes without saying you'll be entered for this year's college competition, you'll blow them away.'

She shakes her head. 'I don't know what to say. I'm shocked.'

'You knew this was good, didn't you?'

She slides the work back into her portfolio, 'Not sure.' She thinks back to her sessions with Edward, how excited she'd felt, 'Yes, I suppose I did.'

'*Phenomenal!*' The word keeps bouncing around in her head as she waits at the bus stop. '*Phenomenal!*' She is so excited, she has to tell someone. Claudette? She will ring her when she gets in. It hits her then like a wall of sadness: The one person more than anyone else in the world that she wants to tell. Couldn't she have waited just a few more months? She kicks the bottom panel of the shelter. The metal dongs back at her.

The trees on the skyline are still thin black bones in the sky. Her granddad dead, Claudette dead, how can she leave her gran and go to London? If only Claudette were still alive she would have come up with a solution. She thinks back to the funeral, staring up at the crows circling the black trees. Glancing across the grave and being captivated by Edward and his mother. Claudette had given her Edward. Without her dying she would never have found Edward. She must find him again.

CHAPTER FIFTY-TWO

Rachel gets up that morning with the intention of giving the back room a good bottoming, and cleaning the French windows so the whole garden gleams back at her.

She doesn't bother getting washed or dressed, but instead slips her old housecoat over her nightdress. When she has finished cleaning, she intends to pack herself some lunch and catch the bus into town; maybe go to the gallery above the library. She hasn't been there in years. She could see if Edward is back at work. She stands back from the window, searching for any rogue traces of Windowlene she may have missed.

She hears a knock on the door, perhaps the milkman. She looks at the clock, 11.30. It can't be, maybe the postman. She scoops the slumbering cat off the chair and goes to open the front door. There is no one there. She looks up and down the street, no one. She hears the side gate banging against the catch. Holding the cat closer to her, she steps outside onto the wet concrete in her bedroom slippers. She waits. Someone is knocking on the side door.

'Hello?' she shouts.

The gate clicks shut and, from behind the overgrown Buddleia bush, Angela emerges. Rachel steps back onto her threshold, stroking the cat harshly between the ears. She says nothing.

Angela looks up at her from the garden path and smiles shyly, 'Sorry. I forgot you used your front door.'

Rachel nods.

'I'd have rung only I've lost your number.'

Rachel looks down at her cat, 'I see.'

The girl advances towards her, then hesitates. 'Do you mind if I come in?'

Rachel wants to refuse, but instead steps aside, her back pressing against her front door. Angela wipes her feet on the coconut mat. Rachel nods in the direction of the kitchen. She is stunned. Caught unwashed and undressed, she lets the girl enter her kitchen. She motions to a chair,

'Excuse me? I'll just get dressed.' She closes the kitchen door.

Angela sits at the kitchen table. She can hear Rachel moving about upstairs. She wishes she hadn't come. She has spooked the old bird by turning up unannounced and catching her all unawares in her scruffy old housecoat.

Delving into her rucksack she brings out the old-fashioned photo album that she had purloined from Claudette's. She places it on the table, smoothing her hand over its leather surface. She glances around the room. Under the window is an old pot Belfast sink. She stands up and walks over to the window. The sink has a tarnished brass plughole and a large rubber plug in swirls of green and white like the inside cover of an old book. She remembers the Belfast sink her gran had before her modernisation purge. It had the same plug but with pink swirls instead of green. Her gran would fill the sink to brimming and place her in it. The water would spill over the side and her gran would always tell her off for being careless.

To the right of the window is a rack with willow pattern plates, blue on white, the bridge where the lovers meet, the willow tree hanging low. The cups are on white hooks under the cupboard. The kitchen has the smell of an old person about it; old people, food, cabbage and the linger of pork dripping. A slight draught comes in through the cat flap at the bottom of the door. Angela can feel it around her ankles. It lifts, ever so slightly, a white envelope lying on the coconut mat. She crouches to pick it up, Edward's handwriting. She shakes her head, what a funny pair. She props the envelope against a small glass vase of snowdrops in the centre of the scrubbed pine table and then sits back down again.

She hears Rachel coming back down the stairs. She turns in her chair, waiting, a cautious smile on her face. 'I hope you didn't mind me coming.'

Silence.

Angela feels she should say something else but the words stick in her throat. She hesitates and then stands up. 'I'm sorry. I shouldn't have come.'

Rachel looks at her, mouth pulled tight. She has on a beige

dress and a necklace of tiger-eye beads. She's put on her armour, Angela thinks.

'Come unannounced, I mean. Sorry, I'll go.' She picks up her rucksack.

The cat jumps out of Rachel's arms. She smiles a cold hard smile, 'Why did you come?'

Angela blushes, stammers, 'I wondered if you'd seen anything of Edward, or you'd got his new address.' She flumps her shoulders, 'I can't find him anywhere.'

Rachel's voice is icy. 'I think that is my business, don't you?'

'Sorry, I don't understand.'

'My son's whereabouts are my business. If he wanted to see you he'd contact you.'

'Yes, but I need to see him. It's important.'

'What, so you can take further advantage of the poor man? Tell me, why on earth do you want to draw his poor deformed body,' she pauses for breath. 'What do you intend to do with the pictures when you have completed them? Parade them in front of the whole world?'

'But it's not like that.'

'Isn't it? It looks very much like it from where I'm standing.'

Angela looks down at the black and white tiles. She presses her teeth hard together. Don't cry, she says to herself, for God's sake, don't cry. 'I thought you of all people, Mrs Anderson, would've understood.'

'Oh, I understand. I understand very well.'

'I see his body as something different, a thing of beauty.'

'Yes, that's it, isn't it? A thing!'

'I didn't mean it like that. I didn't force him to do it,' she ends on a plaintive note.

'No, you didn't have to. Any man like Edward would be flattered to receive the attentions of a young girl like you.'

'But we are good friends.' She looks up, still gritting her teeth, willing herself not to cry. 'I really like him.'

Rachel snorts, 'Oh, I bet you do. I'm sure he suits your purpose admirably.'

Angela says nothing but takes the two short steps to the back door, putting her hand up to the Yale lock. She tugs at the latch. It does not open. She struggles in silence, eventually yanking it free.

By the time she reaches the garden gate the tears are already dropping from her jaw. 'What a bitch! What a bitch! What a bitch!' She repeats to herself over and over again.

There is a woman with a perm and a prim face coming towards her along the street. Angela crosses the road and sees a footpath that leads down to a small river. The bank, spread with weeping willows, slopes steeply to the water's edge. Over the other side of the river she can see the main road and the tops of buses and lorries. She sits down on her rucksack and cries in huge, self-indulgent sobs.

Why had Rachel been so horrid to her? Edward was right about her; she was a bitch. But why had he told her about the sittings? When he'd asked her not to mention it. She shouldn't have gone to see the old cow in the first place. Why had she wanted to be friends with an old witch like that anyway? She starts to cry again.

She remembers in her rucksack the present she had bought for Rachel, two handmade chocolates in the shape of cats, one each for them to have with their cup of tea. The cellophane bags are tied with little yellow ribbons, the ends stretched so that the ribbons curl back on themselves. She tears the bag open and eats both the cats, heads first, then smiles to herself thinking, had she really been so insensitive?

Was that how other people would see it? That she was using Edward? Alex hadn't seen it like that. In the first instance, her reason for drawing him had been his deformity, she had to admit that, but after a while it all sort of linked, became part of him. She'd never thought to study the deeper reasons for the deformity. She recalls his analogy of a basket and smiles. It would be interesting to see the inner workings. She could even do some sketches.

In the university library she searches for a book on spinal deformities. She finds pictures of spines writhing like the skeletons of snakes. X-rays of backs pinned and rodded and straightened and yet, still left scarred and imperfect. She makes lots of quick sketches. For the first time, she feels the enormity of what Edward has to put up with. She had never imagined for one minute the twisting and turning that had gone on in Edward's body to create the shape he is. Had it ever really impacted on her that he might be in real pain and not just grumbling in his usual way? Had she ever really taken his disability into account, tried to make things more comfortable for him? He was always going on about how awful she was. Well, he was right. All she had cared about was drawing him, as if he were little more than an odd-shaped vase.

She looks down at the sketches she has made. These could work in really well with the charcoal drawings. It is dark outside. She hopes she has not missed the last bus.

Angela clutches her pink hot water bottle and snuggles further down the bed. She listens to the rain lashing against the window. What would Paul be doing now? Would he be out at sea, in the dark? She wonders if he has even given her a second thought, whether he had those sort of encounters all the time. That night it had felt as if something inside her had been unleashed, but it wasn't just that night was it? It had it happened once before, in the studio. Maybe she should have stayed in Cornwall an extra couple of days, seen Paul again, banished these stupid thoughts she's had of Edward. She is mixing her art up with her emotions.

CHAPTER FIFTY-THREE

That morning on his way to work, Edward is gripped by a sense of trepidation. It increases as he walks along Surrey Street. When he reaches the library steps he pauses. Already, there is a beggar in place between the pillars.

'Spare any change, mister?'

It is a young girl with a black and white collie. *Just acknowledge us,* he'd read in the Big Issue. *We don't mind if you don't give us any money, just don't pretend we're not there.* Edward has never given money to a beggar before,

'Good morning, young lady.'

She looks up at him. Her face is very pale, her eyes are grey; her voice, flat and low. 'Can you spare any change?'

Edward wants to know what she will do with the money if he gives it to her. 'It's a bit cold to be sitting out here, isn't it?'

'Can you spare any change?' Like a stuck record, he thinks. He feels in his pocket for a few coppers but it's empty. He takes his wallet out of his breast pocket and looks in the note section. There are two ten-pound notes and a blue five-pound note. He gives her the five-pound note. She looks up into his face. Her eyes are grey, clear, like Angela's.

'Thanks, mister.' Her voice is still flat. He looks for more response, but she is busily stroking her dog.

Edward's new-found sense of generosity sits like warm bread on his chest. He doesn't go straight down to the archives but takes the lift to personnel. Stick in hand, he waits to be seen.

'Yes, Mr Anderson, what can we do for you?'

'I was wondering,' he coughs, 'it being my first day back from sick leave, whether I could apply to work in a different department.'

'Why, may I ask?' The man peers at him over his glasses. 'You are very much valued in the archive department you know?'

'It's just that, well, it gets a bit claustrophobic working down there in the archives.'

'Usually we would be able to offer you a job in another department, even if only temporarily, but one of the women in your section,' he looks down at the papers on his desk, 'Janice Brown, has just gone on maternity leave. So I'm sorry, but you'll have to fit back into your old slot.'

Edward wants to say, 'Please put me somewhere else. I don't want to be down in the archives. I don't want to be looking up to the light.' But he says nothing.

It's as if he's never been away. He is appalled. His pencils, his files, everything is still on his desk just as he left it. Everyone is still the same. He wants to stand on his desk and shout at everybody: *you may all be the same, but I'm not! Can't you see I'm different now*? Lucky Janice. She'd got away, and yet she was the only one who'd ever really bothered with him.

The rain falls all morning, straight and loud. It falls from everywhere into the small enclosed courtyard, overflowing from the gutters and spurting from holes in the rusty downpipe. Edward watches it from the basement window, searching for the sky through the bars, but there is only a grey blur. He looks down and sees the raindrops dancing on the wet concrete.

The bell on the book-lift dings a request. He walks away from the window, still listening for the sound of the rain.

At twelve o'clock, the rubber ferrule of his stick is pressing into the top step outside the library entrance. The beggar girl is still there.

'What's your name?'

She cocks her head like a bird, 'Why?'

'No reason.' He shakes his head and hobbles off down Surrey Street, stopping on the corner to take a deep breath. The wind is cool on his face. He must find a refuge. In the churchyard he sits on a bench dedicated to Lily Appleyard 1924-1984, the dates are somehow satisfying.

The blue hands on the face of the church clock move gradually around to one o'clock. It is cold. He could go home now and no-one would notice. *You have to go back. Come on, Edward, this is not like you*. He makes a pact with himself. If the girl is still there between the pillars then he will go back in. If she isn't, well, he isn't quite sure.

Her dog looks up and whimpers at him. He wonders how Tabitha is getting on, all on her own. Would she be asleep in his chair? He wants to say to the girl: I gave you five pounds this morning, why couldn't you have gone home? But would she reply, *'I haven't got a home to go to'*?

And he knows he doesn't want to hear that.

CHAPTER FIFTY-FOUR

Rachel comes back from town and lets herself into the house just as the clock in the hall chimes four. She sighs as she thinks of the events of that morning, and the short shrift she'd given that poor girl. If only she hadn't turned up like that, so unexpectedly, smiling her intrusion into the house and demonstrating to Rachel the triviality and yes, even the loneliness of her own existence.

The cat puts its head in through the flap and quickly surveys Rachel and the kitchen before squeezing the rest of its body through. Rachel laughs at it and feels comforted. 'You fat thing.'

She decides on a ham sandwich for her tea. She places a willow pattern plate on the table and sees the letter propped against the vase of snowdrops. At first she thinks it must be from Angela, and then she recognises Edward's handwriting. The girl must have picked it up from the mat.

> *80 Hancock Place*
> *Sheffield*
> *Dear Mother,*
> *I'm glad, after your initial reserve, that you liked your bird egg book. I would love to see a picture of a bullfinch egg. Will you bring it with you next time we meet?*
> *I have bought another book for you, although I shouldn't really tell you, should I? I got off the bus, glanced into the charity shop window and there it was, staring back at me, and I thought, I have got to get that for Mother. I'm sure this time you will like it.*
> *Tell me, I want to know what colour kingfishers' eggs are? What do they make their nests from? This is a fascinating subject I have discovered isn't it? If you were a bird, what sort of bird would you like to be? I think I would like to be a cuckoo. King of the heap, and telling of spring.*
> *Love,*
> *Edward*

But that was ages ago. Confused, she studies the date. It was a couple of weeks after they had met for lunch at the Blue Moon cafe. How can this be? Has it been lost in the post all this time, to end up like a ghost dropping through her letterbox?

She sits down heavily on one of the kitchen chairs and puts her head in her hands. Why has he disappeared without telling anyone where he was going? She is struck by how much she cares. After all these years, he has managed to penetrate her inner skin. She must be getting old and silly. No, she only wants to know he is safe and happy, nothing else. If he wants to be left in peace that is alright. She knows how it is to yearn for peace. She reaches over to place the letter safely into the second drawer, where she keeps her papers. On the worktop she notices a dark maroon cover like the menus from Henrys, but of fine leather and much, much thicker. She picks it up. It is a photo album. To see the photos on each page she must first peel back the tissue paper. All the photos are in black and white.

There is a strangeness about them that at first she cannot comprehend until she sees a shop in the background. The board above the shop is in French. Claudette. This must be Claudette's photo album. The girl must have brought it to show her as she promised she would. She feels mortified. The girl hadn't just come for her ballet ticket, or to find out where Edward was, she had brought her this as well. But that still didn't excuse the way she'd treated Edward. She still deserved a flea in her ear.

There is a photo of Claudette looking younger and yes, there is her own grandmother. She has the same picture in her father's old photo album.   She scans Claudette's face and that of her grandmother, looking for a likeness, maybe in the shape of the mouth. She must write to the girl and apologise.

6 Acorn Cres.
Sheffield
Dear Angela,
I have been looking at the photo album. Thank you for bringing it. I'm sorry if I snapped at you and I hope you will find it in your heart to forgive me. I am still not sure how I feel about Edward modelling for you, but I suppose I should accept that he is a grown man and the decision rests

with him. To be honest, I am very worried about him. I do not know where he is either. I arranged to meet him for lunch a few weeks ago and he didn't turn up so I went to his place of work. They said he was off sick, so I went to his lodging and his landlady said he had moved out and I have heard nothing since. If you do hear from him, could you please let me know?

I will fully understand if you don't want to, but I would very much like you to come to tea next Thursday at 3.30 so that I can give you back the photo album and discuss it with you.

In case you decide you can't face me again I am enclosing the Ballet ticket I got for you.

Regards,

Rachel

If she didn't come to the house but went to the ballet would she realise that she would be sitting next to Rachel? The best seats in the house, and all for free.

She had once received a single ticket through the post to see *Giselle* performed by a Russian dance company. In the envelope had been a slip of white paper; *From an admirer*. Nothing else. She used the ticket and found herself sitting in the front row. So close that she could hear the padding of the dancers' shoes above the music. The whole ballet was performed behind a muslin curtain. She'd loved it. The music, the dance, everything about it gave her a feeling of great longing.

She stood outside the theatre afterwards, blinking in the sunshine. She wished it was dark so that she could have let the feeling linger, perhaps kept it with her all the way home on the bus. She felt someone lightly touch her on the elbow. She turned and looked up into the face of a young man. He smiled. She knew that smile. It was the shy boy, the artist who used to visit her house. He worked at the theatre now, creating stage sets. He had seen her in town one day and knew he wanted to thank her for what she had given him. The ballet always reminded him of her, he'd said. It had the same ethereal quality.

Rachel runs her hand across the leather cover of the photo album. She opens it up from the back. On the last page is a photo of Claudette's mother with a boy of about thirteen. He is distinctly odd around the face. *'Not quite the full shilling,'* as her father would have said. Is this who Claudette called the deformed boy? She takes a closer look. Her blood runs cold. His back, like Edward's, is hunched to one side.

CHAPTER FIFTY-FIVE

The branches of the beech tree are tapping against the window to the side of the balcony. He has watched the tips gradually change from a dark russet to a pale brown. On his balcony the tubs are spiked with a glimpse of crocuses and their promised colours of yellow or purple. A secret they've shared with the dark earth all winter.

Edward sits back down in his chair. He must go to see Angela. He must take back power over his life. However awful the truth is, it can't be any worse than this limbo in which he exists. He imagines her face, the softness of her contours, and then, when she sees him, the distortion of that loveliness as she recoils in horror at the old man she has made love to. Who would have thought that single act could shatter the crisp white shell he had placed around his life for so long. In fact, cracked it so wide open that the pain of it, the intensity, cuts through him like a knife. He would like the dullness of his old life back. At least that was safe. He didn't have to endure this pain. He presses his hands to his ears and listens to the turmoil in his head. Behind his eyes he can see a blue light through which drift sea-horses, with their strange questioning faces. He is he losing his grasp on reality. Tabitha brushes up against his bare legs and meows. He puts his hand down and strokes along her back, pulling her tail.

'You're right, girl. It's about time I got a grip on myself.' He will get a newspaper and a writing pad, and then he'll write to her. He feeds the cat, readies himself to go out.

The sun is shining through his bedroom door. Soon it will be up over the roof and this afternoon it will strike the balcony. He picks up his stick and, forgetting his coat, goes out. He walks down the high street. It is alive with shoppers all enjoying that same Saturday morning feeling. He stops outside the greengrocers and admires the tilted display of apples and oranges. There is a fresh wind that brings a chill to the air and Edward wishes he had brought his jacket. He notices people sitting in the window of the German Coffee House reading the Saturday papers. He enters and looks around. The table in the bay window has just been vacated. Someone else's crumbs are still there, scattered around a half-empty cup of weak tea. A single daffodil with a sprig of catkin in a little glass bottle sits in the centre of the table. The waitress comes to clear up and take his order.

'I'm sorry to be a nuisance,' says Edward. 'Perhaps I should have sat at one of the prepared tables.'

'This table is always popular in the morning when the sun's on it. What can I get you?'

Edward studies the menu board. 'May I have a cafetiere of – I think I'll try the Moroccan. And can I have hot milk with it, please?'

He leans over and picks up a copy of *The Guardian* from the table next to him, scanning the front page for an interesting article. He doesn't open the paper. It is too difficult for him unless he has an empty table to lay it out on.

His cup, made at the local pottery, sits perfectly in his hands leaving the little saucer redundant on the table. He feels a little better now. The sun is on his back warming him through, and he has found a good cup of coffee. What else could a man want?

The door opens, letting in a cold draft. He looks up to see Angela standing there.

Oh, my God. He picks up *The Guardian*, takes a sly sideways look. Yes, it is definitely Angela, heavily muffled against the wind, but it is her. He would recognise that stance anywhere. Her hair has grown since he last saw her, it is wisping out from the bottom of her scarf and he is comforted to see that it is still her natural colour. He tries to focus on the photograph on the front page of the newspaper. It is of a woman, her face contorted in pain. He listens for the door opening, for Angela making her escape. He has made it easy for her.

'Edward? How are you?' She smiles down at him, a shy smile.

He stares back at her. The paper falling from his grasp. 'I'm fine, thank you.'

She glances around the coffee shop as if looking for an empty table.

'Will you join me?'

'Thanks. I'd like that.' She hesitates, 'If you're sure.'

He looks up at her and nods. She slides into the window seat next to him and then proceeds to ease herself out of her coat. He watches in silence not knowing what to say, but realising how much he has missed her.

She tilts her head to one side and studies him. 'You look different, somehow,' she says. 'I like the chinstrap beard.'

They smile at each other. How well she looks. Her skin is so lucent he wants to reach out his hand and softly stroke her cheek. The waitress comes over.

'Can I have a pot of tea for...?' Angela looks over at him and sees his cafetière.

'Just for one,' he interjects, 'and please, could I have another cafetiere? This coffee is very good.'

They both watch the waitress as she walks away.

She stammers. 'I'm sorry. I've spoilt your peace, haven't I?'

He is reassured to see that she looks nervous.

The waitress returns with their drinks, placing the tray on the table.

'It's strange meeting you here,' he pauses. 'I was just thinking this morning that I should contact you.'

'Alex said he'd seen you in here, so I thought I might find you.'

She doesn't look up but concentrates on stirring her tea. He doesn't answer. He can feel tears trickling down his cheek. She has sought him out. She looks up and stretches across the table, pushing her blue napkin in front of her.

'Thank you.' He tries to smile.

They sit in silence. Edward closes his eyes. That thrashing monster is there again, crushing his chest. He hears Angela pouring her second cup, a steady stream into her china cup.

'Shall I pour your coffee?'

He shakes his head. 'No, no thank you. I'll let it stand a little longer.'

'Let it stew, eh?'

He gives her a weak smile. 'You must find me a very strange creature.'

'I've missed you, actually. Don't look so disbelieving. You're not the only lonely person, you know.'

'I never said I was lonely.'

'I'm sorry, I just assumed. You do have a certain air about you.'

'Still?'

She puts her head on one side and surveys him, 'Not sure.'

'Are you lonely?' He asks, curious.

'Yes. I suppose I am.' She hesitates, 'I dunno, it feels like I've got this big black hole inside me. The only time it goes away is when I'm drawing. How did you shake off yours?'

'I'll tell you one day'

'Still dodging the issue, I see.'

He smiles and reaches for the cafetière.

'Edward?' He looks up. 'Can I do that?' She indicates the cafetiere.

'What?'

'Press the plunger. I love doing it.'

He smiles and then watches the child-like expression on her face as she presses it down.

He tries to think of something to say but his mind is blank.

She breaks the silence by indicating up the hill with her head. 'The Art College is just up there, you know?'

'So it is. I'd forgotten about that.'

'Are you living around here? Your mother said you'd moved out of your lodgings. She seemed a bit perturbed.'

'Yes, I've got a flat. I love it.'

'Aren't you going to invite her round?'

'I don't want her to spoil it. I don't want her to have any part in it.'

'Don't you think she might be lonely?'

'To be quite honest, I don't care. I used to, but not anymore.'

'What has she done to you to make you feel like this? She's quite concerned about you, you know?'

'Can we drop the subject?'

He watches as she concentrates on stirring her tea, her black lashes stark against her pale skin.

'How have you been, Edward?' She looks up, searching his face.

That one question unnerves him. He sees with surprise the care written in her eyes. He scrapes back his chair. 'I ought to go.' He beckons the waitress, 'Can I have the bill, please?' His voice wavers.

'For everything?' she asks.

'Yes.'

'Thank you,' Angela tilts her head in that way that he remembers so well.

'My treat,' He picks up his stick and notices his hand is shaking uncontrollably. The doorbell tinkles as he pulls it open. He is met by a blast of cold air.

'Edward?'

He turns. Angela is picking up her coat and scarf, making her way towards him. 'Can I come back and see your flat?'

She slows to his pace as they walk up the hill. 'You're not far from the college are you?' She feels impelled to keep up a constant flow of conversation. Strange, seeing him again it feels as if nothing happened, that it was all a dream. Everything will be all right once she has broached the subject of him sitting for her again. He'll be relieved when he sees that she just wants everything to be as it was.

His flat is lovely, the views across the valley breathtaking. They stand on the balcony, leaning against the rail, trying to pick out different landmarks across the city. He falls silent. She doesn't notice. She is watching a single magpie in the tree below, trying to find a second.

'I love you,' he says.

She wonders if she has imagined it. It was no more than a whisper. Then he turns to her and says it louder, his voice choking in his throat, 'I love you.'

His knuckles are white with tension, grasping the rail. 'I can't bear it any more.' She looks up; his chin is beginning to wobble.

'I can't live without you.'

'I have to go.' She picks up her coat and scarf and runs. Away from his voice, pleading like a cracked bell.

As she makes her way back down the hill she is sobbing with anger. How dare he? How can he say something like that to her? As if there was a possibility that there could ever be anything between them. She had felt so hopeful when she'd seen him in the café, hopeful that everything could go back to normal and they could pretend nothing had happened. She could have told him her news, how thrilled Alex had been about her work. They could have continued with the sittings. He had to go and spoil it all.

'I love you,' she mimics.

Well, it wasn't her problem. She will write to his mother, give her his address. She can sort him out.

CHAPTER FIFTY-SIX

Tabitha is waiting on the metal walkway. She meows up at him, complaining.

'I'm sorry, puss. Come on, let's go in and get you a nice saucer of milk.'

Edward had peeled the potatoes for his evening meal earlier that day, placing them in a half-pint Pyrex bowl of water to keep them from turning brown. He opens the soy sauce and shakes the contents of the bottle liberally over the thinly cut strips of pale pink pork. He stretches cling film over the dish and places it in the fridge, pours himself a half measure of red wine into his special goblet of old-fashioned glass and goes to sit in his rocker by the window.

The whole of the valley and the distant hills are captured in the mauve of twilight. He takes a sip of his wine, 'Mmm... perfect.'

The cat stretches, arching its back; its mouth wide to show the thin white stripes of teeth against a pink tongue. It pauses a moment, then pounces onto his knee. He gently scratches her under the chin and she purrs her contentment loudly, nestling up against his jumper and burrowing her face into his neck. He strokes her back and, closing his eyes, he listens to her soft purr, the hum of the traffic on the front and the lone magpie screeching in the beech tree. He hates that magpie.

He thinks of Angela standing beside him, out there on the balcony. He had frightened her, and she had run away like a startled fawn, out of his flat and down the road, dropping her scarf in her haste. He picks it up now and sniffs her scent. She had run from his words. And yet, in his head, it feels better now that he has told her.

There is a loud rat-tat on the door. The cat jerks back and claws his jumper. Putting her gently on the chair he goes to answer the door. Could it be Angela returning for her scarf? He swallows hard.

Standing there, silhouetted in the twilight, is his mother.

'Mother, how are you?' It doesn't sound like his voice.

She is standing there on his threshold looking very frail, and for the first time he sees a vulnerability that perhaps he does not want to see.

'I am fine, Edward, fine. But I was not so sure about you, so I came to find you.'

Edward clears the back of his throat. 'And here you are.' He steps outside and grasps the handle, pulling the door closed behind him.

'It must be three months, Edward.'

'Yes, Mother. I know.'

'It seemed strange not getting your letters. I missed them, and our lunches,' she says, a plaintive note in her voice.

'I'll just get my coat and we'll pop down to the local café, shall we? Wait there.' He closes the blue door in her face.

He picks up his coat and stick from the bedroom and pauses, looking at his reflection in the mirror. He is shaking, his teeth chattering. He does not want to see her. He will tell her to go away.

When he opens the door he sees that Tabitha is arching her body around Rachel's stockinged legs. Traitor, he thinks.

'Edward, is this cat yours? She's lovely.'

He looks down at his cat, irritated by its betrayal. 'No, Mother, it's not mine, it's my neighbours.'

'Shame. It's a lovely cat.'

He prods the treacherous animal with the end of his stick and says nothing.

'How long have you lived here, Edward?'

'A couple of months. Why?'

'Nothing. I was just wondering. I called round at your lodgings you know, met Mrs. Ingram for the first time.'

He taps his stick on the walkway and hears the dull echo of the metal. He takes a deep breath. He must tell her to go away, that he never wants to see her again.

'Edward, would you mind very much, but I don't think I can walk any further. Can I come in?'

'No.'

He hears her gasp.

'But, why not?' she says, weakly.

'I don't want you to. I never want to see you again.'

'Edward, why?'

'Why what?'

'Why are you treating me like this?'

He doesn't reply.

'Why, Edward?' she pleads.

'I know,' he blurts out.

'Know what? I don't understand.'

'About you and Uncle Jack.' There. Finally he has said it after all these years. He looks straight at her. She stares back. He sees a flicker of fear pass across her face.

'Uncle Jack?' Her voice is almost a whisper.

'Don't try to deny it. I saw you. I must have been ten years old. You were in the barn, like a couple of dogs on heat. It was so ugly.' He shudders. 'It has destroyed my whole life.'

He sees her grab hold of the rail to steady herself.

'How could you,' he continues. 'With your own uncle, and look at me, the product of your badness.'

In the light shining from above the door he sees the blood drain from her face.

'How do you think it has felt, knowing all these years?' He goes on, 'To live with that secret. To know that the man that I called father was in fact not my father.'

He sees tears on her face reflecting in the overhead light. It is the first time he has ever seen his mother cry.

She looks up, shocked. 'You thought that Jack was your father?'

'I have my back as proof, don't I?'

'I think I'm going to faint,' she says. Just in time he catches her arm and steadies her. She weighs so little.

She sits at his kitchen table sipping a glass of water, 'Edward? Why now? After all these years?'

He sits down opposite her. She looks terrible, a deathly white.

'I, I don't know.' He holds his head in his hands. 'It's like I built a dam that day. A dam to block out all my emotions and...' he pauses, 'this last year the walls have started to crumble. I think it was Angela that started it off. Damn her,' he murmurs.

She speaks quietly without raising her head. 'I'm sorry to disappoint you Edward, but George was in fact your father.' She snaps open the clip on her handbag and brings forth a black and white photo in a clear plastic cover. She holds it under the light. It is of Edward and George. Edward is about fifteen. They are sitting at a table outside a pub in York. She pushes the photo into his hands and for the first time he sees the truth. In the photo the light is behind them, the shapes of their heads, which are slightly silhouetted, are identical.

She stretches her hand across the table, tries to take his hand. He shrinks away.

'I don't blame you for hating me.' He feels Tabitha brush against his legs. She continues, 'I'm not going to try and explain or justify anything to you. There would be no point. What happened between Jack and myself... started when I was nineteen and went on until he died. All I can say is that I still cherish those moments we had. It has sustained me throughout my life. I only hope that one day you can experience a similar passion.' She looks at him, searching his face for understanding.

He shakes his head, unbelieving. 'Were you in love with him?'

'Yes, but not in the way that I wanted to spend the rest of my life with him. There was just this passion between us, made even more intense by the fact that we knew that what we were doing was wrong. I'm so sorry that you had to see us.'

'And what of father?' He rolls the word around in his mouth. For the first time in many years it doesn't feel like a lie.

'We didn't have that kind of a relationship.'

'Never?'

'No. I never should have married him.'

'Why did you, then?'

'He seemed,' she hesitates. 'It was just one of those things. I knew on our honeymoon that I had made a mistake. That was when you were conceived. One of the few times we ever had... relations.'

CHAPTER FIFTY-SEVEN

When she opens the door, she doesn't know what to say to the girl. She ushers her through into the back room. They both stand there a moment, saying nothing. Angela glances around the room as if she is expecting to be asked to sit down, or even if she would like a drink, but Rachel does neither. Instead she sits in her own chair and pretends to be absorbed in stroking her cat.

'You mind me coming?' Rachel hears the girl ask, thinking she can detect a slight tremor in her voice. This child is scared. I really hurt her. Rachel looks up and studies her face.

'I'm sorry,' the girl stutters. 'I thought from your letter you wanted to see me.'

Rachel sighs, 'I need to talk to you. Sit down. I'll put on the kettle.' She gets up from her chair, letting the cat fall easily to the floor. 'You're very contrite today, young lady.'

Angela laughs nervously, 'Sorry. I just, well, sort of feel a bit awkward, after last time.'

Rachel sits back into her chair and examines her hands, 'I'm sorry I was so very hard on you. Not that you didn't deserve it.' She looks up. Angela is staring out of the window. She nods, but does not look at her. The cat, seizing an opportunity, tries to jump back onto Rachel's lap. She stops it with her hand. It meows loudly. 'I don't know what's wrong with this cat lately, meow, meow, meow. It never shuts up.'

When Rachel comes back into the room with the tea, Angela is standing by the window, staring out into the garden. Rachel places the wooden tray on the table and observes, as she has many times before, that the grains and colours of the wood are remarkably similar.

She goes to stand next to the girl and points to a rustic bird table. 'I bought that yesterday from the pet store on the front. The man in the shop said I would have to wait up to a year for the birds to get used to it. But do you know what? I dangled some bacon rinds from it, the cat was most annoyed at me for giving away his precious bacon rinds, and this morning when I drew back the curtain there was a blue tit clinging to it. I felt so privileged. It sounds silly doesn't it, especially when I can remember when birds were so abundant that they used to drop out of the sky dead on the pavement in front of you. And now we even get excited if we see a sparrow. I noticed in the local paper that they are planning on having a dawn chorus meeting in the cemetery once the birds start nesting. I'm tempted to go along.'

'I thought,' Angela stares down the garden, 'that after my first visit we had become friends. I know I shouldn't have called round without warning, but even so, you were very hard on me.' Her voice wobbles, 'You really upset me.'

'You want to be friends with an old woman? Why?'

Angela shrugs. 'I just like talking to you. It's like still having a link to Claudette.'

'I'm not sure I'm worthy of the comparison, my dear.' She pushes the cat away with her foot. 'Especially after the way I reacted to Edward modelling for you. I'm sure Claudette wouldn't have reacted like that. But thank you for the comparison, and thank you also for sending me Edward's address.'

Angela turns from the window, 'Have you been to see him?'

'Last night. He was very funny with me. I don't know what's up with him these days. Do you?'

Angela shakes her head. 'Shall I pass you your coffee?'

Rachel takes the cup and saucer. Her hands shake, making the teaspoon chink against the cup. 'I don't know what's wrong with me, either. Look at my hands. I can't stop them shaking.'

The cat meows, wanting to get onto her lap. 'Shut up, cat. Shut up.'

Angela sits down in the chair opposite, 'Thank you for the ballet ticket.'

'One week to go, I'm really looking forward to it. We have the best seats in the house. You don't mind going with me, do you?' Rachel adds as an afterthought.

Angela shakes her head and smiles.

'That was the other thing,' Rachel continues, 'I knew there

was more than one reason why I was cross with you, young lady.'
Rachel points a finger at her. 'You told Edward about me modelling
at the college.'

Angela blushes a deep red. 'Yes, I know. I'm really sorry. It
was wrong of me.' She glances up at the portrait. 'It was looking at
him made me remember where I'd seen you before.'

'Did you know the first time you came here?' Rachel asks.

Angela nods, her blush deepening.

'You little minx,' Rachel tuts.

They both sit silently sipping at their coffee.

'You know,' Rachel puts down her cup. 'I really miss it. I
think that's one of the reasons I was annoyed at Edward modelling
for you. I was jealous.'

'Why did you stop?'

'I'm not sure really. I think I began to lose confidence in my
body.'

'I'm sure they'd love to have you back. There's always a
shortage of older models.'

Rachel shakes her head. 'I couldn't, not now. Suddenly I feel
very old.' She looks down at her hands, noting the liver spots. 'That
reminds me, go and get the photo album off the kitchen table will
you?'

They leaf through the photo album one page at a time.
Pointing to the last page, Rachel asks, 'Did you notice anything
about the boy?'

Angela takes a closer look, 'He looks a bit, well, retarded.'

'Look at his back.'

'Oh yes. How peculiar. It's just like Edward's. How odd.'

'Maybe not so odd. You see, if this boy is who I think he is,
he would have been my father's half-brother. Maybe it is just as
well that Edward never had any children.'

Angela gets up off her haunches and stands beside Rachel's
chair,

'He could still have children.'

'Who? Edward?' Rachel shakes her head. 'I doubt it very
much.'

'Have you told him about it?'

'No, not yet. Like I said, he's a bit tetchy with me at the
moment.'

'But you don't know for sure who this boy is, do you?'

Angela asks.

'If only Claudette were alive.'

'How many times did you meet Claudette?'

'Only the once. Strange that. It's as if we had nothing else to say to each other after the first meeting.'

'Did she never meet Edward?'

'No. All the time I was married, and even after George died, I kept parts of my life sectioned off. Edward's father and I, well, we had a very dull marriage, and the only way I managed to survive was by leading a double life. But I think, looking back on it, it was a bit unfair on Edward. I wish now I had done things differently, included him more.'

'May I?' Angela takes the album from Rachel and sits down on the chair opposite. She gently prises the photo from its corners and turns it over. 'Edward Pascal and Madame Pascal.' she reads.

'Then I was right.' Rachel leans forward and takes the photo from her. 'I've gone all shivery. Even the same name. Come to think, it was my father who suggested I call him Edward. How very, very strange. I wonder if he's still alive?'

Rachel is glad that she didn't turn the girl away a second time. Although this time she might have been gentler. She might have told her she felt unwell, which was partly true. She had lain awake all night thinking of Edward, remembering his face contorted with hatred for her. She shivers. All those years he had kept that terrible secret. He had intended to cut her out of his life completely. She suddenly feels very cold. She thinks back to when he was eleven or twelve but she can't remember any real change in his behaviour. Any minor ones she must have put down to his adolescence. Theirs had never been a terribly close relationship. She'd never, even when he was a tiny baby, felt much of a bond towards him. It was nobody's fault, just one of those things.

She washes the willow pattern cups in the white froth of too much washing up liquid, raises up her yellow rubber hand and gently blows. A single bubble lifts, holds and then pings against the window. She thinks back to why she used the willow pattern set. She knew that the girl would take pleasure from them, that's why. She'd remembered the first time she'd come, and how they'd talked of the way she used to make up stories about the figures on the bridge. A mere skit of a girl and yet – Rachel blows another bubble – and yet something about this girl intrigues her. Rachel is glad that she had given her a big chunk of the ginger cake to take with her. She had told her it wouldn't keep, which was a lie, because ginger cake got better with keeping.

She hooks each cup back into place on the white hooks under the cupboard. She will write to Edward, and ask him if he would like them for his flat. She doesn't want them any more. They will go nicely in his kitchen.

Angela shivers, hoping that a bus will soon come round the corner. The ginger cake is still slightly warm. She puts the package inside her coat to warm her.

'I love you,' he'd said. How could he do that to her? Standing out there on his balcony, just as she'd thought things were returning to normal. She thinks back to that moment in the studio and finds it is held there in her memory like a bubble, glistening in blues and greens; a perfect moment. But it couldn't be. It had spoiled everything, like a single cup smashing to the floor. Like the willow pattern cup of her gran's; the way it had fallen from her hands. She hadn't told Rachel the full story about her gran's willow pattern cups that had sat unused, in pride of place in her glass cabinet. One day, after Angela had nagged her incessantly for months, her grandmother had relented and let Angela get them out: 'but only the once, mind.' But when Angela was carrying them back to the cabinet, each cup and saucer carefully washed, one cup had slipped from her grasp. She had watched in horror as it fell and shattered onto the red quarry tiles of the kitchen. Jagged pieces lay on the floor, sharp as her gran's tongue. Her voice, Angela shudders at the memory, ran through her like ice. She shoved her out of the way, ignoring her wobbly lip and, crouching down, lovingly brushed up each fragment before carrying the dustpan out to the garden. Angela watched from the kitchen window, as she carefully trowelled the fragments in around the roots of her beloved roses.

When she came home from school the next day the whole set had gone, and in their place was a polka dot set. Each cup and saucer a different colour: pink, blue, maroon, bottle green, yellow and lilac.

She huddles against the cold and wishes she were at home in

bed in her dingy room that never gets the sun. Some days she sees the sun bouncing off the brick wall at the end of the yard. She wants to reach out and touch it, and drag it back into her room. It seems so unfair that there are some places that never see the sunlight.

CHAPTER FIFTY-EIGHT

> *4b, Crow Edge Flats,*
> *Sheffield*
> *Dear Mother,*
>   *I don't know what to say to you anymore. I'm sorry I treated you so badly when you came round to visit, but thank you for being honest with me about you and Uncle Jack. For years that image has echoed in my head. Sometimes I wondered if I had imagined it.*
>   *I went to visit father's grave yesterday. I know this may sound silly but he has a marvellous view. From up there you can see for miles, right over the moors and onto the other side of the valley where the landscape is woven with the ancient pattern of small fields.*
>   *Do you ever visit the grave? Why did we decide only to put his name and date of birth on the head stone and not mention me and you? Are we to be added later? I hope so. I would like to lie there and listen to the crows in the trees.*
>   *Love,*
>   *Your confused son,*
>   *Edward*
>   *PS. Yes I would like the willow pattern crockery please.*

He puts the letter in the envelope and licks the edge before sealing it.

She had given him the photo. How strange her having a photo of them in her bag. He would never have imagined it. He picks it up from the table and walks over to the window where the light is better. He smoothes his hand over his father's face remembering that day, way back then, when his mother had taken the picture. Even then he was carrying the burden of his mother's secret. He looks closely; yes, his back had already begun to contort. It was as if the secret he couldn't divulge to anyone had grown and solidified itself on his back.

Later, when he started university, he remembered, with shame, how his father had begun to irritate him. He'd thought that this man who is so proud of me is not even my father. This man who is satisfied with so little, is never hungry for knowledge; so unlike myself. It had never entered his head that his quickness of mind, even his curiosity, could have been inherited from his mother. He thinks of Uncle Jack and remembers him as a man with a dark presence, a man who walked through life with few words and who spent long days out in the fields, and long nights out shooting rabbits. And his aunt, like a starling, sniping at them all constantly, and the photo on top of the redundant piano of a boy with dark hair like his father's. And why, Edward laughs to himself, had he never thought of the colour of his hair? It was not dark like Uncle Jack's; it had tints of ginger like his father's. How could he have been so stupid, so blind? All these years he had nurtured this thing, growing it inside him, feeding it fresh coals, and now suddenly it was gone.

He shudders with pleasure, suddenly remembering Angela and the touch of her skin. He shuts his eyes. If only he could transport himself back to that moment and live it forever. Is that what his mother had felt? That exquisite feeling of being wrapped in warmth, in ecstasy, and knowing that every year she could go back and tap that feeling, like harvesting sap from a tree.

A sudden thought occurs to him; the shock of his revelation could have killed her. He had been so bound up in his own sense of outrage, he had not given her welfare a second thought. He'd felt all that pent up fury flow from him and now the only feeling he has for her is pity. Why, he is not quite sure. For God's sake, she ruined his life, and she hadn't even been sorry for what she'd done. She was sorry he'd seen them, but not for what she'd done.

'*Edward, those few snatched moments were more precious than a lifetime of contentment. I will cherish them always.*'

Was she right?

He watches the men further down the hill spraying yellow lines on the road. Down below him a man is making his way up the garden of a terraced house. He is leaning heavily on his stick, pain etched deep in his face, grey hair falling lank against his head. Edward wonders what his name is. He watches the rain coming across the valley. He sits down in his chair and waits to hear it lash against the window. He is in the mood for rain. He sighs, and realises that tomorrow he really must return to work.

He had gone back for one day and the following morning he had waited at the bus stop and, when the bus arrived, a young woman had stood aside to let him get on first. He'd shaken his head and turned away, gone back up the hill to his flat, shaking with fear, with anger at himself. And now tomorrow he would slink back in. Maybe it would be like before; his desk exactly as he had left it. Maybe they didn't need anyone to do his job. He wishes he had the courage and the money to give it all up so that he could sit here at his window all day, watching the weather and the encroaching seasons.

He can hear Tabitha scratching at the living room door. He opens it an inch or two, teasing her as she curls her paw around the frame; one perfect white paw that he could crush with one movement. He shudders and opens the door further. The cat, oblivious of his thoughts, presses up against his legs. He crosses to the chair and sits down, knowing that she will jump onto his knee and nuzzle into his neck.

'I don't deserve you, puss. Fancy telling my mother you weren't mine and yet here you are.'

The rain has come at last. He closes his eyes and strokes the purring cat. He decides to unseal the envelope; ask his mother if she would like to meet him for lunch.

'Hey, what a to-do, puss? What a to-do. A cup of coffee and a saucer of milk are in order, don't you think?'

He begins the ritual of the coffee by breathing in the smell of the freshly ground beans. He is glad that he has not gone to work, glad that he is alive and at home with Tabitha. He watches transfixed as the milk rises up the pan.

CHAPTER FIFTY-NINE

Rachel has gone to a lot of trouble in the garden. The soil is rich and black beneath the orange berries that have spilled from the bush above and now lie scattered like children's sweets. She can hear the phone ringing in the house. It stops when she gets to it and she is glad. It may have been Edward ringing to cancel their lunch tomorrow. If he can't reach her he will have to turn up, won't he? She would understand if he had changed his mind. In fact, part of her would be relieved. She is not sure what he wants to say to her. He has been to visit his father's grave.

Although the border is only half dug, she has had enough of gardening. She had planned to go to the shops on the front tomorrow and buy some new bedding plants, instead of leaving it too late in the season like she normally does, when only the dishevelled ones are left. She peels off her gloves and eases her ankles out of her gardening shoes. Tomorrow she will finish the border.

But in the house she feels empty, restless, isolated from the world. She wishes she had stayed outside. She was all right outside. She goes into the front room. Through the window, the street is empty. She has always relished her isolation, but now she suddenly feels... she shakes her head, *Snap out of it, Rachel*. But she can't.

She sheds her coat and makes a cup of tea. The rain hits against the French windows; unusual, the wind must be from the east. She watches as the dark comes in up the garden. She sits down in her chair, lets the cat jump onto her knee and picks up her cup. Her hands are shaking. Clasping the cup tightly with both hands she allows the warmth to seep into them. The cat suddenly lets out a loud yowl. She tries to shove it off her lap, but it digs its claws in. She stands up and it jumps down, complaining loudly. She walks over to the window, Wallflowers. That's what she should have planted last autumn. If she had, the deep velvet russet of the flowers would soon be dancing outside her window. She presses her face against the cold glass. And then, in summer, her deep red climbing rose would bloom. She turns and looks into the room. In the centre of the table is a thin glass vase, supporting a tall blood-red rose, crystalline in death. George had wanted to get an Albertine, a frothy, frivolous pink, but she had held out for the blood red.

All these years Edward had known. How he must have hated her, blamed her for his deformity, and all those same years she had never suspected a thing, thinking it was just Edward being Edward, and all that time he was carrying around so much pain. The thought of it makes her want to retch.

She sits back down in her chair. Come on Rachel, she thinks to herself, make an effort. Go and sort some clothes out for tomorrow. He wants to meet you. Maybe he has forgiven you, but God knows why. If only he hadn't discovered her secret, how different his life might have been.

Rachel is dressed in her pink candlewick dressing gown, and the slippers with a pom-pom of white fur on the toes. She is sitting in her high back chair; her head resting against the wing, her mouth slightly open. Next to her on the table is a book, open and placed face downwards.

It is quarter to three in the morning. Upstairs, an electric blanket warms the bed. In the bathroom, the bath is squiggled with green liquid soap, so that in the morning the scum will lift easily and leave the enamel gleaming white.

In the spare bedroom Rachel has laid out the outfit she will wear for lunch with Edward. A light brown jersey dress with sleeves that finish at the elbow and a neck that is rounded, slightly scooped. Shaped into the waist, the skirt is slightly flared. On top of the dress, laid in a twist, is a long string of tiger-eye beads and a pair of newly opened chocolate-brown stockings. On the floor is a pair of black-patent court shoes.

In the living-room, the gas fire on a low setting hisses and blows with the wind outside. The cat stretches and yawns, catching its claws in the white sheepskin rug. The wind moves the dark maroon curtains drawn across the French windows. It is black outside. The climbing rose scratches against the glass.

On the side in the kitchen, next to the kettle, stands a cup, a present from the Isle of Wight. Inside is one solitary dry teabag, ready, waiting to be taken upstairs.

The pond is almost completely covered with duckweed. Tiny, perfectly shaped little beads of flat pale green. The russet coloured leaves from the beech tree above float down and, like an embroidered collage, make a pattern with the weed.

Rachel stirs the weed with her fingers and it drifts apart, showing clear, secret water, and the rusty reflection of the tree above. How odd she should remember, after all these years, the boat, and herself wanting the courage to sit in it, to perch on the centre bar and row across the silent pond. And now here she sits in the nose as the ferryman, whom she has paid full in silver, sculls the oars through the water.

Edward waits for his mother for half an hour. He even orders a coffee to fend off the circling waitress. Maybe she is doing to him what he had done to her; getting her revenge.

Half way along Surrey Street, Edward realises that he is not at work today. He stops on the corner feeling hungry and wishing he had been able to bring himself to eat something. He catches the number fifty-six bus, it stops beside the park. There are ducks on the lake. How often, when he was living at home, did he pass along this road?

Edward pushes the red button and waits until the bus has come to a complete standstill before getting up and shuffling down the aisle, 'Thank you.'

The driver grunts and as soon as Edward has let go of the rail he closes the doors with a hiss and sets off.

Edward steps up onto the pavement and rests on his stick. He can see his mother's house from here. Still with the red sills and the green door that he remembers his parents arguing about so long ago.

'You can't have a green door and red sills. You have to have them matching.'

'Why?' his mother had asked.

His father, eventually, as in all their arguments, had given in.

After all these years he'd thought somehow he would find it shabby, yet the house appears well-maintained. Why has he kept away? He smiles to himself. Can he forget so easily?

He knocks on the door. A cat is yowling from the back of the house. He makes his way through the green gate at the side of the house and round to the back. The sun is glistening on the frosted lawn and in through the French windows. The rose hips, stark red, tap against the glass. He presses his face up against the window and shields his eyes to peer in.

CHAPTER SIXTY

Edward looks around his mother's attic. He is seated on a chair under the skylight. There is nothing else in the room except an old trunk and the chair on which he sits. Even the floorboards are bare.

Angela groans, 'I can never undo locks.'

'Pull the key out slightly, and then turn it,' he advises. The lock springs open in her hand. She places the padlock on the bare floor, puts her fingers to the rim and tugs.

Inside is a wooden tray, separated into small shallow sections, spanning the top of the trunk. In each section are little packages of tissue paper. Edward comes to stand beside her. She hesitates. 'Go on then,' he says.

She picks one up and unwraps it. Nestling in the paper is a coral necklace. She gasps in delight, 'Isn't it beautiful? Like small twigs of terracotta.' She holds it to the light. 'It's exquisite.'

'I remember now where I've seen that trunk before.' He pulls the chair over towards her and sits down. 'It belonged to my uncle. It used to be in the attic at the farmhouse. How on earth did she get it up here?'

Angela opens another package. Each parcel holds a fresh treasure: turquoise, cornelian, jade, and egg-shaped beads of amber, glistening like barley sugar. Edward remembers Rachel wearing some of them, but some he has never seen before. The last package contains a perfectly matched string of river pearls.

'Where did she get them all from?' Angela asks, letting the pearls run through her fingers.

'I haven't the foggiest idea. See what's on the next layer.'

She prises out the tray. 'Nothing, except,' she leans into the trunk, 'an old piece of newspaper with strange foreign looking writing.'

Edward stands up and peers into the trunk. 'It's Russian. Fancy that, it must have been my maternal grandmother's trunk.

She came from Russia when she was a little girl. I remember my mother telling me.'

The cat yowls loudly up the stairs. 'You'd think it'd come up, wouldn't you?' Edward says.

'Her pewter pearls aren't here. I loved them. They were so… her. I remember she was wearing them at Claudette's funeral.'

The cat's cries become more plaintive, echoing up through the house. They try to ignore it, but it seems only to get louder, more complaining.

'Do me a favour will you?' He stands up, 'Go and put that bloody thing out.'

'Aren't you afraid it will wander off?'

'To be quite honest, I don't care. I just can't stand that noise any longer.'

The corner of the bed is folded down. The pillows are plumped and ready, waiting for Rachel. Edward sits down on the edge of the bed and is surprised to find it warm. He pulls back the covers and places his hand on the bottom sheet.

'The electric blanket has been on all this time. She must have put it on the night she died.'

Angela comes over to the bed and, like Edward, places her hand on the bottom sheet. 'How wonderful, it's as if it's been waiting for you.'

He says nothing, feeling suddenly overcome. While they have been in the attic it has grown dark outside. The heavy damask curtains are still open. Angela tugs at them and they slide together easily, the curtain rings jangling against the brass rod.

'There, that's better.' She sits down on the bottom corner of the bed.

Edward prises himself up and opens the middle drawer of the dressing table. He takes out a drawstring pouch made of crimson velvet, 'I want you to have these,' he says, sitting down on the bed next to her. He places them in her lap. She picks up the pouch and gently presses it between her hands. 'What is it?'

'Open it and see.'

With her index fingers she draws open the top of the pouch and, turning it upside down, empties its contents onto her lap. She gasps, and picks up the pewter pearls. The first thing she does is put them up to her cheek. Edward sees how the light catches them, dappling her skin.

'They're so beautiful.'

'I want you to have them.'

'They must be worth loads, I can't accept them.'

'Mother has left me everything. Thank you, Mother,' he looks upwards, 'I might even be able to give up my job, so please accept them.'

'But why, Edward? Why are you giving them to me?'

He wants to tell her that he has dreamed of placing them around her neck, of bending and kissing the blue vein running down to the softness of her breasts.

'I want to thank you for your kindness over this last week, and for coming to the funeral with me,' his voice cracks. 'I'm not sure I would have got through it without you.'

She had been the first person he had thought of. He'd leafed through his notebook for her number. He'd heard her voice. That was almost enough, just to hear her voice.

'What are you going to do with the house?' Angela holds the pearls cupped in her hands.

'I honestly don't know.' Edward is silent for a moment, trying to contain his emotions. 'I feel so confused.' He pauses, trying to gather strength, 'As you know, mother and I had rather a fractious relationship.' He thinks back to the last time he had seen his mother alive, sitting at his kitchen table. He covers his face with his hands. A tear trickles out from between his fingers and down his arm, disappearing into his jacket cuff.

He feels her hand on his shoulder. 'Please don't cry, Edward. You'll set me off. Shall I make us a cup of tea?'

'You're wise for your years, you know?' he says, smiling, brushing the tears away with the palm of his hand. 'I've just remembered, there's a bottle of whisky downstairs in the cupboard under the sink. Will you go and get it?' Give me time to compose myself, he thinks.

Angela lies on her stomach, legs bent at the knees, bare feet waving in the air. He wants to put his hand out and hold the plumpness of her calves, squeeze the flesh gently between his fingers.

'You know,' she says, sipping at her whisky. 'I keep getting this irresistible urge to draw you.'

'Oh,' he says, 'if only. Oh, for those times back again. When life was less complicated.'

She smiles sadly. 'Nothing seems black and white anymore does it? I should have known that I couldn't just stick with charcoal.' She laughs at her own joke, and gets up from the bed to pour them another drink.

'I don't mind, you know?'

'What?' She waits, bottle in hand.

'Mother has a sketch pad downstairs.' He watches her face, frowning, as she tries to comprehend his meaning. He imagines lying naked with her here, in-between his mother's best cotton sheets.

She pulls a face. 'I'm a bit drunk!'

He rattles the ice in the bottom of his glass. 'Just think, mother prepared this ice for us.' He hiccups. 'You hadn't thought of that, had you?'

'I did actually, clever clogs. As I was running the ice tray under the tap, I had the very same thought.'

'Shifting sands.'

'Pardon?'

'Shifting sands.'

'Are you drunk?' she grins.

'That's what life seems like lately.'

'You're right, nothing seems quite safe anymore, does it? I mean, fancy you moving out of Mrs Ingram's. I thought that you'd end your days there. What are you going to complain about now you haven't got her to ruin your clothes, or serve you up salty food?' She begins to giggle. 'Oh, Mrs Ingram? Look. You've ruined my best socks,' she mimics.

He pokes her in the ribs.

Outside in the garden, they hear the cat yowling.

He must have nodded off. He wakes in the middle of the night propped up against the pillows. Angela is asleep with her back nestled up to him, snug against his body. He leans forward and, marvelling at his new-found courage, kisses the vein on her neck, letting his lips trace it down to her collarbone. She turns her head slightly and smiles up at him, her eyes still closed. If he wasn't so drunk he could get up and turn the light off. He lays there wishing they were both naked.

And now it is the next morning and she is pacing back and forth in the kitchen.

'Angela?' She stops pacing long enough to look at him. 'Do you want any sugar in your tea?'

'No.'

'No, thank you, Edward,' he reprimands.

'Any chance we can go in the back room yet? It's so dingy in here.'

He nods.

On the side are little packages wrapped in old newspaper. He picks one up and peels back a corner to find a willow pattern cup. She must have wrapped them up to give him.

He finds it strange to be in his mother's kitchen, using her things. He has found only one mug – a present from the Isle of Wight. He will have that. It already has a tea bag in it. He unwraps one of the willow pattern cups for Angela. He will need a tray. He finds it tucked under the sink where it always lived. He waits for the kettle to boil and smiles to himself, thinking of the night they spent together. He is beginning to feel better. He will ask her if she will come to the grave with him today. They could even go for lunch afterwards.

If he is careful he can manage to carry the tray through with one hand. He props open the kitchen door. Angela has opened the French windows. The sunlight is stippling the lawn. A bird is on the bird table. He notices his mother's stone birdbath and remembers all those years ago when he and his father bought it as birthday present for her and how, for once, they'd got it right.

Edward watches Angela as she sits slumped in the chair. She is miles away, her finger twisting a coil of hair.

'Penny for them.' He expects her to smile, but she doesn't. She removes her finger, letting her hair uncoil.

'I decided earlier, whilst you were making the tea, that I'm going to Cornwall later this morning. If I can get a train.'

His voice is toneless, 'But I thought we were going to the ballet this evening.'

'I have to see someone.'

'Who? A man?'

She snorts, 'No.'

She is lying, he thinks. 'Please don't go, not yet,' he pleads. 'I love you.'

'Fuck off! Just fuck off, will you?'

He hears the front door slam, the stained glass rattling in its lead.

He sits staring out into the garden, numb with shock. He holds his hands prayer-like up to his face. His grandfather, Richard Appleyard, stares kindly down at him.

CHAPTER SIXTY-ONE

As the train makes its way southwards, the tension in Angela's jaw lessens. She absorbs the sounds of the train: the clack of the wheels on the line, the softer roll of the tea trolley making its way towards her. The image of Edward's face that morning is beginning to fade. She presses back into the headrest, closes her eyes and feels the warmth of the sun on her eyelids.

Once upon a time, she thinks, there was a man and a woman. The man was old and crippled, and the woman was young and... she opens her eyes long enough to study her reflection in the glass, cocks her head to one side – lovely – that would do. Why not beautiful? She looks again, smiles. She has always liked her teeth; the colour of fine porcelain, the perfect balance of translucence and pearl; neither too big nor too small. No, she doesn't want to be beautiful, that would be too ordinary. Will Paul, her Cornish fisherman, think her lovely when he sees her again? She closes her eyes. She must be mad, but what wouldn't she do for another night like they'd had?

He is there when she enters the pub, sitting on a stool along the bar with his mates. He glances over at her and then looks away. She sees that he is studying her in the mirror behind the bar, a gradual recognition dawning on him. As she crosses the room towards him she sees he is still watching her. Her heart is banging against the inside her rib cage.

'Hi.' She can feel her face turning red, 'Fancy meeting you here.' How trite she sounds.

His mates smirk and nudge one another.

'All right, Maid?' He looks her up and down, still unsure, 'What are you doing down here?'

'And there's me thinking you'd be pleased to see me.' She

tries to gauge him. Is he just being like this because he's with his mates?

He takes a drink of his beer. 'I never usually `spect to see Emmets again.' He laughs, 'Suppose you want a drink?'

She nods her head towards the door. 'Do you want to go for a walk?'

He descends reluctantly from his stool. 'Okay.' He finishes his beer and follows her out.

As they come out of the pub, a cold wind blows in across the cove and she shivers. He stands awkwardly, looking down at the incoming tide.

'Down here with your fancy feller, are you?'

She doesn't reply. He follows her to the top of the slate steps, to the edge of the quay where they'd first met.

She sits on the wall and picks at a limpet. 'I don't know what to say now.'

He sits down beside her. 'What is it, Maid?'

She remembers how funny she'd found it to be referred to as 'maid'.

'I was just down at the cottage again,' she lies, 'and I thought I'd look you up. See if you wanted to relive our one night of passion.'

He grins, and she remembers some of the attraction she'd felt for him.

His grin widens. 'Oh, I see,' he sticks his hands in the front pockets of his jeans. 'It were good, weren't it? In fact, it were fuckin' fantastic.'

She laughs.

'Can't go tonight, though. If this weather holds, we're going fishing. First bit of good weather we've had in days. Can't miss it, not even for you.'

He takes her hand and turns it over, studying her palm. 'How about tomorrow night?'

She shakes her head. 'No can do. I'm going back tomorrow.'

'Well, how long have you been down here?' he asks.

'A week,' she lies.

He turns to face her. 'How about now?'

'Now?'

He shrugs, 'Yeah. Why not?'

Her inner self is saying no, but she has come all this way just to see this man. 'Where?' She asks.

'No reason why we can't go back to the Keep House,' he replies, holding his hand out. 'Come on.'

She remains seated on the wall. 'I'm not sure. It all seems a bit rushed.'

He leans forward and kisses her. It is a good kiss. She searches his chapped lips with her own, trying to bring back the feelings she has coveted for weeks.

The evening light is shining through the diamond panes of the window and patterning the wall opposite. Angela turns and watches the last of the sun as it sinks into the sea.

Paul comes and stands behind her, clasps his arms around her waist and sniffs the hair at the back of her neck. 'Your hair's grown,' he whispers. 'I like it.' His hands move up to her breasts. 'God, have these grown as well.'

Under her jumper, she is wearing the bra Edward gave her.

She can feel him, pressing into her from behind. She pulls away. 'Just let the sun set first.' She puts her elbows on the windowsill and stares out to sea.

He copies her and grins, 'Same old floor show every night.'

'What?'

'The sun going down.' He pulls her towards him. She feels his tongue pushing her teeth apart, and the sudden strangeness of it all.

She pulls away. 'I'm sorry. I can't do this. It was good that night, really good, but I should have left it there.'

'For fuck's sake!'

He stands there enraged. She holds her breath quite still, looks down at the floor, her eyes tracing the rust veins in the slate tiles. He turns abruptly, leaves the huge studded door wide open behind him.

She sees his headlights wander down into the cove and the red rear lights weaving up the hill opposite.

She watches as the darkness creeps in off the sea. She is afraid to turn on the lights in case someone comes. She lies down on the bed. She must have dozed because when she wakes the room is pitch black. She listens to the constant song of the sea and for strange noises; imagining that Paul, after his fishing trip, might return to try again. At first she sleeps like a cat, wakeful to any sound, but the wind and the constancy of the sea soothe her and she is surprised when she wakes to find the sun shining brightly through the window, her arms cut into a diamond pattern by the shadow of the leaded bars.

The screeching of seagulls drives her from the bed. She has slept all night in her clothes and her body feels gritty and unwashed.

She looks down into the cove. Hilda's cottage still sleeps. The sick room window is half open, the pale green curtains lapping on the grey slate window ledge. A woman is sitting on the wall, her face raised to the sun and her palms pressing into the slate slabs. It is not Hilda. She takes a closer look and wonders if it is Alex's mother. Up the valley the faith healer's chimney is already spiralling smoke up into the air.

She leaves the bed unmade and hides the key back under the stone. She remembers there is a phone box down in the cove, an old fashioned red one, the only contrast against the greys and greens of the landscape.

She picks up the receiver. It is dead. She rests her elbows on the scratched black shelf, her head in her hands.

What is she going to do now? For no apparent reason an image of Rachel comes into her head, the image Edward had painted of Rachel sitting in her chair; head resting against the wing, her mouth open. She shudders and thinks of her gran. She suddenly feels very alone.

She sits by the stream, looking down into the clear water, a picture keeps drawing itself in her head. Two black figures, silhouettes, are loping across the page. They are thin with rounded shoulders, their hair straggly and unkempt. A man and a woman; her parents, they are moving towards her.

'Ange? I thought it was you I saw coming down the hill. What on earth are you doing down here?'

She looks up. Alex is leaning over the bridge studying her. She gets to her feet.

'Are you all right? You look terrible.' He is making his way towards her.

'I didn't see your car parked in front of the house or I'd have come over.'

'It's in the boat shed.' He nods up the valley. 'Do you want to come and have a cup of tea and meet my mother?

'Is that who I saw sitting on the wall earlier?'

'Yes, she's doing really well. Did you come down to see me?'

'No.'

His mother is still sitting on the wall in front of the cottage. She is younger, gentler than Hilda.

'Mum? This is Ange. You remember? The girl that came down with me so I could keep working while I was visiting you.'

The woman looks into Angela's face, her head tilts slowly, taking her eyes out of the light. 'Yes, I can see she would be a good model.'

'Are you an artist?' Angela asks.

The woman smiles, 'Only of life. Alex tells me you're his star pupil. He keeps talking about your work.'

Angela shakes her head, not knowing what to say.

Alex sits down on the wall beside his mother. 'Yes. Right now, some of your work is hanging on the wall in the hall at college.'

'Oh shit! I wanted to ask Edward for his permission before I displayed them.'

'Too late.'

'Shit!' She puts her hand to her mouth and looks at Alex's mother, 'Sorry.'

He waits with her at the station. She flicks a spot of water off the slatted seat and sits down. 'How long are you here for this time?'

'Just a week. I've got another term to do at college. I didn't tell you, did I? I'm leaving permanently. I've had enough of teaching. I'm going to concentrate on my art. Move down here, be nearer my mother.'

'What brought that on?'

'Lots of things, you partly, seeing your work made me realise I better bloody get on with it.'

'That good, huh?' Her work had impacted on him that much? 'You're really leaving then?'

He nods, looks down at her with an expression of curiosity on his face. 'You never did tell me what you were doing down here.'

She shrugs, 'The truth?' She squints up at him. 'I met

someone the last time I was down here.' He shakes his head, puzzled. 'We've been writing to each other,' she lies. 'I arranged to come down, but it didn't work out.'

The train pulls into the station. 'But I don't understand...'

'Thanks for the lift.' She grins, 'Let's leave it as one of life's little mysteries, shall we?'

'Angela?' She is just about to place her foot on the first step of the train. What is he going to say? He looks a bit miffed. 'Look after yourself.'

She smiles, turns back towards him and, surprising herself, kisses him on the cheek.

'I've just remembered something.' He takes her hand, 'Will you do me a big favour? I left a new canvas and all my oil paints in that studio you use. Will you put them somewhere safe for me?'

'One, two buckle my shoe,
Three, four knock on the door,
Five, six...'

The small boy sitting opposite her on the train is waiting to be prompted by his mother.

'Pick up sticks,' Angela wants to say.

The boy, disinterested, pulls his coat sleeve over his knuckle and wipes the window, staring out at the countryside rushing past.

The mother sighs, 'Pick up sticks, Seven eight, the garden gate, Nine ten...' She pauses. The boy turns and grins, 'A big fat hen. Can we stop now? Are we nearly there?'

She remembers her gran teaching her that rhyme. There is more but she can't remember it. She must go and see her. Tell her she's going to London. See if she will go with her when she goes for the interview. Then she will be able to see for herself that it's not a million miles away.

'Eleven twelve... dig and delve' That's it.

Angela checks her watch. 3.30. She feels drained. When she gets home, she will go to bed. But first she has to do that favour for Alex, she owes him that much.

In the studio, Angela wedges the canvas between two chairs. It is stretched and ready like Alex had said. She smears red vermillion, gauging the proud line of Edward's back with a small palette knife, slashing it with the straightness of his stick. His head is bowed, rimmed by blue and yellow; ribs limned in green, arched as a fleshless basket, weaving and expanding around and around; swirling until they fill the whole of the canvas; spreading like ripples on a pond, encasing the head, the back, the legs, until even the stick is encircled within the basket.

From these fresh reeds, fresh green will grow into new white willow; pliable, without flesh and muscle to contort and twist it like before. Through the centre she plots a backbone snaked in blue, twisting and secretly meandering like an underground river.

She is panting for breath, not through exertion but through anger; anger at herself, anger at Edward.

She remembers him on Surrey Street. Himself, his stick, and the wind, carved against the light like a black thorn tree. But now spring has come and she has carved of him a rainbow tree, like all the colours in his mother's trunk.

She can no longer see him in black and white.

CHAPTER SIXTY-TWO

Edward enters the house, uninhabited now except for his mother's cat that skulks under the table, mewing at him accusingly.

He hears the snap of the letterbox. On the coconut mat is a pale blue airmail envelope. Leaning heavily on his stick he bends to pick it up. Staring back at him is his own name – Mr Edward Anderson. A letter from Uncle Ruben. Surely it can't be his birthday, not today. He works out the date in his head. It is.

He pokes at the mat with his stick, digging down into old dust. If only Angela hadn't gone off like that. He flinches, remembering the expression on her face when he'd told her again that he loved her. He places the willow pattern cups and saucers carefully into one of his mother's old shopping bags. He looks for the egg timer from Bridlington. She must have forgotten to wrap it. He opens the cupboard to the right of the draining board and – there it is. He pulls it forward and then notices something dark behind it. He reaches further in and lifts it out. It is the china bird that his mother once used to prop up the centre of her steak and kidney pies. He runs his fingers down its extended neck and the slimmed-down body, and wonders what sort of bird it is. It seems too slender to be a blackbird. It could be a cormorant; sleek-necked as it dives into the sea. He sighs, if only he could transport himself back to the studio and the time when he and Angela had laughed about his own 'china bird'. Perhaps they could stay there; both of them locked in time. If only she were a bird, he could put her in a gilded cage and keep her there forever.

He wanders from room to room, consumed by an aching restlessness. On the landing he pauses. The spare room, once his, is lit by the late morning sun. On the narrow bed his mother's clothes are laid out, exactly as she left them, in preparation for their luncheon date: a light brown jersey dress with sleeves that finish at the elbow; slightly old fashioned, Edward thinks, but, like his mother, rather elegant. On top of the dress a twist of tiger-eye beads catch the light from the window. Newly opened and placed next to the dress as if to check the match, the soft texture of fine denier, chocolate-brown stockings. On the floor, placed ready to step into, is a pair of black-patent court shoes.

He turns and makes his way along to his mother's bedroom. Seeing his mother's outfit on the bed like that has given him a pang of regret. He thinks of her in the earth, encased in her coffin in her candlewick dressing gown and her bedroom slippers. When he'd read the instructions she'd left for her funeral, he'd flown into a rage. She was to be dressed in her lilac suit and her pewter pearls, and to be cremated, her ashes to be scattered on the old pond down on the farm. As if to state finally that he and his father had been nothing in her life. As he had watched her coffin being lowered on top of his father's he had felt a moment of triumph, but all he feels now is the emptiness of his revenge. He wishes he was down on the farm scattering her ashes, standing on the edge of the waterlogged ditch they had called a pond.

He is overcome with an overwhelming sense of loss. It washes over him in waves, feelings that he had never felt for her whilst she was alive. He buries his head in his mother's pillow, folding it around him, shutting off the outside world. He can smell the scent of Angela. He lifts his head and out of the corner of his eye he sees something glisten. He glances over at the dressing table. Laid in a twist, as if discarded carelessly, is the string of pewter pearls. Angela hadn't taken them. He snatches them up and crushes them between his fingers. How he hates them. All his life they have been there. The pure translucence of what should be cream, turned to grey. He squeezes them tighter and feels them crunch against each other. From the bottom of the stairs he hears the cat yowl. He goes out onto the landing.

'Shut up, shut up!' He hurls the pearls down the stairs. They smash against the wall and the whole necklace comes apart, shattering like silver rain on the hall carpet. The cat bolts into the kitchen and he hears the cat flap snap shut.

As he makes his way to the front door he pokes the pearls aside with his stick. He is glad that he has broken them apart. It feels is as if a grey cloud has lifted. He closes the front door and puts the key in his pocket. The sun is still on the front of the house and the cat is sunning itself on the top step. He pokes it gently with his stick and makes his way to the bus stop. From the bus he can see the river and the willow trees. He feels in his pocket and takes out his uncle's letter. He slits open the envelope with his finger. 'Oh, God!' It suddenly occurs to him that he hasn't told Uncle Ruben about his mother's death.

He scans the letter. As always, his uncle signs it in the hope that, this year, Edward will make it across the pond. Edward shakes his head, always the same ending. Why did he never give up? Maybe he should go to America. Get away from here. He could even take his patterns, see if Ruben could run him up some new jackets. He thinks of the pink cardboard pattern pieces lying flat beneath his mattress, but no – he has left them at Mrs. Ingram's. No matter, he shrugs. He can go and visit her. Maybe, Mrs Ingram would be interested in his mother's fat cat.

He gets off the bus a stop early. He had seen the sign this morning: *Exhibition of Students Work.*

Edward will see whether the other students' work is as good as hers. For the first time he enters through the gates.

The walls are flat mushroom and beige. The light reflected around the hall is exquisite, midday sun on a clear winter's day. Pictures have been hung around the walls at different heights.

He sits down on the leather seat in the centre of the hall and gazes around him, awed by the silence.

On the far wall, in pride of place, he notices a drawing that looks familiar. A woman is gazing up at it. He stands and moves closer. It can't be. He walks away, turns around and looks again. It can't be him – and yet – he tilts his head, and there is his face staring back at him. He smiles; there is such care drawn into it. He studies his own spine, a contorted black line across the paper. He wants to touch it, put his finger to the curve of his back and run his hand down the full length. She has given him a grace of form he would have once found unimaginable; like a proud bird, one wing lifted, ready, as if preparing for flight.

***

From the author

■■

I would like to thank Yvonne Barlow of Bookline and Thinker to whom I owe a huge debt of gratitude for bringing to fruition her Hookline Novel Competition.

I would also like to thank the book groups who participated in the competition for all their hard work and dedication. I feel honoured and humbled to have been chosen.

Keith Jafrate of Word Hoard, Huddersfield.

Livi Michael, Lesley Glaister, Lynne Alexander, Mike Harris, and Steve Earnshaw.

Julia South, Siobhan Osborne, Karen Davies, Ruth Valentine, Joan Deitch and Michael Elliott.

Chris Johnson of the Osteopathic Practise, Sheffield.

My son, Tim.

■■

Credits

The Observer's Book of Birds' Eggs
Frederick Warne & Co. Ltd, 1937

Egon Schiele by Wolfgang Georg Fisher.
Published by Benedikt Taschen Verlag, 1995.
English translation: Michael Hulse, Cologne

Quinquireme of Nineveh poem by John Mansfield

∎∎

Other Hookline Novels chosen by book groups are:

A Young Woman's Guide to Carrying On by Jilly Wosskow

After a row with her mother, Kathryn collects her belongings and slams the door for the final time. It's 1974 and the beginning of a new life – but how much can Kathryn really leave behind?
She takes a live-in job as a waitress at a country house, working alongside the outrageous Dee-Dee. Both 17, and both with their own tragic past, they learn how to bag a bloke, get through testing times and even how to get on the property ladder.
A Young Woman's Guide to Carrying On is a tender, witty and wise novel of love, adultery, second chances and questionable parenting.

Readers' Reviews:
'This was a fantastic book. Well written, the author did a fantastic job of carrying you through all the emotions of the characters and didn't let them do the 'right thing'. Nothing in real life is straight forward and we often go down a path that we regret later.'

'Fantastic book! I will definitely recommend it to my family and friends.'

'Made me laugh out loud – reminded me of my own family in many ways.'

The Half-Slave by Trevor Bloom

The year is 476 AD – the Roman Empire is disintegrating and
Germanic tribes are moving south. Among them are the Franks.
Their ruthless young Overlord, Clovis, plans to build a new empire
that will eclipse Rome's fading power, but his hope is jeopardized
by the massing forces of a seaborne Saxon uprising.
One young man is sent to find out where the Saxons will strike.
Ascha is the son of a Saxon warlord and a Roman slave mother, a
half-slave, locked in the limbo between slave and free. As a hostage
of the Franks, Ascha struggles to survive. But when the Overlord
offers to make him a free man if he will spy on his own people
Ascha must summon all his resources and his courage to discover
where his loyalties lie.

Historical Novel Review said:
*'I found the realism in the characters, situations, and deftly
woven plot strands made this a gripping story.'*

Readers' Reviews:
*Thoroughly convincing recreation of an entirely different
era which kept me fascinated by the characters and wholly
involved in the fate of the hero, with some gripping situations
and moral dilemmas. I found it increasingly hard to put
down, so a lot of midnight oil.*

*A refreshing lack of idealisation – even of the hero; I
believed in the characters.*

I'd happily read the sequel!

Village Fate – A Country Tale of Cooks, Crooks and Chickens by PJ Davy

Neville would love a woman in his life – until three turn up at once! Cynthia believes Neville is her soul mate. Fliss just wants him to wake up and smell the chickens. Lucy, well, no one is sure what Lucy wants, but it is unlikely to be Neville in his bicycle clips. And then there is Baby Behr and Mummy Behr, who would be happy if Daddy Behr did not spoil their domestic bliss. Nettlecombe Hatchett villagers come together as strange creatures stir in the undergrowth.

Readers Reviews:

'Exuberant writing style! The climax had me roaring with laughter.'

'An amusing take on a serious subject ... an enjoyable read.'

'A light-hearted modern morality tale.'

■■

Lightning Source UK Ltd.
Milton Keynes UK
UKOW03f0011311013

220103UK00001B/16/P